The Eight Bench Walk

Patrick C. Walsh

The Eight Bench Walk

The tenth 'Mac' Maguire mystery

Garden City Ink

A Garden City Ink ebook
www.gardencityink.com

ISBN 9781674691923

Cover art © Patrick C Walsh 2019
Garden City Ink Design

"If you want to know what God thinks of money, just look at the people he gave it to."
— ***Dorothy Parker***

This once again is for my readers Kathleen, Jean, Kay and Patricia. Without their suggestions and eagle-eyes this book would have been much poorer.

The Quest

He was old and sick but he kept telling himself that his will was indomitable. He'd been feeling really ill that morning yet, just a few hours later, here he was once again scrambling around the rocky countryside. The prize was so great that he'd keep looking even if it killed him.

He was looking for the place that had been described in the letter. Unfortunately, the description was vague to say the least. He knew from the hand-drawn map that it must be somewhere around here but where? He had been on the island for some months now and, while he'd originally thought that his quest would be easy and would only take a few weeks, he was not about to give up.

The little car jolted up a mountainous road and he drove to its very end. He got out and, using his stick, he walked as far as he could. Even though it was late in the day the intense heat bounced off the rocks and he had to use a handkerchief to wipe the sweat from his eyes.

He got a copy of the letter out and read it for probably the thousandth time. He then carefully folded the letter, put it back in his pocket and looked around him. The sun's rays were low in the sky and that was how he finally found it, by its shadow.

He walked over to the large rock and touched its surface. It looked as if it was part of the rocky outcrop but, when he looked closely, he could see that there was a gap around every edge. His hand caressed the stone and the sign that had been chiselled into the rock nearly two hundred years before. It had weathered now but the sun's rays had shown it in relief – the trident of Poseidon!

He almost fainted when he thought of what might lie on the other side of the rock.

He could now start to put his plan in motion.

He would now be remembered when he died, he thought with some satisfaction, and everything and everyone else could happily go to hell in a handcart.

Chapter One

Mac was glad that he'd booked assistance at Larnaka airport. After four and a half hours in the air his back was feeling very stiff and the wheelchair was more than welcome. A nice young man pushed him through the fast lane at passport control and then rolled him to the luggage carousel before rescuing his suitcase. He then dropped him right by the taxi rank. Mac wished that he could have given him a tip but he wasn't sure if that was allowed. He gave him his best smile instead.

He blinked for a moment as he stood and luxuriated in the warmth of the sun. It had been a dank dark Tuesday morning when he'd left Luton and the dry midday heat was wonderful.

'Whereyougoing?' a large man at the taxi rank shouted as one word.

Mac didn't quite pick it up and wondered if he was speaking Greek.

'Hotel? Hotel?' the man asked again impatiently as if repeating the word would make it more intelligible.

'Oh yes, it's the Libretta Apartments, St. Lazarus Square,' Mac replied.

'Ayiou Lazarou,' the man shouted.

An old dark blue Mercedes detached itself from near the back of the taxi rank and glided towards Mac. The driver was short and balding and around the same age as Mac. Like Mac he was also somewhat pear shaped. He wore a white shirt with the sleeves rolled up and black trousers held up by a pair of bright red braces. He hefted Mac's heavy suitcase into the boot with ease. Mac got in and admired the polished wood of the dashboard as the taxi moved off.

'English?' the taxi driver asked.

'Yes,' Mac replied.

The man went quiet for a moment and Mac began to wonder if being English might not be such a popular thing in Cyprus.

'My father told me what it was like when all this was run by the English,' he said as he waved his hand at the passing countryside. 'It was better then. The English, they knew what they were doing, and everything worked. Now it's...'

The driver made a sound like air going out of a punctured tyre.

'On holiday?' the driver asked.

'Oh yes, I'll be here for three weeks. I'm really looking forward to it,' Mac said with some enthusiasm.

They left the airport and then drove alongside a large body of water. This confused Mac. It was flat and shallow and was obviously not the sea. The driver must have seen his puzzled look.

'That's a salt lake,' he said. 'Towards the end of the year that lake turns red as thousands of flamingos come to eat the shrimp. It's something to see.'

Mac guessed that it must be. It just looked flat and drab at the moment although he did catch an intriguing glimpse of a building as they sped by. He saw a large white dome and next to it there was a slim tower. Mac guessed that the tower was a minaret and therefore the building must be a mosque. It seemed a strange place to have a mosque.

Before long he started seeing other buildings. At first, they were just industrial and business premises but soon the road narrowed and houses with a hodgepodge of building styles, colours, sizes and shapes lined either side of the street. New buildings were mixed in with some that seemed to be in the process of falling down and clearly hadn't been occupied for years. The road narrowed even further and the taxi driver had to weave in and out as cars were randomly parked along the side of the road as if they'd been left behind by some great flood.

The taxi eventually stopped, and Mac looked up. 'The Libretta' a tasteful sign said next to a set of double doors. He was finally there!

He looked at the taxi meter. It said fifteen euros which, as airport taxis go, Mac thought was more than a fair price for the five miles or more that they'd gone. The driver helped him out with his bag and Mac gave him a twenty euro note telling him to keep the change. He also asked for the driver's card. He knew from experience that an honest taxi driver in any country was well worth hanging on to.

Opening the taxi door had been like opening the door of an oven. The afternoon heat hit him with some force, and he could feel rivulets of sweat trickling down his legs. Wearing trousers might not have been such a good option. He'd noticed that most of the men on the flight were wearing shorts and he now knew why.

As instructed, he phoned a number and waited outside the apartment for someone to come. A few minutes later a smiling woman in her thirties holding a bunch of keys in her hand strolled over and introduced herself.

'Hello there, I'm Sonia. Welcome to the Libretta, Mr. Maguire. I'll show you to your apartment. Is there just you?' she asked.

'Yes, my friend, Mr. Teagan, has been delayed and I'm afraid that he won't be here until next week now,' Mac replied.

'That's no problem. Just ask him to come and bring me his passport when he arrives. You'll normally find me behind the reception desk at the Libra Hotel just over the other side of the square.'

He followed her inside as she walked towards the lift. The lobby had marble floors and white walls and

5

it felt wonderfully cool after the heat of the street outside. His guide was dressed in a brightly patterned sun dress. It was made of material so light that it wafted around her body as she swayed from side to side when she walked. She was a very attractive woman but, even so, Mac was surprised that he'd noticed it. He decided that it must be the heat.

She stopped at the lift.

'You're on the second floor,' she said with a smile as she pressed the lift button.

Mac noticed that there was just one more floor above his. The lift was small and slow but it was fairly new and looked robust enough. With his suitcase inside they had to stand close together which he found a little embarrassing. Sonia didn't seem to notice. With some relief the lift doors opened and Sonia took him to the room at the end of a short hallway. She opened the door and invited him inside.

The room was beautiful. The walls were painted white and large colourful canvasses featuring flowers were hung on the walls.

She gave him a quick tour and, most importantly, showed him how to work the air conditioning. Mac was impressed by the little kitchen and even more so by the size of the walk-in shower. He was absolutely dazzled though when she pulled back the curtains and opened the double doors so that he could walk out onto the balcony. There was more than enough room for a small table and two chairs and there was a tasteful wrought-iron balustrade that went right the way around in a semi-circle. It wasn't the ironwork that made him catch his breath though.

The view was incredible.

He looked out over the square which was more of a triangle really. It was dotted with trees and lined with cafes outside of which people were sitting and drinking and talking. In the middle of the square there was a church, the Church of St. Lazarus. It was like no other church that he'd seen before with its barrel shaped roofs and its high bell tower. It was made of a beautiful honey-coloured stone and the tower had elaborate carvings all the way up.

Mac smiled and shook his head. The pictures that Bridget had shown him looked wonderful but being here was so much better.

'Is the apartment okay?' Sonia asked.

'I should say so,' Mac said with some enthusiasm.

'I'm glad you like it,' Sonia said. 'The housekeepers will come and clean the room every day but if you want to sleep late there's a 'Do not disturb' sign behind the door. Please note that if the fire alarm goes off don't attempt to use the lift. You'll need to access the fire escape but please only do so in the event of a fire. The fire escapes are alarmed as, unfortunately, guests in the past have used them to smoke outside and then they forget to close them afterwards. Have you any questions?'

Mac couldn't think of any.

'Very well then,' she said. 'I'll leave you the keys but don't forget that, if you need any help or advice, just come over to the hotel where we'll be happy to help you.'

She took a photo of his passport with her phone and then they shook hands and she was gone. He spent a few minutes poking around the flat before he started unpacking his suitcase. The little kitchen seemed to have just about everything he'd ever need and the two twin beds were of a good size. He sat on one to try it out. It seemed quite firm for which he was grateful.

He put his suitcase on the bed nearest the balcony, which he'd decided was his, and started hanging his clothes up in the wardrobe. It didn't take him long to unpack which was just as well. He was desperate to get

7

outside and have a look around. He had a quick shower, put a loose T shirt on as well as some shorts and sandals and he was ready to go. He looked at himself in the mirror on the way out and decided that he looked like a big jessie with knobbly knees.

As it was far too hot outside for trousers, he decided that he would just have to do.

Chapter Two

He stepped out of the apartment lobby and into a different world. The entrance led onto a narrow side street with just the post office separating him from the square. He walked the few yards into the square and just stopped and stared.

People were sitting and talking or just sitting and looking about them. No-one was in a hurry and even the odd car that went by drove slowly. He stood there for a moment and smiled as he felt the stress of the long flight ooze away. He ambled across the narrow road and took a closer look at the church. A ginger cat crossed his path.

A tour group was being spoken to by a guide near the entrance to the church. Mac couldn't understand a word of what was being said but he guessed that they might be Russian. Even though it was hot the women wore long dresses and hats and the men all wore trousers. A few minutes later they disappeared into the church. Mac went over and had a look at a notice near the door. The church was open to visitors most days until five thirty. He was curious about what it might look like inside and he decided that he'd give it a try tomorrow.

He turned away from the church. He knew from hours of looking at the map of Larnaka that the beach was just a short walk away down the street in front of him.

He wanted to see the sea.

As he walked back through the square, he glanced at the people around him. They were of all types and ages with knobbly-kneed middle-aged men in shorts being quite well represented. They didn't seem to be bothered about it so he decided that he wouldn't be either. Again, he noticed a couple of cats going from table to table seemingly begging for food. He was glad that he hadn't been able to bring his dog Terry with him, seeing this many cats around the place would have driven him crazy.

It was certainly hot though and he was more than glad for the ventilation afforded by his shorts. He'd looked at the weather forecast before he left and they were saying that it was going to be well over thirty degrees. He hadn't taken his old fedora hat along, as that would have been too warm, but he'd given little thought as to what he should wear on his head. He was only halfway down the street when he felt the top of his head heating up. His thinning hair provided little or no protection from the unrelenting sun. By coincidence he found himself standing next to a shop that sold shoes, bags and hats.

He went in and looked at some baseball caps as just about everyone else seemed to be wearing them. It took him some time to find a cap that had a design on the front that he could live with. He finally settled for a navy-blue cap that had the Barcelona FC badge on it.

It wasn't Aston Villa, he thought, but they weren't bad.

Back on the street the top of his head felt immediately cooler. He smiled, not at his balding pate's relief but because he could now see the sea between the buildings at the bottom of the street. He hurried on.

As he turned the corner the whole world opened up in front of him. Under the vault of a vast light-blue sky the beach arced away into the distance on his left. It was dotted with hundreds of sun loungers most of which appeared to be in use. A wide pavement and a narrow road separated the sun worshippers from the brightly coloured shops, bars and rest-aurants that lined the beach. To his right there was a short stretch of sand behind which an ancient fort jutted out into the sea. Behind it a minaret, looking like an ancient space rocket ready to be launched, spoke of the island's Islamic past. The fort was built using the same honey-coloured stone as the church but they had used a paler stone for the minaret and the adjacent mosque which somehow set them apart.

Mac noticed that there were no sun loungers on the little beach by the fort, just people lying on towels. A middle-aged man with a pronounced paunch got out of the sea and started drying himself off. Mac decided that this was where he would go swimming too, well away from the gaze of those seriously topping up on their tans.

He remembered what his daughter had told him. She'd said that if he went to his left it was a nice walk along the beach but the bars and restaurants were a bit generic. She said that the nicest walk was on the other side of the fort. Mac had the distinct impression that his daughter was trying to get him to exercise more. However, he could well understand why this might be the case. The long winter seemed to have seized up his back for long periods and he hadn't gotten out and about as much as he normally would have. He could understand his daughter's concerns and, in a way, he was only here because he knew it would please her.

He sat on a bench and watched the waves and the comings and goings on the beach. He wondered at how he'd been worried about looking foolish in his swimming shorts and whether everyone would look at him when he went in the sea. However, here there were more than enough pale skinned men who were well past their prime going about their business. He'd fit right in.

Of course, there were also lots of younger people on the beach too. He particularly noticed a girl in her early twenties. She had long hair, curves and a beautiful smile. She was walking along the beach with a friend, waving her hands as she talked. She was wearing a very small red bikini and Mac could see every curve gyrate as she moved.

He tore his glance away and felt quite silly for a moment.

'An old man like you!' he said to himself. Followed closely by a guilty thought. 'What would Nora think?'

He thought of what his wife Nora would have said and he laughed out loud. He hadn't felt any sexual urge or desire when he'd looked at the girl, she'd just been very beautiful that's all. He realised that he'd enjoyed looking at beautiful women even when his wife was alive. He had a short conversation with his dead wife in his head.

'Looking for a newer model?' she asked.

'Now, why would I be looking at a Mini when I've already got a Rolls-Royce at home?' he replied. 'Anyway, I'll bet that she can't cook cabbage the way you can.'

For some reason him saying this had always made her laugh.

Thinking of her made him smile. If he told people of the daily conversations that he had with someone who'd been dead and buried for nearly two years now, they'd have put him in a madhouse. He didn't care, talking to his Nora made him feel less alone.

There was a sort of walkway going out into the sea. Mac was curious to see what lay beyond the fort and so he roused himself and headed for it. He walked out as far as he could and looked around him. Finikoudes Beach swept away to his left while, on the other side of the fort, a sort of esplanade ran alongside the sea. It arched away and, at its tip in the far distance, he could just see a cluster of masts. Mac guessed that there must be a marina of some kind.

The esplanade was on two levels. The lower level, which was a few feet below the street, seemed to be for pedestrians only, while the upper level had a narrow road and, alongside that, a pavement. Mac could see two benches on the pavement from where he stood. Bridget had told him that there were benches at regular intervals all along the esplanade and that's why she'd suggested it.

He could now understand why his daughter had recommended the esplanade as a nice place to walk. However, after all his recent inactivity, he wasn't sure how far he could walk without it increasing the pain levels in his back. He guessed that he was about to find out.

He carefully walked around the fort as the path was a little uneven and then went up a few steps. He was now on the esplanade at street level. Whoever had designed it had done a good job. Instead of a wall separating the two levels they'd installed clear glass panels. The first bench was around a hundred yards away or so. He decided to give it a try.

He passed by a group of massive boulders that stood on the pavement. They were smooth and polished and he guessed that they were some form of artwork. However, they were also quite practical as a young couple came by and sat down on one. He walked on and reached the first bench quite easily. He looked further up the esplanade and noticed that there was another group of boulders between him and the next bench. He liked this esplanade.

He turned and looked at the sea. The glass panels allowed him an uninterrupted view. White crested waves washed up on the rocks below while the sea, green and blue with every shade in between, receded into the far distance. It was only punctuated by the odd ship. In the foreground a small tourist boat that bore the legend 'Glass Bottom' trundled by while on the horizon a cargo ship seemed to hang unmoving in the blue haze.

He sat there watching the sun bounce off the sparkling wavetops. He didn't think, he didn't feel. For a moment he just was.

When thought resumed he had no idea how long he'd sat there. He felt at peace as he roused himself and eyed the next bench. He made that quite easily too and he began to wonder if the dry heat was loosening up something in his back. He again stared idly at the sea for some time but this time he also took note of the people who walked, ran and cycled by on the lower level. Then there were those who sped by on all sorts of electric powered scooters and tricycles. He was beginning to wonder if he'd finally found a hidden talent for doing nothing. He eventually got himself up again and made for the third bench.

He could see that it was just opposite a restaurant that had an old windmill near the entrance. His back was grinding a bit as he neared this bench so he decided to make that as far as he'd go today. A three-bench walk.

There was no back to the bench so, after gazing at the sea for a while, he was able to swivel right around and look at the restaurant. It was now mid-afternoon and it seemed quite full. The tables, covered in red and white checked tablecloths, were being buzzed about by waiters who expertly balanced multiple plates of food on their arms. A little band of cats waited on the pavement below looking upwards for any scraps that might be dropped to them by the diners.

Bridget had told him that the restaurant was a lot bigger than it looked from the front so, even if it seemed to be full, she said that he should still give it a try. She'd told him to go on a Sunday and order the Lamb Kleftiko. It was now only Tuesday so he'd only have to wait a few days before he could see if it was as good as Bridget said it was.

He also remembered something that she'd said about the cats. She'd mentioned that some wild cats roamed the streets of the town but Mac hadn't been expecting to see quite so many. Again, he thought of his dog. If he was honest, he was already feeling a little guilty at leaving Terry behind for such a long time.

He hadn't wanted to put Terry into kennels for three whole weeks so he thought about asking his neighbour Amanda if she could take him. However, he'd been more than apprehensive about this in case she thought that he was taking liberties. She already did enough in taking Terry out for a long walk every day but he just didn't want to leave him with anyone else. Terry really liked Amanda and her dog and Terry had become good friends. He was relieved when she said that she'd be happy to look after Terry and, in return, she hoped that Mac would be able to look after her dog for two weeks later on in the year when she went on holiday. The fact that he could reciprocate made him feel a lot better about the arrangement. Of course, he'd need to hire a dog walker but he'd cross that bridge when he had to.

He made it back to the fort after stopping again at both benches on the way. His back was now telling him that it had had enough for one day, so he decided to head back towards the square and home. He stopped when he reached the fort and looked back. He'd walked a fair distance, for him anyway.

As he walked up the side street towards the square, he realised that he was getting thirsty. He once more stopped and stared as he entered the square. It was now late afternoon but the day was still hot. The ground floor of his apartment block was a café and it had tables and chairs dotted about on either side of the narrow road. He saw a young lady come out of the café door carrying a tray that had a single pint glass full of an amber coloured liquid. That decided him.

He sat down and waited for her to come around.

'I'll have one of those,' he said pointing to the large glass of beer she'd just delivered to a nearby table.

'A pint of Keo?' she asked.

'Yes, that's it,' Mac said hoping that he'd ordered the right thing.

He fell into a sort of relaxed reverie as he sat and looked at the people around him. There were old married couples who sat in silence as all the words had already been said. There were younger couples, freshly in love, who couldn't bear to be more than an inch away from each other and who said everything with their eyes. Some locals were talking animatedly at a table nearby over small cups of coffee and he could hear a backgammon game going on somewhere behind him. Two tables away a group of five middle-aged women were drinking cocktails and laughing at their own jokes. He couldn't help noticing that a couple of them were eyeing up a young waiter as he went past. There were also a few men who, just like him, were sitting by themselves. Some of these, the lucky ones, seemed happy in their solitude while a few just looked plain miserable.

Of course, he hadn't planned to be by himself for the first week of the holiday. His best friend Tim was supposed to have been there too. After a long winter they were both looking forward to a lengthy stay in the sun. It was a simple mistake, a single letter, that had forced Tim to change his flight and delay his holiday for a week. Work had been a bit scarce which was another reason why Tim had been happy to go away for three weeks. Then, just a couple of weeks before they were due to fly out, he got the offer of a job which he snapped up. Tim was never happy when he was idle.

He'd taken it on thinking that it was going to be a reasonably quick job. He was a furniture restorer and antiques dealer and he knew pretty much every stately home in the area but he'd never heard of this one before. He assumed that it would only take him a few days at the most.

His mistake had been an easy one to make. He'd read 'Hertfordshire' in the address but it had, in fact, been 'Herefordshire' which was on the other side of the country. Once he'd been and had a look, Tim realised the scale of the job and he'd been very apologetic when he'd called Mac to let him know. Mac had told him not to worry and to go ahead and take the job. He'd use the first week of the holiday to find out where all the best bars and restaurants were so that Tim could hit the ground running when he finally arrived.

A whole week by himself. He'd thought that it would be nice but he now wondered how he'd get on. One thing was for sure, he hoped that he wouldn't end up sitting alone and looking miserable.

His musings were interrupted by the arrival of his beer. A tall slim glass was placed before him. The bubbles streaked through the amber liquid terminating in a fluffy white head. He touched the glass and found that it was cold, so cold that they must have kept it in a fridge before filling it with beer. He found that he was more than thirsty but he restrained himself and just looked at the beer for a while. As he raised the glass, he was hoping that it tasted as good as it looked.

It did.

It was light, refreshing and perfect on a hot day. Mac smiled. He now knew what he'd be drinking for the rest of the holiday. He'd only been in Cyprus for a matter of hours but it had already changed him. He was more than happy to be doing absolutely nothing which was quite unlike him.

He had a snack with his second beer but, as he came to the bottom of the glass, he could feel the tiredness creeping up on him. It was nearly five o'clock so, after a very long day, he decided that an hour or two in bed might be just what he needed before going out again in the evening.

He had no trouble getting to sleep and he woke just before seven. After another shower, he felt amazingly refreshed and ready for whatever the evening might bring.

By chance Mac found himself back at the same table in the square. He'd had a little walk but he didn't go too far as his back was still complaining. The sun had almost set behind the square and the cafes were all filling up. He'd checked out a restaurant just down the road that Bridget had highly recommended but every table had already been taken. He was almost glad in a way as he didn't feel all that hungry. He wondered if he should just stay at the café and have something light to eat.

The decision was taken out of his hands when loud music came out of a speaker just to his right. He'd seen the notice saying that they had live music that night and, as luck would have it, he'd picked the worst table to sit at. He wondered if that was why it had been free in the first place. He stood up and had a glance inside the café where three men, two playing bouzoukis while the other played a guitar, were belting the tunes out. He liked Greek music but not quite at that volume.

He got up and ambled around the square for a while before sitting down on the low wall that ran around the church. From this distance the music was fantastic. He looked around and noticed that there was a little café situated in the opposite corner of the square. A sign said 'Za'atar Lebanese Bakery'. Mac was curious, he'd never tried a Lebanese bakery before.

He looked inside and a man behind the counter smiled and said, 'Eat here or takeaway?'

Mac noticed a large fridge full of fruit juices, cokes and, luckily for him, cans of beer. This gave him an idea.

'What do you do here?' he asked.

The man gave him a leaflet which had photos and descriptions in English of everything they did. He opted for the vegetable pizza solely on the basis that it looked nice and he knew what it was. He got himself a cold can of beer from the fridge and watched the man as he made his pizza.

This was no exercise in taking the plastic packaging from a factory-made piece of dough and then shoving it in a microwave. Mac watched with something like awe as the man took a ball of dough. He then expertly stretched it and rolled it flat before showering it with assorted vegetables and then covering it with cheese. Mac knew from the menu that this was 'kashkaval' cheese but he had no idea what that might be.

He then put his creation on a big metal paddle and carefully placed it into a big baker's oven. Even though he was busy with other orders and chatting to other customers he still kept a close eye on Mac's pizza. When it was deemed to be perfect, it was removed from the oven and placed into a box where he expertly cut it into eight pieces using a curved blade with two handles. Mac got a couple of beers to go as well and he was surprised to find that he still had change from a ten euro note.

He smiled all the way back to his room. From the vantage of his balcony he sat and enjoyed the music from a safe distance. He watched the people come and go in the square below while stuffing his face with the most amazing pizza he'd ever tasted. Mac's sense of well-being reached a peak.

This, however, was not to last.

He'd just finished eating his last slice of pizza when he heard something from the balcony directly above his head. It sounded like chairs or a table being knocked over, he thought.

Then he heard a man shout, 'Help! Help!'

A few seconds later Mac saw something fall past him. He looked over the balustrade and saw an old man spread-eagled on the road below. His body was broken and blood was seeping from his head. A walking stick lay on the street beside him. He was lying on his back and his eyes were wide open.

He seemed to be staring up at Mac with horror.

Chapter Three

Mac reacted quickly. Within a couple of seconds, he grabbed his room keys and he was out of the door. He walked the few paces to the lift as quickly as he could. He pressed the button and the lift door opened immediately. It looked as if no-one had used it since he'd returned with his pizza. He wedged his crutch in between the doors so that they couldn't close. There was a little two-seater sofa opposite the lift so he sat down and waited.

Like many buildings the stairs spiralled around the lift shaft. He sat and stared at the stairs that ran down from the floor above. He pictured someone bounding frantically down the stairs trying to flee a murder scene but no-one appeared. If someone had pushed the old man to his death, he'd either used the fire escape to get away or he was still up there. He sat and waited as he heard the police sirens grow louder. He kept his eyes firmly on the stairs.

He had no idea how long he'd waited before a detective appeared on the stairs coming from the first floor. He was in his mid-forties, had combed back jet-black hair that was going grey at the sides and he had a thick black moustache. He wore plain clothes, a dark blue polo shirt with light beige trousers and a dark blue windcheater. Mac knew instantly that he was a policeman. This was confirmed when he caught a glimpse of a gun cradled in a leather holster hanging from his belt. He was followed by a younger man who wore a black T shirt with a grey hoodie and blue jeans. They both stood there for a moment and stared at Mac. They then turned and looked at the crutch propping the lift doors open.

The older one said something to the younger one in Greek. Mac would have bet on it being something like, 'And there we were, wondering why the lift wasn't working.'

He first spoke to Mac in Greek and, on seeing his incomprehension, tried English.

'Is that your crutch?' he asked.

'Yes, it is,' Mac replied.

The policeman didn't need to ask the question as his face said it all.

'The man who fell, his balcony is right above mine,' Mac explained as he stood up. 'I heard the sound of a scuffle of some sort and then someone shouting for help. A second later he was flying past me on his way down to the street. I came straight out here and pressed the lift button. The doors opened instantly so, if there was anyone upstairs with him, they couldn't have gotten out that way. The lift is quite slow so they wouldn't have had time. So, I wedged the lift doors open, sat here and kept watch on the stairs but no-one's come down.'

'Come on, someone could still be up there!' the older policeman said to his partner. He then turned to Mac. 'Can you go back to your room and we'll come and talk to you when we can. Don't try going outside, there's a policeman guarding the entrance. Oh, and you can take your crutch with you, we might need the lift.'

Mac did as he was told. He sat on his balcony and had another beer as he watched the police cordoning the area off. The forensics team arrived next and eventually erected a little white tent over the body. The uniformed police had just started interviewing the people who were sitting outside when he heard a knock on his door. It was the two detectives.

The older one showed Mac his warrant card. It was mostly in Greek and he didn't have enough time to read the name which was quite long.

'Chief Inspector Christodoulou, Larnaka CID,' he said.

For some reason the name sounded familiar to Mac.

The Chief Inspector looked at Mac with great interest as he sat down opposite him. The younger detective had to sit on one of the beds as there were only two chairs.

'Can I see your passport, please?' the Chief Inspector asked.

Mac took it out of the little safe in the wardrobe and gave it to him. He looked at the photo page and then looked up at Mac. He then passed it to the younger detective.

'Take a photo of it,' the Chief Inspector said. He then turned back and looked at Mac for a few seconds before he continued, 'That was really quick thinking on your part, Mr. Maguire, or something else perhaps.'

Although the Chief Inspector spoke English with a slight foreign inflection, Mac thought that there was something very familiar about his accent too. For some reason he couldn't quite put his finger on it.

'What's the something else?' Mac asked.

'Well, you said that no-one could have used the lift or the stairs to escape from the crime scene...'

'It's definitely a murder then?' Mac asked.

'It looks like it,' the Chief Inspector replied. 'There were clear signs of a struggle of some sort, chairs were overturned and glasses smashed. The table and chairs on the balcony were pushed into a corner too. So, it looks as if Mr. Jones might have been trying to get away from his attacker when he went out onto the balcony. Unfortunately for him it looks like his attacker followed him out there and pushed him to his death.'

23

'I take it that you found no-one in the dead man's apartment then?' Mac asked.

'No, we didn't.'

'Perhaps he used the fire escape to get away?'

'No-one used the fire escape,' the Chief Inspector stated. 'It's alarmed and the staff at the hotel have told us that no alarm went off. We checked the door and the alarm is working as it should.'

'So, it must have been one of the other guests on his floor then,' Mac suggested.

'We've checked out all the other rooms and only one was occupied. All the other guests were out for the evening.'

'And?' Mac asked.

'There were two people in the room, both quite elderly. The man is in a wheelchair and his wife has just had a hip operation. They're with their daughter and son-in-law who are staying at the hotel.'

'Not particularly good suspects really, are they?'

'No, but we have a better one,' the Chief Inspector said.

'Who's that?' Mac asked.

'You.'

Mac gave the Chief Inspector a bemused look. He hadn't thought of himself as being a suspect but he could see how it might make sense from the Chief Inspector's point of view.

'Did you know the dead man?' the Chief Inspector asked.

Mac shook his head.

'The first time I laid eyes on him was when I saw him flying past my window.'

'It's strange though, isn't it? You arrive here this afternoon and, within a matter of hours, the man in the room above yours is dead. Unlike most people, you're not stunned at seeing a man fall past your balcony to his death. No, instead you run straight out to check the lift and then keep watch on the stairs in case a murderer appears.'

The Chief Inspector gave him a look that underlined the improbability of it all.

'Yes, I can see how that might look a bit strange,' Mac admitted.

'What do you do, Mr. Maguire?'

'Do? Not much these days, I'm retired,' he answered.

He didn't want to admit to being a private detective for some reason. He still felt a bit silly when he told people.

'And what did you do before you retired?' the Chief Inspector persisted.

'I was a policeman.'

This was obviously not an answer that the detectives had expected. They gave each other a look before the Chief Inspector carried on.

'Really? What did you do in the police?'

'I was the head of the London Metropolitan Police's Murder Squad for a time.'

Mac could see the wheels going around in the Chief Inspector's head before a light went on.

'You're not Mac Maguire by any chance?' he asked.

Mac nodded.

'My real first name is Dennis. Mac is a nickname.'

The Chief Inspector got his phone out and spent a little time on the internet. Eventually he seemed to find what he was looking for. He showed the screen to his colleague who read for a while. He gave Mac a surprised look as he handed the phone back.

'Okay, now I understand why you acted in the way you did,' the Chief Inspector said. 'It's exactly what I would have done but you had me puzzled for a while.'

'But I'm still a suspect,' Mac said.

'Of course, but you knew that anyway.'

Mac nodded.

25

'I'll need you to make a formal statement at the station tomorrow,' the Chief Inspector said as he stood up. 'In the meantime, I'll need to hang on to your passport. You'll get it back when you come to the station.'

Before he left, he gave Mac a card which had his name and the address of the station on it.

Mac let them both out and then suddenly felt tired. As he lay back in an unfamiliar bed, he ran the day's events through his mind. It was indeed unlikely in the extreme. He arrives in the afternoon and a matter of hours later there's a murder. He remembered Tim commenting about the time he'd found a murdered man at an airport while he was waiting for a plane.

'You're getting just like that woman on the TV in 'Murder She Wrote'. She can't go anywhere without there being a murder too.'

He began wondering if he was somehow attracting murderers by his very presence. He was just thinking how silly this was when he fell into a deep sleep.

Chapter Four

Despite the events of the evening before Mac had slept well. That was until a stray ray of brilliant laser-like sunlight woke him up. He looked over and realised that he hadn't fully pulled over the black-out curtains the night before. He was about to turn over and go back to sleep when the bells in the church tower started ringing. He knew then that he might as well get up.

Although it was only seven fifteen, he found that he didn't mind being woken up too much. He remembered that he had to go to the police station and he thought it might be best if he got it out of the way as soon as possible. He had a holiday to get on with.

He had a quick wash and got dressed before stepping out onto the balcony. He smiled as the sun hit his skin and he feasted his eyes on the church and the scene in the square below. The café was still cordoned off and closed for business and he could see that a uniformed policeman was guarding the entrance. He could still see the dried blood pool on the road's surface. Obviously, the cleaners hadn't arrived yet.

He went down, walked to a café on the other side of the square and ordered orange juice and coffee. For some reason he wasn't hungry but, then again, it was only eight o'clock.

He waited until it was nearly nine before he took out the card that he'd been given by the taxi driver. He read it. It appeared to be a one-man business and the owner's name was Michalis Andreou. That name rang a bell with Mac. He'd met someone called Andreou who was from Larnaka before but he supposed that there might be thousands of people here called that.

He rang the number on the card and was told to wait where he was. Ten minutes later the big old Mercedes pulled up in front of him.

'Where to?' the driver asked.

'The police station,' Mac replied.

As they pulled away the driver asked with some concern, 'You haven't been robbed or anything?'

'No, nothing like that,' Mac replied. 'There was an incident last night at the apartment house that I'm staying in.'

'Yes, I saw the policemen. A man fell from a balcony, or so I heard. It sometimes happens, people drink too much on holiday,' he said with a shrug.

'My name's Mac by the way, Mac Maguire.'

Mac thought it would be good if they were on first name terms if he was going to be using him regularly. The driver looked a little surprised by this.

'Michalis Andreou,' he replied.

When he stopped at some traffic lights Michalis leaned over and shook Mac's hand.

The car turned into a back street and before long they were driving down a long narrow road lined with shops, most of which seemed to be selling clothes and handbags. The street looked quite familiar as a lot of the names on the shop fronts were the same as those back home in England. A minute later and they were at a busy crossroads waiting for the lights to change.

'That's the police station there,' Michalis said.

Mac looked over the road at a two-storied building on the corner. It was rendered a cream colour and had gothic arches around the sides topped with a circular look out post over the main entrance. It didn't look all that inviting. Michalis pulled up outside.

Mac paid him and asked if he'd be free to take him back in a while.

'Of course, just call me when you're ready. Be very careful though,' he said. 'There are people who go in there just to pay a parking fine and they're never heard of again.'

He said this with a twinkle in his eye so Mac hoped that he was just joking.

Inside the lobby was busy. Uniformed policemen came and went and there was a small queue at the reception desk. Luckily Mac didn't have to wait long. The young detective from the evening before walked by and noticed him standing in the queue.

'Mr. Maguire, you don't need to wait. Come with me and I'll take you to see Dave.'

Mac was glad that he didn't have to wait but he was wondering who on earth Dave might be as he was ushered down a corridor and into a large office. The Chief Inspector was sitting at a corner desk. He stood up and smiled as Mac walked towards him.

'Mr. Maguire, I'm so glad you could make it. You'll be happy to know that you're no longer a suspect and, that being the case, you can have your passport back.'

'How come?' Mac asked as he put his passport in his pocket.

'We have several witnesses who saw a man fitting your description looking down from the balcony of your apartment just after the old man fell to his death. One of them also conveniently filmed the scene just after the event and that confirms that you couldn't have been the killer.'

'Well, thank God for that then,' Mac said with some relief as he started to stand up.

'Before you go, I'd like to ask you for a favour,' the Chief Inspector said quickly.

Mac sat back down again.

'You might actually be in a position to help us if you'd be willing. At the moment all we know about the dead man is his name, Harold Maurice Jones, his age and his address in the UK. It was the first time he'd visited Cyprus as far as we can tell and he'd travelled alone. He'd been here for around four months by the time he met his end but he'd paid for his apartment up until the end of August.'

'That's unusual, isn't it?' Mac said. 'I mean that someone would book such a long stay on their first visit.'

The Chief Inspector gave this some thought.

'He originally booked for two months and then extended his stay but you're right, it is unusual. We've already started asking questions about him but we've learned next to nothing so far. It looks as if Mr. Jones didn't go out much and that he kept himself to himself for the most part so perhaps it wasn't a holiday that he was here for after all.'

'Where did he live?' Mac asked.

'Knebworth in Hertfordshire. That's where they have the rock festivals, isn't it?' the Chief Inspector asked.

'That's right,' Mac replied.

Although it wasn't far from where he lived, he'd never actually been to the festival. All he could remember about it was the truly monumental traffic jams he'd sometimes got caught up in when driving home from work.

He continued, 'I take it that you've discovered that I've worked with the Police Major Crime Team that covers the Knebworth area quite a few times before.'

The Chief Inspector nodded and smiled.

'I'll need to go through the formal channels in contacting the police in the UK but that usually takes some time. I'd be grateful if you could help us to get the ball rolling a little more quickly.'

'So, you want me to contact the Major Crime Team in Hertfordshire on your behalf?' Mac asked wanting to be sure.

'If you wouldn't mind. You'll be all too aware that the first few days of an investigation can be crucial and I don't want to waste time while we wait for everything to go through official channels. I'd really appreciate your help in this.'

'That's no problem. Just give me a minute,' Mac said.

He pulled out his phone and got Dan Carter's number up.

'I'm calling Detective Superintendent Dan Carter, he's the head of the team,' Mac said.

He calculated that it would be about seven thirty in the UK and he guessed that, as it was a Wednesday, Dan would be up and about. He was. Mac explained the situation to him.

'Yes of course, we'll kick off an investigation straight away,' Dan said. 'We're all quite busy at the moment but I can put Kate and Tommy on the case for a week or so and then see where we are.'

'Kate and Tommy? That would be great,' Mac replied. 'Tommy's been to Larnaka fairly recently so he'll have an idea of what the place is like.'

'Can you put me on to the detective who's running the case?' Dan asked.

Mac handed the phone over to the Chief Inspector. He and Dan had a short conversation which left the Chief Inspector smiling. At the end of their little chat the Chief Inspector scribbled down some email addresses and phone numbers.

'Thanks Mr. Maguire,' the Chief Inspector said as he gave Mac his phone back. 'DS Dan Carter's assigning a team to deal with the case at his end and he's also volunteered his computer specialist who he said could have a look at any information that your government might have on Mr. Jones.'

31

'His name's Martin Selby and he's very, very good,' Mac said. 'If there's anything out there on this Mr. Jones, he'll find it.'

'We were going to go back and have another look at the crime scene in the daylight. We can drop you back at your apartment if you like,' the Chief Inspector said.

Mac was more than happy to accept his offer. They got into a white car that had a wide blue stripe and the words 'POLICE' and 'ΑΣΤΥΝΟΜΙΑ' on the bonnet and the sides. They drove back down the road that ran right alongside the beach. The sun worshippers were already out in their hordes and the cafes and bars on the other side of the road were doing good business. They turned right just before the fort and emerged into the square. The road directly outside the café was still closed off so the young policeman parked the car just in front of the police crime scene tape. They nodded to the uniformed policeman who was guarding the cafe. Another policeman nodded them into the apartment building.

'Well, at least the lift's working,' the Chief Inspector said with a smile.

'Would you mind if I had a quick look?' Mac asked.

He'd promised himself that he wouldn't get sucked into the investigation, after all he was on holiday. However, he was curious about the case and his curiosity won out, as it usually did.

'Yes, of course,' the Chief Inspector said as he pressed the button for the third floor. 'I'd be glad to hear what you think.'

'I take it that forensics have already been through the place?' Mac asked as they walked down the hall towards the crime scene.

'They have but they told us that it would still be best if we put these on,' the Chief Inspector said as he handed out some latex gloves and shoe covers. Seeing that Mac was having problems bending down to put the covers on his sandals the young detective bent down and slipped them on for him. Mac didn't quite know what to make of the Chief Inspector as yet but he was definitely warming to the young detective.

Another policeman let them into the apartment. Mac looked at the door as he opened it for them. There was no sign of damage around the lock or the door jamb. He stood in the doorway and looked at the room before stepping inside. At first sight it was very like his own except that the paintings were different and there was a large double bed instead of two singles. The bed had only a bare mattress on it. He guessed that the sheets and covers had been taken away by the forensics team.

The two chairs were both on their sides and the mirror had been knocked to the floor. It was in one piece but it had a single long crack in the glass running from corner to corner. The floor by the little kitchen was strewn with broken glass. As he could see a slim stem in among the fragments, he guessed that they were once wine glasses. To confirm this a puddle of red wine also lay on the laminate flooring. It had dripped down from an empty bottle that was on its side on the work surface.

He took a few steps inside. A bedside lamp lay on the floor on the other side of the bed and the curtain rail on one side had come away from the wall.

Mac could almost see the struggle that took place. He wondered if the old man had used his walking stick to defend himself. That might explain why it was in his hand when he fell. He walked over and had a peek out onto the balcony. The two chairs and the small table had been wedged into the right-hand half of the balcony. He went out and looked over the balustrade.

The balcony was more than high enough up to ensure that anyone who fell would meet their death.

Mac stood in silence for quite a while. The young detective looked at the Chief Inspector. The Chief Inspector shrugged.

'Do you have any thoughts?' the Chief Inspector finally asked.

Mac woke up. He'd been running the assault through his mind again and again.

'Well, it would appear that Mr. Jones knew his attacker. There are no signs of forced entry and, from the amount of glass there is on the floor, I'd guess that there were at least two wine glasses in use. So, it could have been a social visit of some sort. By the way how old was he?'

'He was eighty-one,' the Chief Inspector said.

'Really? I was thinking that it might have been a romantic liaison of some kind but at his age, who knows? I take it that forensics are checking the bed sheets for signs of sexual activity?'

'Yes, but we've not heard anything from them yet,' the Chief Inspector replied.

'Did he have a laptop or tablet with him?' Mac asked.

'If he did the killer took it with him. All we found was a cheap phone. It had no stored numbers on it so it was probably a burner.'

So, either Mr. Jones hated technology or the killer was smart and had taken the evidence away with him, Mac thought.

'Anyway, my guess is that things soon turned nasty and the old man then tried to defend himself with his walking stick,' Mac said. 'He backed off and eventually retreated out onto the balcony where he shouted for help. He was then pushed over the parapet to his death, or in other words, pretty much as you said yesterday.'

'Of course, it could have been someone local who killed Mr. Jones,' the Chief Inspector said, 'but, as it was Mr. Jones' first visit, it's more likely that it might have been someone he knew from the UK. We've got a large ex-pat community here in Cyprus but we'll need to work the case in both countries.'

'Well, if there's anything I can do to help...' Mac said making a polite offer.

'Thanks, I'll take you up on that,' the Chief Inspector quickly said with a wide smile. 'I know that you're on holiday but it would really help us if you could liaise with your colleagues in Hertfordshire. It should hope-fully only mean taking a few phone calls now and then.'

'Okay,' Mac said wondering if he should have kept his mouth shut. 'Have you got any leads yet?'

'Just the one so far. One of the cleaners told us that she saw Harold Jones talking to a man in a café near Psarolimano a few weeks back.'

'Where's that?' Mac asked.

'It's a little marina at the end of the Piale Pasa. It's used mostly by local fishing boats.'

Mac remembered that this was the name of the esplanade he'd walked along.

'Yes, I think I've seen it from a distance. I had a walk along the Piale Pasa yesterday but I only got as far as the restaurant with the windmill.'

'Anyway, the cleaner was able to give us a detailed description and so we've got a good idea who the man is. Let's just say that we've had dealings with him before,' the Chief Inspector said.

Mac briefly wondered why the cleaner had been so interested in the man that Harold Jones had been with. She'd seen him once some weeks before but she was still able to describe him in detail. It was probably nothing but Mac made a mental note of it anyway.

They all got back into the lift and Mac held the door open at the second floor while they said their goodbyes.

He went back to his room and sat on the balcony while he figured out what he wanted to do next. It didn't take him long. He started thinking about how inviting the sea had looked as they drove back along the beach. He decided that it was now or never.

He changed into his swimming shorts, crammed a towel and some flip-flops into a bag and set off. He didn't hesitate when he reached the beach. He took his T shirt and sandals off, balanced his crutch on his bag and carefully walked towards the sea.

It felt cold at first but, as he got further in, he found that it was just the right temperature. The beach had quite a shallow incline and it took him quite a while to get far enough out so that the water was up to his shoulders. On this first time, he didn't do much swimming. He just bobbed about in the water, revelling in its weightlessness. The ever-present pressure in his lower back started to ease off a little and it felt wonderful.

The waves lapped at his back with an occasional higher one breaking over his head and surprising him. The water massaged him and the constant tension he felt in his back started to float away on the waves. He stayed in the water for quite some time and only came out when he saw that his fingertips were wrinkling up. As he carefully walked through the water back to the dry sand of the beach, he thought that this was something he should do every day.

He dried himself off as best he could and then sat on a bench, letting the sun do the rest. He found the people going in and out of the water, or just passing by, to be of great interest and he'd have sat there for longer if his stomach hadn't started grumbling. He suddenly realised that he was hungry.

He'd brought enough money with him to buy breakfast so he hauled himself up and crossed the road. He decided on a pub that was on the corner. They had a picture of a Full English breakfast outside and it looked inviting. He was so hungry that, while it may not have been the greatest breakfast he'd ever had, it still went down very well.

He was in holiday mode and slowly ambled back to his apartment, stopping on the way to look in some of the tourist shops. Once back he had a quick shower and changed. Only after that did he think of checking his phone. There was a missed call from Tommy. He went out onto the balcony, sat down and looked out over the square. The café downstairs was still closed but the other cafes were doing brisk business. The church looked subtly different in the late morning light but it was still as beautiful and intriguing as ever. Outside another large tour group was being spoken to by a guide. He finally managed to tear his gaze away and make the call.

'Tommy, how are you?' Mac asked. 'Have you found anything?'

'Kate and I have just been to Mr. Jones' house. It's in Knebworth on the London Road, one of those big houses behind the hedge.'

Mac knew the area that Tommy was referring to. One side of the London Road consisted of detached houses that were big enough in their own right. However, on the other side, a long high green hedge, interrupted only by driveways, hid everything from the gaze of the riff-raff. Some of the houses behind the hedge were truly enormous.

'Although he lived in an eight bedroomed house, he apparently only used two rooms downstairs, one as a study and the other as a bedroom,' Tommy said. 'We found no computers, tablets or phones, in fact there wasn't even a television just a small radio. At first, we thought that his house might have been cleaned out by someone. However, we managed to interview the woman who regularly cleaned for him and she said that, as far as she could tell, nothing was missing. Mr. Jones apparently wasn't into technology. She also said that he was well known for being very tight with his money. She'd worked for him for nearly twenty years and in all that time he'd never given her a tip once, not even at Christmas.'

'Was that because he didn't have any money though? I've come across people who, while they might live in big houses, are basically broke,' Mac said.

'Well, Martin's done some digging and his financial activities seem to be complicated to say the least. He's only scratched the surface but it looks like Mr. Jones was worth many millions.'

Harold Jones was rich then. While the Libretta was a nice enough place to stay, you'd expect someone who had millions to find somewhere a little more upmarket.

'If Martin is finding Mr. Jones' finances hard going ask him to contact DI Colin Furness at the Met,' Mac said. 'He's with the Fraud Squad and he's a bit of a genius when it comes to murky financial dealings. If he's not too busy then he'll lend you a hand.'

'Thanks Mac, I'll do that,' Tommy said. 'We've taken away lots of documents and boxes and boxes of card indexes from the house. I must admit that I haven't seen any of those for quite a while and they'll take some going through.'

'Mr. Jones seems to have been quite old fashioned in his ways. They only found a cheap phone on him here. They think that it might have been a burner.'

'Well, as he seems to have been on the stingy side, that might not be the case. He might have bought it just because it was cheap. Anyway, how are you enjoying Larnaka?' Tommy asked.

'It's great, apart from the odd person being pushed to his death from a balcony that is,' Mac replied. 'I even had a dip in the sea just now. It was wonderful.'

'I'll tell Bridget, she'll be made up.'

'Oh, and tell her that I've tried out that walk too,' Mac said. 'I made three benches yesterday and walked as far as the restaurant with the windmill.'

'You sound as if you're enjoying it. By the way, before you go can you confirm what the phone number is for Chief Inspector Christodoulou? I tried to call him earlier but I couldn't get through.'

Mac read the number out.

'Thanks, I wrote one of the numbers down wrong. I'll try not to bother you again,' Tommy said.

'No, you can keep me in the loop if you like,' Mac said quickly.

He immediately wondered why. He was on holiday after all. He heard Tommy chuckle.

'I know you too well, you're getting hooked, aren't you? Okay, I'll keep in touch but try to fit in some holiday around the investigation or you'll get it in the neck from Bridget.'

Mac thanked him and said goodbye. He then smiled. Tommy did indeed know him too well.

He rang the Chief Inspector and said that he had some information. He agreed to meet him around six o'clock at a little bar just the other side of the fort.

He felt thirsty and, without thinking, he opened the fridge. It was, of course, empty. He needed to do some shopping. He rang Michalis who drove him to a small supermarket. There he bought some supplies. Perhaps more than he should have. However, Michalis was good enough to help him bring them up to his room. Without him doing this Mac would have been really stuck. He made sure that he gave him a good tip.

He felt better knowing that he could have a drink or a snack whenever he wanted to without needing to go out. To Mac's surprise it was already two o'clock. He'd been up early and it had been a busy morning. He set his alarm and gratefully lay down on the bed. He went to sleep almost instantly.

Chapter Five

He woke up an hour and a half later and felt better after his nap. All he needed was another quick shower, a shave and a change of clothes and he was ready. As he was meeting the Chief Inspector at six, he still had a couple of hours to kill. He took a cold bottle of water out onto the balcony and sat down.

It was late afternoon and the square below was relatively quiet. He sat and looked at the scene below while he thought. It didn't take him long to decide what he should do next. He'd try a four-bench walk!

Instead of going around the front of the fort, which had a stone path that was a bit bumpy in places, he decided to try walking around the back. The sun was low in the sky but it was still incredibly strong so he was glad to be able to walk in the shade for a while. He passed by some little shops and a souvlaki restaurant. A group of cats lying indolently in the shade kept a close eye on him as he walked past.

There was a bar at the back of the fort and he briefly wondered if this was the place that the Chief Inspector had mentioned. He decided that it couldn't be and walked on. He'd been told that it was near the corner just as you turned onto the esplanade and that it overlooked the sea.

As he turned around the corner of the fort, he could see the start of the esplanade and beyond that the shimmering sea. He walked a bit faster until he reached the glass wall. He stopped and looked out at the sea as though he'd never seen it before. When he'd convinced himself that it wasn't going anywhere, he turned and started looking around for the bar.

Two men were loudly playing backgammon just a few yards away from where he was standing. One of the players got up, crossed the road and disappeared into a doorway. He returned with a can of beer. There were a few plastic chairs and tables scattered on the pavement on either side of the doorway and there was a small sign in Greek over the door. Mac guessed that this must be the bar where he'd be meeting the Chief Inspector a little later.

The esplanade was now mostly in the shade for which he was thankful. He walked on and sat down on the first bench and looked at the waves crashing on the rocks below. As before he just let the time go by before readying himself for the walk to bench number two. He was more than aware that his back pain usually flared up a day or so after he'd done too much, so he kept monitoring how he felt.

To his surprise he felt okay. Of course, the pain was still there, as it always was, but it was bearable. He wondered if the time he'd spent weightless in the sea had helped him. He easily made bench number two and bench number three after that. The restaurant wasn't quite as full at this time of day but there were still a surprising amount of people eating.

He glanced up the esplanade to his target for the day, bench number four. It looked to be a manageable distance away so he roused himself and went for it. He was surprised to find that there was only a slight increase in pain by the time he finally gained the bench. Having attained his goal, he sat and watched the sea and the people passing by in a state of utter relaxation.

Only minutes had seemed to have passed when he finally looked down at his watch. He was amazed to find that it had gone five thirty. He got up and headed back towards the bar, stopping for a short rest at each bench on his way. Stepping inside the doorway Mac found that the 'bar' consisted of a little shop which sold sweets, ice cream, some tourist souvenirs and a few other items. A white-haired man in a short-sleeved shirt stood behind a counter and smiled at him.

'Beer?' Mac tentatively asked.

The man smiled and pointed to the wall behind Mac where two massive glass-doored fridges stood. They contained a vast variety of fruit juices, iced teas and other soft drinks. While he took note of these it was the right-hand side of the second fridge that Mac headed for. It contained nothing but beer. He opened a door and selected a giant bottle of Keo beer. The man smiled again as he took the cap off, handed him a glass and then charged him a ridiculously small amount for his drink.

'Enjoy your beer,' the man said.

Mac assured him that he would and took his bottle and glass outside. He sat down on one of the plastic chairs. It was quite sturdy and remarkably comfortable. He sat looking at the sea for some time. Eventually, he looked to his left and gazed at the high stone walls of the fort. He was intrigued and resolved to see if he could get inside and have a look around. As he saw people on the battlements taking photos, he surmised that it must be open to visitors. Beyond the fort he could see people walking into the sea from what he now thought of as 'his' little beach. From this vantage he was surprised at how far out they could walk.

The sound of a commotion brought his attention back to the men playing backgammon. Another man had joined them and he was watching the game with great interest. He guessed that they were locals when the loser of a game shouted something in Greek. It sounded as if an argument was about to break out but then both men burst into laughter. Greetings were shouted out as they were joined by two other players who brought out another backgammon set and a small table from inside the bar. Mac smiled as he listened to the counters being slammed down and the animated banter of the players. Even though he couldn't understand a word, he felt that he could hazard a guess as to what they were saying from their body language alone.

'I'm sorry, I'm a bit late,' a voice from his left said.

It was the Chief Inspector and he looked a little hot and bothered.

'I'll be with you in a minute,' he continued before he went inside.

Mac could hear him talking to the white-haired man. It sounded as though they knew each other. There was the sound of laughter before he returned with a bottle of coke and sat down next to him. He took a long swallow from the bottle before he said anything else.

'It's been a long day,' he said before taking another swallow.

'Any luck with the man that Harold Jones was seen with?' Mac asked.

'Not yet,' the Chief Inspector replied. 'He's still out in his boat somewhere but we know who he is. His name is Costas Skarparis and he owns a fishing boat that's usually moored in Psarolimano. He does a little fishing and some tourist trips, in fact anything that will earn him a few euros and that's why he's known to us. He's been caught smuggling twice in the past year.'

'Smuggling? Was it anything serious?' Mac asked.

'Not really, cigarettes the first time and counterfeit clothes and trainers the second. He pleaded innocent both times but he was found guilty anyway. He got fined but no prison time. We suspect that he's been involved in more serious smuggling activities but we've not managed to catch him at it so far.'

'So, what on earth was an English tourist doing talking to someone like Mr. Skarparis?' Mac asked.

'That's what we'd like to know,' the Chief Inspector replied. 'We spent the afternoon chasing up a few of his known associates but we learned next to nothing. Oh, apart from the fact that Mr. Skarparis had come into some money. The man who owns the bar he usually drinks at told us that he'd paid up a three month old bar tab not too long ago.'

'That's interesting. Did you get anything from the people at the apartment?' Mac asked.

'We've got a team interviewing the staff and guests but they've not come up with much so far. From what I'm hearing forensics aren't doing any better either. How about you?'

Mac told him what he'd learned from Tommy.

'I'd never have guessed that he was rich,' the Chief Inspector said. 'From his clothes, his personal items and where he was staying, I'd have thought that he was a pensioner on fairly limited means. We get quite a few ex-pats who live here part of the year to make their money go a bit further.'

'It seems that he was a bit of a miser by all accounts. Any luck with the phone?'

'Not yet. We've contacted the local comms company and they're checking for any calls,' the Chief Inspector said before taking another gulp from his coke. 'So, it looks like we're no further ahead.'

'Well, it's only the first day of the investigation, I dare say that something will turn up before long,' Mac said.

'Let's hope so, we're already getting quite a lot of attention from the press so I'd like to get this one done and dusted as soon as possible.'

Their conversation was interrupted by the Chief Inspector's phone. He listened for a while and then looked at his watch.

'Okay, I'll go there now.' As he put his phone away, he looked at Mac. 'One of the receptionists from the

Libretta says that she saw Harold Jones driving a car. She said that it had a sticker on from a local car hire company. I'm just going to check it out before I knock off. Fancy coming?'

Mac should have said 'No' to the Chief Inspector's request, after all he was on holiday and he was supposed to be relaxing, not getting sucked into a murder case. However, if he was being honest, he'd admit that this thought never even entered his mind.

'I'd love to. Just let me finish this beer.'

They climbed into the Chief Inspector's car which was parked at the back of the fort. He turned right and then right again and drove back towards the beach. He pulled into a side street and stopped outside a brightly coloured office. A loud red and yellow sign said, 'Stentor Car Rentals.' As he got out of the car, Mac could see a thin strip of beach, sea and clear blue sky at the bottom of the street.

An electronic beep welcomed them as the Chief Inspector opened the door. A young man with slicked back hair and a slick smile looked up at them from behind a desk. The smile vanished when he saw who it was. It was obvious that he and the Chief Inspector had met before.

'What now?' the young man said before continuing in Greek.

He was interrupted by the Chief Inspector who said, 'Please speak in English. This is Mac Maguire, a policeman from England. Mac, this is John Petrou, late of East London.'

The young man looked at Mac with a mixture of worry and interest.

'What can I do for the filth today?' he asked in a broad London accent.

Petrou's attempt at an insult didn't seem to affect the Chief Inspector's composure in any way.

46

'We've been told that your company hired a car to this man,' the Chief Inspector said as he showed him a photo on his phone. 'His name is Harold Jones.'

'Never heard of him. Look I've got things to do...' the young man said petulantly.

'Just a moment, I have to make a call,' the Chief Inspector said just before he went outside.

Mac looked at Petrou with interest. He'd come across some criminals from the Cypriot community in his time, a few of who had been fearsome indeed. This one was uncomfortable just being looked at. Mac had already marked down John Petrou in his mind as a lightweight.

A few minutes later the Chief Inspector came back in. He was smiling.

'Okay, now, where were we?' he said. 'Oh yes, the man whose photograph I just showed you, did you recognise him?'

Petrou gave this some thought and decided it would be no skin of his nose if he cooperated.

'Yeah, he used us quite a few times over the last four weeks or so.'

'Is there anything else you can tell me about him?' the Chief Inspector asked.

Petrou shrugged.

'Not really, he paid in cash and the vehicles always came back without a scratch.'

'Okay then, thanks,' the Chief Inspector said as he turned for the door.

'Don't you want to see the records?' Petrou asked with a puzzled expression.

Before he answered the Chief Inspector looked out of the door.

'Not really, in a few seconds you'll be visited by a team of three police officers who'll be going through all of your records. They'll find anything related to Mr. Jones but, in order to do that, they'll need to look at everything else that you've got. I'll be more than interested to see what they find.'

'Oh no, please Chief Inspector…' Petrou groaned.

The Chief Inspector held the door open for the three uniformed officers.

'Go through everything,' he told them.

Mac followed him out of the door. He was beginning to get the idea that the Chief Inspector was not a person to be messed with.

As Mac got into the car, he saw that his colleague was smiling.

'We've been hearing that Petrou's been up to some of his old tricks, ripping tourists off mostly, but a few nastier things as well. I've been wanting to have a look at his books for a while and Mr. Jones's murder has just given me the perfect excuse.'

Mac laughed.

'I thought it was because he'd called you 'the filth'.'

'If I did that to everyone who insulted me the jails would be overflowing,' the Chief Inspector replied. 'Fancy a drink?'

Mac did.

'I'll take you to my local, we can get something to eat as well if you like,' the Chief Inspector said.

Chapter Six

The Chief Inspector drove him towards the outskirts of town and into a neighbourhood where the houses seemed to be a little more spread out. Most of them seemed quite new and a few were quite impressively big. He parked the car in front of one of the more modest residences.

'It's just around the corner, if you're okay to walk that far?' the Chief Inspector said.

As the corner was no more than fifty yards away Mac assured him that it would be no problem. It had now gone seven o'clock and some of the heat of the day had gone leaving the evening pleasantly warm. He followed him around the corner and into a doorway below a sign that said, 'Η Ταβέρνα Γωνιά'. They stepped into a cool dark room that had a few tables and chairs scattered about, all of which were unoccupied. The Chief Inspector waved at a barman who was pouring a beer. The barman waved back. Mac expected him to sit down but he kept walking. He went straight through of a set of double glass doors that were propped open and into a garden.

The large open space was filled with greenery and tables covered in green checked tablecloths. Most of the tables here were in use and waiters were busy flitting from table to table carrying drinks and food one way and empty plates and bottles the other. The Chief Inspector found a table and invited Mac to sit down. He did. He looked up and could only see the darkening sky above his head. The whirring sound of cicadas and the movement of the evening breeze told him that he was outdoors. Due to the changeable English weather sitting outside at night was not something he did all that often at home.

'It's quite a lot bigger than you'd think from the front,' Mac said as he looked around. 'What's it called?'

'In English it's the 'Pub on the Corner',' the Chief Inspector replied with a smile.

Mac laughed.

'I thought that it was going to be something exotic.'

'Shall I order us some beer and snacks?' the Chief Inspector asked.

'That sounds good to me.'

The Chief Inspector spoke to the waiter who glanced over at Mac and nodded.

'I've ordered us some meze as you're on holiday.'

'Meze?' Mac asked.

'It's lots of little snacks, like Spanish tapas but better,' he replied with a smile.

Mac gave him a quizzical look.

'You know there's something very familiar about the way you talk,' he said.

The Chief Inspector laughed out loud.

'I was wondering when you'd notice. I'm a Brummie the same as you. I lived in Birmingham for nearly nineteen years. I was brought there from Larnaka when I was three years old. I went to school there and joined the police there too.'

So that was it! Now that Mac knew he could hear the Birmingham accent clearly. He just hadn't been expecting it and because of that he hadn't been able to tune in to it. He was now more than intrigued.

'What part of Birmingham did you live in?' Mac asked as a waiter appeared with two large beers.

'Bordesley Green, opposite the Broadway pub. My dad and his brothers ran a fish and chip shop there.'

Mac was about to have a sip from his drink but instead he put it down and looked at the Chief Inspector with utter astonishment.

'It wasn't called 'The Three Brothers' by any chance?'

It was now the Chief Inspector's turn to look surprised.

'How on earth could you know that?'

'Every Friday evening my mum used to walk from our house on Palace Road and pass by two fish and chip shops on her way to the Three Brothers,' Mac said. 'I remember asking her why and she always said that Cypriots, being from a Mediterranean country, really know how to cook fish and, besides that, Cyprus spuds were the best potatoes in the world. I remember when I was a kid, she always used to look out for them in the greengrocer's shop. If they didn't have red clay sticking to them then she wouldn't be interested.'

'It's a small world,' the Chief Inspector said with a huge smile. 'I used to work in that shop from when I was about ten or so. I don't suppose they'd allow it now but I used to love it.'

'We've probably met before then,' Mac said. 'I used the Three Brothers right up until I went to London when I was twenty-two. I still think that they were just about the best fish and chips I've ever tasted. Tell me, what made you join the police?'

The Chief Inspector shrugged.

'God knows, too much TV I suppose but it was all I ever wanted to do.'

'I take it that you worked out of Digbeth Police Station?' Mac asked.

'That's right and that's where I got my unfortunate nickname.'

'Nickname?' Mac asked.

'Yes, Dave,' the Chief Inspector said with a grimace. 'I turned up on my first day and told the Sergeant that my name was Panayiotis Christodoulou and he just gave me this blank look. Okay, we'll call you Dave, he said and that was it. I've come to terms with it now but I found it really annoying at first.'

'It wasn't that Sergeant with the big nose by any chance?' Mac asked.

'I take it that you've met him too then.'

'Yes, he was my sergeant when I started out just over ten years before you. When I said my name was Dennis Maguire, he took it as being 'MacGuire'. As far as he was concerned if a name had 'Mac' in it then it must be Scottish and so I was christened Mac. He used to make lots of Scottish jokes when I was around and I must admit that I didn't like it much either.'

Mac remembered something.

'Your partner mentioned something about 'seeing Dave' but I didn't have a clue who he was talking about at the time. Do they still call you that here?'

'Unfortunately, yes,' the Chief Inspector said with a rueful smile. 'I made the mistake of mentioning it to one of my colleagues over a beer when I first started with the police here and the next day everyone started calling me 'Dave'. I suppose it started out as a joke but somehow it stuck. Everyone except my family calls me Dave now.'

'How long were you in the police in Birmingham for?' Mac asked.

'Only three years, then my dad got really ill and wanted to go back home to die. So, myself, my mum and my sisters all packed up and went with him. I took some leave from the police but he lasted a lot longer than everyone told us he would. I should have known that anyway, dad never gave up anything without a fight,' Dave said with sad smile. 'Anyway, I ended up having to resign from the police and then I decided to do my military service while I was over here. I enjoyed it, well most of it, but I was

52

still determined to go 'home' to Birmingham once dad had gone but then something happened.'

'That 'something' wouldn't be female by any chance?' Mac asked.

Dave nodded.

'About four months after I joined the army, I was on patrol and we'd stopped for some lunch. We were sitting at the bar of a cafe when I noticed this girl. She was sitting outside with her back to me so I couldn't see her face. She was talking to a friend of hers and waving her hands around as she described something. Even though I couldn't see her face I found her mesmerising. A few minutes later she said goodbye to her friend and walked off. I then had the strangest feeling and I knew that I had to follow her. My partner was surprised when I left my meal half-eaten and ran off without a word. She had a good head start but I still managed to catch up with her. I didn't even stop to think, I tapped her on the shoulder and she turned around.'

Dave gave Mac a misty-eyed look.

'Even though she seemed shocked at being stopped by a soldier she still looked so beautiful. Then I amazed myself by asking her out on a date. She smiled at me and after that I knew that I'd never be able to leave Cyprus again. She gave me a long look up and down before she finally said okay. That was twenty years and three kids ago.'

Mac laughed out loud.

'Yes, life has a way of making the decisions for you sometimes.'

'You're right there,' Dave replied. 'I still have friends and family in Birmingham so I go back from time to time but I've never regretted a second since I met Eleni. I belong here now. However, not everyone on the island thinks that people like me can ever truly belong here. They call us 'English Cypriots', when they're being polite that is.'

'I know exactly what you mean,' Mac said. 'There are people who were born in Ireland and have lived there for decades and, just because they spent some time working in England, the locals still call them 'blow-ins'. I wouldn't mind so much except that it was the people who went to England and sent money home that kept the place afloat when I was young.'

'It was pretty much the same for us,' Dave said. 'The three brothers who went over to England helped to keep a farm and an extended family of eight or nine going over here. I think that people gave up more than they knew when they left to work abroad.'

'That's true...'

Mac was about to say something profound when he was interrupted as plates began arriving at their table. Then more plates came. And yet more.

'We'd better start eating,' Dave said, 'or we're going to need a bigger table.'

Mac's eyes lit up and he was suddenly hungry as plates of dips, olives and vegetables arrived followed by a mound of hot pitta bread. The waiter then brought out a big bowl of salad, bright red tomatoes, red onion and cool green cucumber cut into big chunks and topped with small cubes of feta cheese. He started eating.

He could identify the dips but everything else was a mystery to him. He didn't care, it all tasted wonderful. As plates were emptied more replaced them; potatoes in lemon, aubergines, small Cyprus sausages, meatballs, moussaka, pork in red wine, squid and several varieties of fish were brought in before Mac finally raised his hands in defeat. His taste buds were buzzing with the intensity of the flavours but his stomach was near to bursting.

'You can have more if you want,' Dave said as the waiter brought more beers.

'If I eat another crumb I'll explode,' Mac said truthfully. 'That was just about the nicest meal I've ever had.'

'I can promise that you won't go hungry while you're on the island,' Dave said. 'I don't think that nouvelle cuisine ever really caught on here.'

Dave's words only made Cyprus all the more delightful as far as Mac was concerned.

'So, how did you end up in London?' Dave asked. 'I heard some gossip about you when I was stationed at Digbeth but it all seemed a little unlikely.'

'Well, that's a long story,' Mac said.

'We've got all night,' Dave pointed out.

Mac looked intently at Dave. He found that he was beginning to like his new colleague. Some of this might have been down to him being a fellow Brummie but he suspected that it was his obvious passion for the job that was tipping the balance.

'Okay,' Mac shrugged. 'I've only told this story in its entirety to a few people before. So here goes…

I'd only been a detective for a year or so and hadn't got much further than making the tea when our boss was mysteriously replaced. A new Detective Chief Inspector was appointed and he turned up a few days later from London. His name was Rob Graveley and he brought two new Detective Inspectors with him. To say that this was unusual was to put it mildly. After a few weeks, things seemed to settle down a bit but I think that it would be fair to say that there was still some tension within the team. They didn't like the idea of having detectives from outside foisted on them and especially detectives from London. I think it would also be fair to say that another reason for the tension was that at least a third of the team were on the take in one way or other. While their old boss had more or less tolerated their corrupt scams, they were worried that their new boss might not be the kind who would look the other way.'

'Unfortunately, we've got a few like that here too,' Dave said.

'So have we but, thankfully, not so many as we used to have. Anyway, Rob Graveley quietly did his job and no-one had an inkling that he might be up to anything other than running the team. He was a tall, slim man who was almost totally bald and he had one of those faces that only ever seemed to have one expression. It was impossible to tell if he was happy, sad or angry. I found out later, to my cost, that he was also a terrific poker player.

Anyway, about six weeks or so after he'd arrived, he invited me out for a drink. He drove me to a pub that was well away from where we worked. I guessed that was because he didn't want anyone from the station to see us together which intrigued me. He bought me a pint and explained that he needed my help. I was surprised by this, after all he was a DCI and I was just a lowly detective constable who was still wet behind the ears.

He told me that he'd been looking at every member of the detective team and he thought that I might be the only one he could trust. He said that he needed someone on the inside who could tell him what the team was thinking and who could also provide him with some local knowledge. He also told me the real reason why he was in Birmingham.

The Chief Constable at the time was as lazy as they come. He loved doing all the ceremonial stuff but he was quite happy to leave all the operational matters to his deputy so that he could maximise his time on the golf course. The Deputy Chief Constable was still young, very efficient and, on the surface at least, he seemed to be a model policeman. However, the Home Office had received information from an informant in another case that the Deputy Chief was dirty and that he'd been bought and paid for by the Legge crime family some years before.'

'The Legges?' Dave said. 'I remember hearing some of the older coppers talking about them. They were quite a vicious bunch from what they told me.'

'They were and Ronnie Legge, who was the head of the family, was both very vicious and very smart. He figured that the only way to beat the system was to have it in his pocket. He'd made it his business to seduce politicians, policemen and even local magistrates and judges with free holidays and expensive gifts and then use this as a weapon to blackmail them. This is exactly what he'd done to a young and very promising police inspector who, with Ronnie's help, quickly became Deputy Chief Constable. In effect, Ronnie had the whole of the city's police force in his pocket. That was why the Home Office had sent Rob Graveley to take over the detective team. They had no idea who else in the local police force might have been in Ronnie's pocket so they appointed someone from outside the area.

Rob had come armed with some information that revealed a chink in Ronnie Legge's armour. A lot of people wanted him dead and, in case any of them succeeded, he'd placed evidence about his enemies and everyone he'd corrupted with his solicitor. This solicitor had been ordered to send this evidence to the press as soon as he heard of Ronnie's death. So, even though he might be dead, in that way Ronnie would still get some revenge from the grave. Rob had put together a plan to make the solicitor believe just that.

Luckily for Rob this solicitor was very set in his ways and, as you'll hear, this was what made Rob's plan possible. The whole thing relied on convincing the solicitor that Ronnie Legge had indeed been murdered. Of course, this would be impossible today as we can simply look at our phones to get any information we need, but this was before mobile phones and even before the internet, ancient history really. Anyway, this is how we did it.

Rob got some technical people down from London and we broke into the solicitor's house while he was at work. When he came home, we then broke into his office. I remember that Rob was quite impressed by my lockpicking skills at the time. Anyway, everything was then set for the plan to go into action the morning after.

One of Rob's men had been watching the solicitor for weeks and we knew that he lived alone and always got up at seven thirty on the dot. He then listened to the local news as he ate his breakfast using a small transistor radio to do so. In those days most of these radios also had cassette tape players built-in and this is how our little deception started. It had been rigged so that, when he turned on the radio, it would turn on the cassette player instead.

We'd recorded a fake news segment using one of the actual announcers from the local radio station and this is what the solicitor heard. She started reading out a story about an event that the Mayor would be attending that day but then interrupted it with the breaking news that the notorious local gangster Ronnie Legge and several members of his gang had been found shot dead just a few hours before.

Of course, the solicitor immediately tried to contact Ronnie but we'd rigged the phone so, whatever number was called, it would come to us. Rob answered the phone, identified himself as a policeman and asked who was calling. This was enough for the solicitor. He called for a taxi and one arrived very quickly. It was being driven by a friend of mine, a real taxi driver for authenticity. As he drove off, he mentioned hearing about Ronnie Legge's death on the radio and had a small rant about how all criminals should get the same treatment.

Then, just to keep the ball rolling, as the solicitor arrived at his office, I was standing on a street corner selling newspapers and shouting 'Read all about it, Ronnie Legge dead.'

He tried once again to reach Ronnie from his office but he just got another police officer. He then had to a decision to make and, thankfully for us, he made the right one. A few minutes later he came out with a small suitcase and several bulky envelopes which he placed one by one in a nearby post box. He then climbed back into the taxi and told the driver to take him to the airport. Of course, he drove him straight to the police station instead while we opened up the post box and retrieved all the evidence.

We sent a lot of people to jail using that evidence, including Ronnie Legge and most of the other leaders of the gang. The gang's territory was then carved up amongst its rival gangs and the Legge crime family became history. Ronnie himself died in jail a year later after being stabbed with a shiv. The Deputy Chief Constable and a local magistrate also went to jail but most of those mentioned in the evidence were allowed to quietly leave public life. These included at least a quarter of the detective team. I guess that the breadth of Legge's corruption was too much even for the Home Office to admit to publicly.'

'And what happened to you?' Dave asked.

'I was sent to Coventry.'

'What? No-one would talk to you?'

'No, it was even worse in a way, I was actually sent to Coventry,' Mac replied. 'I worked on the detective team there for four months, the most miserable four months of my life...well, until recently that is.'

'Why did they make you work there though?' Dave asked.

'It was felt that there might be some animosity in the team towards me,' Mac explained. 'It's that stupid idea that some policemen have that you must cover for your mates even if they're dirty and on the take. Rob was very much of the opinion that anyone who breaks the law, even a policeman, is a criminal and should be treated as such. I've taken that very much to heart myself.'

'So, how did you end up working at the Met then?'

'After four very long months I got a call from Rob Graveley. I thought that he'd forgotten about me but he hadn't. He offered me a job on a new murder team he was putting together in London and, of course, I jumped at the chance. Within a few years I'd started rising through the ranks but I wasn't all that ambitious at the time believe it or not, it was the job that I loved. Rob had made sure that everyone on his team were clean and he also tried to make it as diverse as possible. I tried to do the same myself when I eventually took over.'

'Well, you've certainly had a successful career. I've read up on a lot of your cases over the years, especially the Perkis investigation. You were really good at your job,' Dave said.

'Thanks for saying that but any success I may have had was mainly down to Rob Graveley,' Mac replied. 'He was the best copper I've ever worked with and I learned pretty much everything I know from him. So, you're now one of the very few people who know the dark secret as to why I left Birmingham for London.'

'Thanks,' Dave said with some sincerity.

When he'd realised that the totally forgettable middle-aged man he'd met was, in fact, the famous Mac Maguire, he'd wondered what he'd be like. He certainly hadn't been expecting someone so open and so self-effacing. Dave realised that he was really enjoying their time together.

They spent the next half-hour sipping beer and comfortably reminiscing about the city that they both grew up in, a city that no longer existed. Then Dave got a text.

'I'd better get going. Eleni's back and our youngest wants a story before he'll go to sleep,' he said.

'Stories are important,' Mac said.

'Do you want me to get Eleni to drop you back home?' Dave asked.

'No, I'm okay. I've got a taxi number that I can call.'

Mac pulled the card from his wallet.

'Do you mind if I have a look?' Dave asked.

Mac passed him the card.

'I know Michalis, I've used him myself from time to time. You're lucky, he won't rip you off like some of the taxi drivers around here would,' Dave said as he handed the card back. 'We're having a catch up at nine thirty tomorrow at the station. Do you want me to pick you up?'

Mac didn't hesitate.

'I'll be sitting outside in the square.'

'I'll see you tomorrow then,' Dave said with a smile. 'Oh, as he mainly works the area around your apartment, it might be worth asking Michalis if he ever picked up Harold Jones and, if he did, where he took him. I'll send you a photo of him before I go.'

'I'll do that,' Mac said.

He rang for his ride as he watched Dave walk away. Michalis told him that he'd be about twenty minutes so Mac slowly made his way outside, found a comfortable wall to sit on and waited.

He smiled as he thought of the alacrity with which he'd jumped at the chance to be at the briefing tomorrow. He knew that it was really an invitation to join Dave's team for the duration of the case. He supposed it wasn't illogical as he was officially the liaison between the Larnaka and UK police forces but he was still glad that Dave wanted him to be part of the investigation.

For himself, he found that he desperately wanted to know why Harold Jones had ended up dead on the street and who had put him there. His phone told him he had a text and he read the short update that Kate had sent him. It was good to hear that the investigation was getting underway back in the UK as well.

He was still thinking about the case when the old Mercedes pulled up in front of him.

'Back to your apartment?' Michalis asked as Mac climbed in.

'Yes please,' Mac replied.

'How was your dinner with Dave?'

Mac gave his driver a puzzled look.

'It was great actually but how on earth did you know about that?'

'I guessed. I know that Dave Christodoulou eats at the taverna a lot as he lives just around the corner,' Michalis said with a little smile.

Mac thought of his old friend Blue McParland who had started out as a taxi driver and had ended up as a private detective as well. Blue always said that if you wanted to know anything ask a taxi driver. They see and hear everything even though many of their passengers seem to think that they're deaf and blind once they're in the back of a cab.

'There's a man who was staying at my apartment, Harold Jones. Did you ever pick him up?' Mac asked.

Michalis gave him a sidelong glance.

'So, it's true then, that you're an English policeman and that you're working with Dave Christodoulou?'

'Yes, that's right,' Mac replied wondering how he'd figured that out.

'I have lots of policemen who are customers,' Michalis said answering the question that Mac hadn't asked. 'I wouldn't have guessed that you were a policeman though.'

'I'm retired mostly these days but I help out now and again.'

'Harold Jones, he's the dead man?'

'Yes, that's right,' Mac replied.

'I don't know the name. Have you got a photo?'

By the time Mac had gotten up the photo of Harold Jones that Dave had sent him they'd pulled up outside his apartment block. Mac passed his phone to Michalis. He studied the photo for a few moments and then looked up and to his left. Mac let him think in silence.

'Yes, I remember him. I picked him up twice I think, both around five or six weeks ago. Once from outside the apartment here and once from outside a bar just off Kalograion, not too far from the police station. I drove him back here.'

'What was the bar called?' Mac asked.

Michalis shrugged.

'I've no idea, I was given the street name and was told that it was an English bar. When I got there, I could see that they had a Chelsea football shirt in a glass case on the wall. You shouldn't have any trouble finding it, we used to have lots of English bars here years ago but not so many now.'

'When you picked him up from outside the apartment, where did you take him?' Mac asked.

'I dropped him off outside a garage. As they mostly sold second-hand cars, I guess that he must have been interested in buying one. It was over on Luther King

Street and, if I remember rightly, it was called Kirios Motors.'

Mac got Michalis to write down the directions for both the bar and the garage in as much detail as he could. He gave him a good tip before he climbed out of the car. As he walked towards the lift, he decided that he was quite impressed by his taxi driver.

He sat on the balcony and thought about what he'd learned as he watched the late evening's comings and goings in the square below. He thought about the bar that Michalis had dropped Harold Jones at and wondered if it was an ex-pat's watering hole. He also wondered at Mr. Jones looking at cars. He'd been hiring quite a lot of them recently so why might he have suddenly felt the need to own his own vehicle?

He was lost in thought until he finally noticed that the square was getting empty. He looked at his watch and found that it was quite a bit later than he'd thought. He went straight to bed and prayed that sleep would come soon.

He smiled as he lay there. He had a briefing to go to the next morning.

Chapter Seven

At the same time that the first plates of food were arriving at Mac's table, Kate and Tommy were sitting in the Major Crime Unit's team room at Letchworth Police Station waiting for the third member of their little team to arrive. It had been a long hard day and they were both feeling tired. Detective Inspector Colin Furness from the City of London Police Economic Crime Department had told them that he'd already started looking into the case but, as he didn't have anything else on at the moment, he'd decided to join the team in person for the next few days at least.

'So, what did he say?' Tommy asked Kate.

She'd been miles away and looked up at Tommy with some surprise. When she'd first met Detective Constable Nugent, he'd seemed so incredibly young but he was starting to fill out a little now and she could see that he was really growing into the job. She wouldn't be surprised if he made sergeant before too long.

'He said that he thought that the case would be fun, believe it or not,' Kate replied.

She pulled a face that made Tommy laugh. He liked Kate. While she had a hell of a temper, she was a good copper and she could be good fun to be with at times as well. He and his girlfriend Bridget had started socialising with Kate and her partner Toni and they'd had some nice evenings out with them.

'Anyway, Mac says that he's got incredible skills when it comes to tracking down dirty money so he sounds like he's just what we need…'

Kate was interrupted by the office door being flung open with a bang. It revealed a diffident man in his late thirties with a very embarrassed look on his face.

'Oh, I'm sorry about that. My bag,' he explained looking down at the small black suitcase he had in his hand. 'I've reserved a room in the hotel just down the road but I thought that I'd pop in here first to see what the lay of the land was like.'

Although it was far from cold that evening, he was dressed in corduroy trousers, a white shirt and a blue tie that was at half-mast, a pullover and a green flecked tweed jacket. Accompanied by his unkempt curly hair, tortoise-shell glasses and slightly dazed expression Kate thought that it made him look like the stereotypical academic. She quickly berated herself for making such assumptions. She held her hand out.

'I'm DS Kate Grimsson and this is DC Tommy Nugent.'

'DI Colin Furness,' he said as he dropped the suitcase and shook Kate's hand.

He then shook Tommy's hand. Besides the small suitcase he also had a backpack. He took it off, pulled out a laptop and sat down.

'I've already started having a look at Mr. Jones's finances and I must say it's been absolutely fascinating. It's been a little easier than most money laundering cases so far as Mr. Jones is dead and part of a murder enquiry. That helps immensely when it comes to getting access to his financial information.'

'Is it true that he was quite rich?' Kate asked.

'Well, yes and no,' Colin replied. 'I need to look at it in more depth of course but, if we put all his holdings together, he was worth well over four hundred and fifty million pounds just six months ago. Here I'll show you.'

He fired up his laptop and showed a slew of graphs and spreadsheets to Kate and Tommy. Although they failed to understand most of it, they managed to get most of Colin's drift.

'So, you're saying that Harold Jones was worth over four hundred and fifty million pounds six months ago and now he's worth absolutely nothing,' Kate said looking puzzled.

'I'll need to confirm a few things but that's about it as far as I can see,' Colin replied. 'He sold his holdings in just about every business he had a finger in, often at a loss. I'm not sure exactly how much he raised by this but I'd guess that it would be around three hundred and twenty million or so. He's taken quite a tanking so there must have been some very good reasons for doing it this way.'

'So, where's all the money gone?' Tommy asked.

'I've no idea,' Colin said with a shrug of his shoulders, 'but that's the crucial question and it's the one that I'm going to be concentrating on for now. I think that it may well shed some light on why he was murdered. After all that amount of money is well worth killing for, in some people's eyes at least. Have you come up with anything new since we last spoke?'

'No, not a lot,' Kate replied. 'Mr. Jones seems to have been a secretive man who had no friends and no relations, or so we were told. We only discovered a couple of hours ago that he does actually have a relation, a granddaughter who lives in Stevenage. We've called her and arranged an interview for tomorrow morning.'

'When it comes to murder cases and money, family members are usually a good place to start,' Colin said. 'Is she mentioned in his will?'

'We've no idea,' Kate said. 'We'll be seeing Mr. Jones's solicitors right after we interview his granddaughter.'

'Okay, as for me I've found a money trail that sort of leads to Australia so I'd like to work from here for a few hours if that's okay,' Colin said. 'It'll be morning there soon so I should be able to start asking some questions from one of my opposite numbers in Sydney.'

'Okay then, we'll leave you to it,' Kate said. 'We can have a catch up here at nine tomorrow if that's okay?'

'Yes, that should be fine,' Colin replied without looking up from his computer screen.

As Kate and Tommy walked towards the door leading into the car park Tommy asked, 'What did you make of him?'

She hesitated and decided not to tell him what her first thoughts of their new colleague were.

'I'm not sure to be honest but Mac rates him and that's good enough for me.'

'I'd bet that he and Martin might get on well together,' Tommy said.

Kate laughed. Martin Selby was the Major Crime Unit's computer and data expert and, for all that he worked through a computer screen, he'd probably helped to crack more cases than any of them. She knew that Mac thought very highly of him too.

'I wouldn't bet against that,' Kate said. 'See you tomorrow.'

Tommy's mention of Mac reminded Kate that a quick update might not be a bad thing. It was a fine light early summer evening so she sat on a nearby wall and put together a few bullet points explaining where they were up to before texting them off to Mac.

She sat there for a while and thought about Harold Jones to whom money seemed to have been everything. She'd had experience of men like him. For most of his life her father had been one of them. He'd only become human once he knew he was dying and, luckily, she'd been able to make her peace with him before he went.

68

Thinking of the misery that her father must have inflicted on so many others over the years in his insane pursuit of money made her feel sad. She tried to shake the negative thoughts out of her head as she walked down the street to the little flat that she shared with her partner. She was late and Toni would be waiting for her. They'd have a glass of wine and cuddle up on the sofa for a chat before dinner. She smiled knowing that all her sadness would soon be forgotten.

Chapter Eight

Mac sat in the square sipping at his second cup of coffee and avidly watching everything that was going on around him. He looked up at the tower of the honey-coloured church, now glowing in the early morning sun, and thought how different it now looked compared to the shadowy and quite sombre edifice of the previous evening.

People were coming and going, some sitting idly outside one of the cafes just as he was, while others clearly had places to be and things to do. The majority, however, seemed to be sauntering slowly into the square before consulting their guidebooks and then taking the obligatory selfies or group photos in front of the church before drifting off to the next item on their tourist check list.

Another tourist group had assembled outside the church. The members of this group looked somewhat different to the ones he'd seen before and their guide didn't seem all that impressed with them. They were dressed in shorts and skimpy tops and looked as if they should be heading for the beach rather than for the inside of a church. He watched with interest as red cloths were handed to some of the women so that they could cover their legs whilst they were inside the church. Some refused and walked away while others were glad enough to take them, even some of the men. He watched as a somewhat reduced group headed inside the church and wondered what they were getting out of it.

He was curious about the church and wanted to get a look inside it himself at some point but he decided that he'd dress for the occasion. It was someone's holy place after all.

His thoughts were interrupted by the arrival of a police car. It wasn't Dave who waved at him though, it was his young partner. Mac realised that he didn't know his name.

'Thanks...er...' Mac said as he climbed into the passenger seat.

'The name's Andreas Kalorkoti, Sergeant Andreas Kalorkoti, but everyone calls me Andy,' Andy said helpfully.

His accent sounded familiar too.

'You're from London?' Mac asked a little tentatively.

'Yes, from Croydon actually. I was born there,' he explained.

It was such a short drive that Mac didn't think it would be worth asking any more questions but he was intrigued. He looked over at Andy as he drove. He was of medium height and had a light beard but his dark hair was cut quite short. He had a slim waist and wide shoulders so Mac guessed that he regularly worked out.

He found it more than strange that, being just a stone's throw away from the Middle East, he'd found himself working with two Cypriot policemen called Dave and Andy.

At the police station the briefing room was full and, despite the ceiling fans and the earliness of the start, it was already quite warm and stuffy. Dave was talking to the team when Mac and Andy walked in. He waved at them without breaking the flow of his words. Although he was thousands of miles from home the scene was incredibly familiar to Mac.

'I'll try and translate as we go along if you like,' Andy offered.

Mac gladly accepted his offer. He sat and watched the body language of the policemen and women around him while Andy supplied the words.

It seemed that the interviews conducted so far hadn't provided much in the way of leads. The teams had managed to interview everyone staying in the apartment block as well as in the hotel on the other side of the square. They'd also spoken to most of the people who worked in the local cafes, restaurants and shops around the square. Apart from one local shop that had regularly supplied Mr. Jones with some basic foodstuffs and the café on the ground floor of his apartment, no-one had recognised his photo. It seemed that he hadn't left much of a footprint on the island during his long stay.

This gave Mac some food for thought. For him, part of the fun of being on holiday was the experience of eating and drinking out but Harold Jones appeared to have holed himself up in his apartment. That didn't sound like much of a holiday to Mac. So, if he wasn't in Larnaka on holiday, then exactly what was he doing here?

Mac was jolted from his thoughts by Dave's voice.

'Former Detective Chief Superintendent Mac Maguire is now our liaison officer with the UK Police,' he said in English by way of introduction. 'Mac, have the team in Hertfordshire come up with anything yet?'

The whole team turned and looked at him with interest.

'Yes, a few things. It seems that Mr. Jones has a relative after all. He has a granddaughter who lives in Stevenage, it's not far from Knebworth where he lived. The team are going to interview her this morning. They're also going to see Mr. Jones' solicitor in order to get a copy of his will. The team has also just been joined by a fraud expert from the London Police, DI Colin Furness. He's had an initial look at Mr. Jones' finances and it would seem that, until recently at least, he was worth well over four hundred million pounds.'

Mac paused and let this sink in.

'It would also seem that all his money has recently disappeared. Finding where that money has gone may play a major part in solving this crime,' Mac said.

'Thanks Mac,' Dave said. 'I've got the number of a financial expert from the Nicosia police who's willing to help us out. If you could let us have DI Furness's number, then they can talk between themselves.'

Dave then told the teams what he wanted them to do next. They were to expand their enquiries to cover businesses further out from the square as well as check on all the local car rental companies in Larnaka just in case Mr. Jones had used more than one company to hire his cars. Lastly, he told them that he would be holding a news conference just after six o'clock and that he'd need everyone to work late to man the phones for a couple of hours.

From the groans Mac knew that this last bit didn't go down all that well with the team. Dave came over to him as his team dispersed and got to work.

'Did Michalis give you anything last night?' he asked.

Mac told him what his taxi driver had said. He then handed him the directions that Michalis had written down.

'Okay,' Dave said with a smile. 'Let's get going.'

They made their way to Kalograion which took all of two minutes. It took slightly longer than that to find the bar.

The 'Tornado Pub' was tucked away down a side street and had a little sign outside showing a jet bomber taking off into a clear blue sky. Mac could clearly see a royal blue Chelsea football shirt in a case on the wall through the glass door. It was only slightly obscured by the 'Closed' sign.

Dave knocked loudly on the door but no-one came.

'I suppose it is a bit early,' he said. 'We'll come back later. Okay, let's try this garage.'

It took them over fifteen minutes to make it through the traffic to Luther King Street. Kyrios Motors was a small garage that only had a dozen or so cars on display. Mac followed Dave and Andy inside. A fat man dressed in a crisp white short-sleeved shirt rose from behind a desk. His smile only lasted for the fraction of a second that it took him to realise that his visitors weren't customers.

'Can I help you?' he asked with no enthusiasm at all.

Dave showed him his warrant card. He asked him something in Greek and the fat man nodded.

'And your name is?' Dave continued in English.

'George Masalis, I'm the owner,' he replied.

Dave got his phone out and showed Mr. Masalis a photo of Harold Jones. He visibly relaxed when he realised that their visit wasn't directly connected to him or his business.

'Have you ever seen this man?' Dave asked.

The fat man looked carefully at the photo and then slowly shook his head.

'Who is he?' he asked as he handed the phone back to Dave.

'His name is Harold Jones, does that name sound familiar to you?'

His reply to Dave's question was another slow shake of his head.

'Are you sure that you've never had any dealings with Mr. Jones?' Dave asked.

'Look around, we're a small garage,' Mr. Masalis said. 'I sell a few cars and repair a few cars, all local customers. We don't generally deal with tourists.'

Dave looked around and he could see what he meant. In all of the cars that were for up for sale

74

there wasn't a single jeep or convertible amongst them.

'Okay, thanks Mr. Masalis,' Dave said.

Mr. Masalis gave them a genuine smile as they headed for the door. Dave stood outside thinking.

'What else is around here?' he eventually asked Andy.

Andy got his phone out and started looking.

'Are you thinking that Mr. Jones might have gotten dropped off here to disguise where he was really going?' Mac asked.

'Yes, as we've learned so little about him, I'd guess that he might have been the type of man who didn't like others knowing what he was up to,' Dave replied.

Mac looked down at his crutch.

'He was old. How far could he walk? Do you know?'

'I'm not sure but, as he used a stick, it might not have been too far,' Dave replied.

Andy passed the phone to Dave and said, 'There's a branch of the Bank of Cyprus just around the corner and next to that there's a brokerage house, DB International Brokers. Just down the road opposite us there's the Department of Lands and Surveys but otherwise it's just the usual mix of supermarkets and shops.'

'Let's try the brokerage house first,' Dave said. 'That sounds like something that Mr. Jones might have been interested in.'

The broker's office was in a tall tower block. It wouldn't have merited a second look in most cities but, as Larnaka didn't have too many tall buildings, it really stood out. They took the lift to the fifth floor and waited in the plush lobby for the firm's business manager to arrive.

A nervous and prematurely balding man in his late thirties eventually joined them and ushered them into an empty office. The building was thankfully air conditioned but, even so, the man was sweating and fidgety. Like the car salesman he visibly relaxed when Dave asked him about Harold Jones and showed him the photo.

'I'm afraid that we can't divulge anything about our clients without their prior approval,' the broker said feeling on more familiar ground.

'I'm afraid that Mr. Jones can't give you his approval,' Dave replied. 'He's dead. We think he was murdered.'

'Oh,' the broker said looking somewhat flustered again. 'I don't...I mean...' He stopped and gathered himself. 'We'd still need some sort of permission from his next of kin...I'd guess.'

'Before we go there could you at least check your records and see if he actually was a customer,' Dave suggested.

'Oh, yes of course. Do you have an address?'

Dave gave the broker Harold Jones' address in Knebworth as well as Libretta House just in case. The broker disappeared.

'He looked a little nervous, didn't you think?' Mac said.

'With the amount of dark money swirling around the island I wouldn't be at all surprised,' Dave said. 'I've heard that one Russian oligarch described Cyprus as his 'personal piggy bank'. I'd guess that just about every broker on the island might have something to hide.'

The broker came back with a smile on his face.

'Our records have told us that we've had no dealings with anyone called Harold Jones from England.'

'Could he have used an intermediary or another name?' Dave asked.

The smile disappeared.

'I suppose he could have but...but how would we know?' the broker said with a baffled look.

'Indeed,' Dave said as he stood up. 'Thanks anyway.'

They tried the bank next and, although the manager was more than cooperative, they got no further.

'Just the Land Office left,' Dave said. 'Mac, are you okay to walk there? I can always get the car around.'

'No, I should be alright, it's not too far,' he replied.

Quite surprisingly his back didn't feel too bad at all.

The Land Office was a large and quite plain five storied building just a few minutes walk from where they'd left the police car. However, the day was starting to heat up and Mac was quite relieved when they walked into the coolness of the air-conditioned lobby. Dave showed his warrant card and asked the receptionist if he could see the District Land Officer.

They weren't kept waiting long. A small woman in her fifties dressed all in black approached them a few minutes later and held out her hand. She said something in Greek and then Dave replied turning to look at Mac.

'Yes, of course we can speak in English,' she said with a smile as she also turned to look at Mac. 'My name is Mrs. Katsaris and I'm the District Land Officer for Larnaka. My office is this way.'

They followed her down a corridor lined with filing cabinets and into a sizeable office which had its fair share of filing cabinets too. She sat down behind a large desk and gestured for them to take a seat.

'So, how can we help the police?' she asked getting straight to the point.

Dave told her about the circumstances surrounding the death of Harold Jones and the fact that he was dropped off not far from the Land Office some weeks ago.

'Would it be possible for you to check your records just in case Mr. Jones visited this office for some reason?'

'Of course,' she said. 'This shouldn't take long.'

She tapped away at her laptop for less than a minute and then looked up at them and smiled.

'I can confirm that a Mr. Harold Jones from Knebworth in the UK paid us a visit just over five weeks ago. He simply had to sign some papers with regard to the transfer of a parcel of land. We could have sent him the papers but he must have wanted the transfer to go through as quickly as possible as he came here and signed them in person.'

'How big was this parcel of land?' Dave asked.

'I'm afraid that I'll need a formal request from you before I can release any information,' she said.

'Of course, I'll arrange that now,' Dave said pulling out his phone.

He made the call while Mac, Andy and Mrs. Katsaris looked at each other in a slightly uncomfortable silence. It was thankfully a short call.

'You'll have an email from our office within the next ten minutes or so,' Dave said.

'Very well, I'll trust you on that,' Mrs. Katsaris said as she looked at her computer. 'Mr. Jones bought a small parcel of land from a Mr. Pitsillides. It's just sixteen hectares in area and it's situated a few kilometres east of Pano Lefkara. From what I can see of it on the map, it looks like it's mostly rocks.'

'Did he say why he wanted the land?' Dave asked.

'No, but that's not something we'd normally ask our clients anyway,' she replied.

'Is that the only transaction he was involved in?' Dave asked.

'It was,' she said as she looked again at her computer screen. 'Your request has arrived. I can put all the information on a memory stick for you if you like?'

It was clear that their time was up and that she had better things to do.

'Yes, that would be fine,' Dave said.

As they walked back to the car Andy said, 'Well, one out of three wasn't bad.'

'It just deepens the mystery though, doesn't it?' Dave said. 'What would a multi-millionaire from England want with a few hectares of mountainside?'

'How far is the parcel of land from here?' Mac asked.

'About thirty kilometres or so as the crow flies,' Dave replied.

'And about fifty by road,' Andy said. 'I've been up that way before. The road to Pano Lefkara itself isn't too bad. The town's supposed to be famous for its lace and silver so a few tourists manage to make their way up there. However, some of the roads in the area where that parcel of land is are terrible, if they're there at all that is.'

'Okay, in that case we'll go back to the station and get a jeep,' Dave said. 'With any luck we'll at least get to see this Mr. Pitsillides and find out why Harold Jones was so keen on buying his land.'

'I think I'll have to sit this one out,' Mac said with some sadness.

While he was sad at having to drop out, even the thought of sitting in a jeep while bumping up a rocky mountain road was making his back hurt.

'No problem,' Dave said. 'You're on holiday anyway Mac, so do a few tourist things and I'll meet up with you later this evening. I'll give you a call.'

Dave dropped Mac back at his apartment before heading back to the police station. He looked at his watch. It wasn't even twelve o'clock yet. He didn't have to think about what to do next. A few minutes later he'd changed into his swimming shorts and was headed towards the beach.

An hour or so of zero gravity in sea water made his back feel wonderful as well as keeping him cool. He dried himself off and then made for a bench so he could put his sandals on. He sat there watching the

79

sunbathers and people strolling by while he dried off some more. He noticed some people coming out of the fort and Dave's suggestion that he should do some 'tourist things' popped back into his head.

He wandered over to the open door and noticed that it was only two and a half euros to go in. As he had to leave his bag while he was in the sea, he only ever kept some loose change in it for a drink. He decided that he'd go in. The fort thankfully wasn't very large and he was able to walk around the interior in a matter of minutes. He decided to chance the steps which led up to the battlements and he was glad that he did so. The view over the bay was magnificent. A few rusty old cannons still pointed out over the water. He could now understand why the fort was where it was. From this point it totally commanded the whole bay.

He walked on and found himself looking down the entire length of the Piale Pasa. The esplanade swung in an arc into the distance with the bottle-green sea on one side and a ragged jumble of buildings on the other. In between was the walkway and road and, dotted along its length, there were small fluffy green trees. From here they looked remarkably like the fake ones that you see on arch-itect's models.

He could also see the bar that he met Dave at the previous evening. The white-haired man was sitting outside. Mac saw him waving at the odd car that went by while a lone backgammon player sat on the pavement opposite waiting for someone to join him.

Unfortunately standing on the battlements also meant he was total exposed to the sun and he suddenly felt as if he were overheating. He carefully went back down the steps and noticed the sign pointing to a little museum. It would probably be cooler in there but, unfortunately, he'd have to climb more steps to get inside. He decided not to chance it. He'd quite enjoyed his stay and learning about how the fort had changed hands from the Cypriots to the Ottomans and finally to the British.

He was about to walk through the exit when he noticed that there was a room to his left. He hadn't seen it when he'd walked in. It looked cool and dark so he went inside. It only took him a few seconds to work out what it had been used for. When he did it sent a shiver down his spine. The floorboards only covered half the room and they ended at a wooden balustrade that was about waist height. Beyond that there was a drop of about ten or twelve feet.

A black and white photo on the wall showed the room as it had originally been in the 1950's. A large rectangular flap was open showing the drop and above it there hung a noose.

A hangman's noose.

Chapter Nine

Mac looked more closely at the photo. A lever could be seen situated at the far end of the room. The flap would be up and locked while the unfortunate prisoner had the noose fitted around his neck. The lever would then be pulled and the prisoner would fall into the void with the noose breaking his fall and, hopefully, his neck.

The last hanging in the UK took place in 1964 so Mac had thankfully been born far too late to witness capital punishment in action. However, he'd spoken to some of his older colleagues about it when he'd first started in the police. Not one of them had a good word to say about the experience.

He turned to go. He felt contaminated by just being in the room. There was a photo on the wall just by the door. It was the head shot of a young man. Mac went over and read the English version of the text below the photo –

'In 1959 Nicos Leonidas was the last man to be hanged in this room. He was just twenty when he was arrested by the British authorities. With several others he was then accused of the murder of a policeman and, in a rushed trial, was quickly found guilty. Evidence was later uncovered that totally discredited the charge and it seems that Nicos Leonidas was most likely killed because of his work as a pamphleteer for EOKA and for his patriotic poems. These were viewed as being seditious by the authorities but he kept writing even though his poems were officially banned. Despite his death his poetry has lived on and it has been read and appreciated by Cypriots ever since.'

Mac looked again at the photo. A dreamy-faced and impossibly young man with black curly hair looked up to the sky with a small smile on his mouth. He managed to leave the room without looking at the drop again. As he walked out the recording of a muezzin calling the faithful to prayer could be heard floating on the air from the nearby minaret. The song sounded sad and plaintive and resonated exactly with how Mac felt.

He stepped out of the shadows and bathed in the sun's rays as though they might act as some sort of spiritual disinfectant. He walked out of the fort and back to the beach without looking back. He sat down on a bench and processed the experience.

In over thirty years of policing that was the first time he'd ever knowingly visited an execution site. He'd never been a fan of capital punishment and couldn't understand how any policeman could be. The job was hard enough without the added pressure of never being able to make a mistake. With capital punishment any mistake would quite literally be fatal.

He remembered one case in particular that had happened quite early on in his career. Whichever way Mac had looked at it, it seemed to be an open and shut case. The accused had previous form for violence and the evidence against him looked insurmountable. The man had never stopped pleading his innocence though, even though he'd been unanimously found guilty of murder by a jury and had been packed off to jail for life. He was cleared two years later when some new evidence emerged that had proved his innocence. Mac had met him when he came out of jail and had apologised to him in person. He'd been magnanimous enough to shake Mac's hand.

He'd learned a lesson from that case and afterwards he always made it his practice to constantly interrogate the evidence and to accept nothing on face value. He'd also tried to be open enough to admit where weaknesses in a case existed and to not brush them under the carpet. He was just glad that, in that particular case, he could apologise in person rather than having to do it by placing flowers on a grave.

He looked around him and immediately felt a little silly. Everyone else was smiling and having fun. This was not a place to be gloomy in. Mac got up and headed back to his apartment. An hour's rest and a shower and he'd be ready for anything.

He slept for nearly two hours and awoke feeling a little groggy but somewhat better. He had a coffee and a sandwich in the square and thought about what he might do with his evening. He knew that Dave would be busy with the press conference and after that he'd be fielding calls from the public. If he was going to catch up with Mac, it probably wouldn't be this side of nine o'clock. However, there was something he could do.

He rang Michalis who said that he'd pick him up in fifteen minutes. As he waited, he wondered how Dave and Andy were getting on in Pano Lefkara. He pictured the jeep jolting from side to side as it made its way up a rocky track and he was more than glad that he wasn't in it. He was still thinking about this when the old Mercedes came to a halt on the other side of the square.

As Mac walked towards the taxi he slowed down as he saw Michalis get out and walk around the front of the car to intercept him. Mac stopped unsure of what to do. Michalis stood looking at him for a few seconds before he hugged Mac fiercely and then kissed him on both cheeks. To say Mac was surprised was putting it mildly.

'Thank you, thank you from all of my family,' he said dramatically before walking back around the car and climbing back into the driver's seat.

Mac stood there nonplussed for a moment until he decided that he'd better get in. Michalis beamed at him and he started to get a little worried.

'I'm sorry Mr. Maguire but I just had to say it,' Michalis said. 'Where are we going?'

'To the Tornado Pub, the bar that you dropped Harold Jones at,' Mac replied.

'Ah, so that's what it's called. I used to see the Tornado jets taking off and landing at Akrotiri when I was young. You couldn't mistake them, like something from Star Wars they were.'

'Akrotiri?' Mac asked.

'It's an RAF base not far from here. It's been there since the 1950s and it's been quite busy over the last few years what with all the trouble in Syria and Iraq.'

The pub sign now made sense to Mac. It sounded as if it wasn't just an ex-pats pub but an ex-forces pub too.

'Do you mind me asking why you were thanking me a couple of minutes ago?'

'As I said, for helping my family. I had a few minutes spare and so I called my cousin George in Luton to catch up on the family news. I told him about the murder and I mentioned you...'

The penny now dropped.

'I take it that you're related to Spiros Andreou and his family?' Mac asked.

'Of course, I'm his first cousin. His father and my father were brothers. The murder of his son Stelios hit us all hard, me especially I suppose with him being a fellow taxi driver.'

It had been Mac's first case as a private detective[1] and one that he'd never forget. It had all started when a young girl's body had been found in the boot of a car after a random collision. Her grieving mother had asked him to try and find out how she died. He'd eventually joined forces with the Luton police detective team but the killer had still managed to carry out two more murders, both due to grudges he'd been nursing.

---

[1] *The Body in the Boot – the first Mac Maguire mystery*

One was a university professor and the other was Stelios Andreou, the joint owner of a Luton taxi company.

'How is Spiros doing?' Mac asked.

Stelios' father Spiros had arrived on the murder scene not long after Mac had. He'd identified his dead son in the ambulance and had then looked up at Mac. It was a look so bleak and so despairing that Mac had never forgotten it. Spiros' whole life had revolved around his eight sons and their families. The murder had affected him so deeply that Mac wondered if he'd ever get over it.

They pulled up outside the bar. The sign now said 'Open'.

'He's okay from what George told me. It seems that little Stelios is keeping him busy,' Michalis replied with a smile.

'Little Stelios?'

'Yes, he was born eight months or so after his father was killed. Stelios' wife, Sofia, is still living in the family house as she's doing a university degree. Spiros has sold the kebab shop and so he now gets to see a lot of his grandson.'

Mac remembered interviewing Sofia just after her husband had been killed. She'd only just learned of her pregnancy that morning and, after years of trying, she was finally going to have a child. Her sister said that she'd laughed and cried at the same time when she'd heard the news.

'I'm really glad, a child will help him to heal.'

'Anyway, when I called George and mentioned your name, he told me that you were part of the police team that found the man who killed Stelios and that also caught the man who was behind the whole thing. Again, I say thank you.'

Michalis wouldn't accept a cent as fare and, short of resorting to violence, Mac couldn't think of any way of making him. He stood on the pavement and watched the Mercedes drive away and wondered at how small the world can be sometimes.

He turned and looked through the glass window into the bar. It wasn't doing great business by the look of it. He looked at his watch. It was only half past five so he supposed it was still early. He pushed open the door and walked in.

A bluff stocky man with iron grey hair looked up from his newspaper. Mac guessed that he was probably in his early sixties but he clearly hadn't allowed himself to go pear-shaped like so many men around that age do, himself included.

'What can I get you?' he asked.

His accent had a slight twang of the West Country about it. Gloucestershire perhaps, Mac guessed.

'I'll have a pint of Keo, please,' Mac replied.

As his pint was being poured, he sat down on a bar stool and looked around the room. There were only four other people there; three men, all around the same age as the barman, and a young woman. They were all sitting at a table together. One of the men had a bushy beard and long hair on top of which was perched a bright red cap with yellow lettering spelling out 'Make America Great Again'. The conversation they'd been having stopped and they all turned and looked at him in silence.

Mac took a gulp from his beer. It was cold and crisp and hit the spot.

'First time in the Tornado?' the barman asked as he wiped the counter.

'Yes, it is,' Mac replied.

'The sign was it? We sometimes get the odd English tourist come in just to see what the sign's about.'

Mac thought for a moment and decided that he might as well be honest. He dug his police warrant card from his wallet and laid it on the counter. Apart from looking a little puzzled, the barman's demeanour didn't change at all. A man with nothing to hide it would seem.

'So, what can we do for the police?' the barman asked.

Mac noticed that the conversation behind him had stopped again. It seemed that he had an audience. He took his phone from his pocket and pressed the 'record' button.

'You don't mind me recording this, I hope?' Mac asked.

'The barman shrugged, 'That's okay with me.'

'Do you own the bar?'

'Yes, together with my wife Sheila,' he said pointing to a sign behind the bar that said, 'Don and Sheila Henderson welcome you to the Tornado Pub'. Below the sign there was a large photograph of a slightly younger barman with his arm around an attractive blonde woman in her fifties.

'So, you're Don Henderson?' Mac asked to be sure.

'For my sins. What's this all about then?'

Mac found the photo of Harold Jones on his phone and turned it around so that Don could see it.

'Do you know this man?' Mac asked.

'Yes, I know him, well not know exactly,' Don replied. 'He's been in about once a week for the last couple of months or so. He's an old man, what would the police want from him?'

'We don't want anything from him,' Mac replied. 'He's dead. We think that he might have been murdered.'

Chapter Ten

The three men got up from their seats and wandered over to the bar. They all had a look at the photo on Mac's phone.

'He was a miserable bastard,' the man in the baseball cap stated flatly in a broad Liverpool accent as he tapped the photo with his finger. 'And a racist miserable bastard at that.'

Now that he was a bit closer Mac noticed that the slogan on his cap actually said 'Make America Grate Again'.

'How was that?' Mac asked.

'He had no time for Greeks, well at least not the ones living today. He called them 'mongrels' more than once. If he'd have done that when my daughter was here,' he said nodding towards the young woman, 'then I'd have had to knock his block off, old man or not.'

'As Jim said he was bloody miserable with it too,' a short round balding man in his late sixties said.

'I'm sorry but can I get your names before we go any further?' Mac asked.

'Jim McDowell,' the man in the baseball cap said.

'Simon Haskell,' the pear-shaped man said.

That left a tall man with grey hair and a pronounced stoop who obviously wasn't the talkative type.

'Paddy McGuinness,' he reluctantly said in a soft Northern Irish accent.

'So, Simon you were saying that he was miserable. What do you mean by that?' Mac asked.

'Well, he never smiled and it was as if he carried his own little black cloud around with him. The only time he didn't moan was when he was going on about ancient history.'

'Aye that's right,' Paddy chipped in with a nod of his head.

They all waited for him to carry on but that seemed to be the sum of what he had to say.

Simon continued, 'He said that Larnaka used to be a great city called 'Kition' that was once ruled by someone called...Oh, what was it now?' he said obviously stumped.

'Evagoras the First,' Paddy said in a near whisper.

'Yes, that's right,' Simon said. 'I'd never heard of him before. Anyway, he said that proper Greeks lived here then and not the mongrels that you see today. Jim got so angry that I had to get him outside. I really thought that he was going to hit the old bugger. You see Jim's married to a Greek lady and the lovely Kat there is half-Cypriot.'

The young woman smiled at Mac and said in perfect unaccented English, 'It's short for Ekaterina. My name is Ekaterina McDowell.'

'But not for long, love,' her beaming father said. 'She's getting married and in less than two weeks she'll be Mrs. Ekaterina Georgiou. We were just talking about it when you walked in.'

'Dad, I'd better get going. I don't want to be late,' Ekaterina said before kissing her father on the cheek.

She waved to everyone and then walked out of the door. Mac thought that she looked very happy.

'She's getting her wedding dress fitted today,' the proud father explained to Mac.

'Kat's wedding's going to be a doozy. Sheila's already bought her dress and I'd bet that it wasn't that much cheaper than Kat's,' Don said with a laugh.

'Have you ever been to a wedding in Cyprus?' Jim asked.

'No, it's the first time that I've visited Cyprus and I've not been here long,' Mac replied.

'Well, you should try it sometime. This one will go on for a least a couple of days.'

'A couple of days? Really?' Mac said with some surprise.

'In Cyprus if something's worth celebrating then they celebrate it properly,' Don said.

Mac decided that he needed to steer the conversation back to the murder.

'Tell me, did Mr. Jones ever say anything to you about why he was here in Larnaka?' Mac asked them.

They all looked at each other blankly.

'It makes you wonder why he came here at all if he didn't like Greeks, doesn't it?' Don said.

Mac was indeed wondering about that exact point.

'Did you ever see him in here with anyone else?' he asked.

There were more blank looks except for Simon who looked thoughtful. Mac said nothing and waited for him to speak.

'I did see him with someone once. They only talked for a few minutes,' Simon said as he turned towards Don. 'It was one afternoon when Sheila was behind the bar. Paddy and I were a bit early and the old man was already here. I thought that we were going to be stuck with him but then this other chap came in.'

'Did you hear what they said?' Mac asked.

'No chance, he and the other chap went up the far end of the bar there and spoke in whispers.'

'The man that Mr. Jones met, what was he like?'

'He was in his thirties I'd guess, dark hair, medium height but quite stocky with it,' Simon replied. 'He was dressed in work clothes, you know, denim jacket and trousers and high work boots. I think that he might have been Russian.'

'Why do you think that?'

'Well, he looked Russian,' Simon said. 'He had that Slavic face, if you know what I mean, but I also heard him when he said hallo to Mr. Jones. He had a pronounced Eastern European accent.'

Mac thought for a moment.

'A lot of work clothes have the firm's logo on them. Did you see anything like that?'

'Yes, I think there was something on the left-hand pocket of his jacket....' Simon said.

Simon screwed his face up while he was thinking.

'And?' Mac asked.

'Er...I'm sorry but I've no idea what it was,' Simon finally admitted.

'It was an 'L'. A capital 'L' and it was red,' Paddy volunteered. 'I thought it looked a little like the sign that learners put on their cars.'

'So, it was just an 'L', nothing else?' Mac asked.

'No there were some other letters after the 'L' but I'm afraid that I've no idea what they were,' Paddy replied. 'It wasn't an English word that's for certain but it did remind me of something.'

Mac gave Paddy time to think.

'No, I'm sorry, it's gone.'

Oh well, Mac thought, knowing that the name of the company that the Russian worked for started with an 'L' was better than nothing he supposed.

Despite asking several more questions Mac learned no more. He decided to change tack and ask them some questions about the bar and themselves. It might give him a clue as to why Harold Jones had visited the bar in the first place and why he kept coming back. Besides that, he had to admit that he was curious about the four of them anyway.

'Have you any idea why Mr. Jones frequented your bar in particular? It's not all that close to where he was staying.'

'When he first visited us, he said that he'd asked a taxi driver for the nearest English bar and he drove him here,' Don replied.

'How long did he usually stay for?' Mac asked.

'I'd guess that he usually stayed for around two to three hours,' Don replied. 'He had the same every time he visited, three glasses of red wine and not our best red wine at that. He certainly made them last though.'

'He was very rich. Did you know that?' Mac asked.

They all exchanged mystified looks.

'Well, I'd never have guessed,' Simon said. 'I thought that he was a pensioner who was feeling the pinch a bit money-wise. I even bought him a drink once. Was he worth a few hundred then?'

'A few hundred million, yes,' Mac replied.

'You're joking!' Jim exclaimed. 'So, he wasn't just a miserable racist bastard, he was a skinflint with it.'

The indignant look on Jim's face made everyone burst into laughter. Jim laughed along with them.

'Well, I don't think his money did him much good then,' Simon said. 'What's the point of being rich if you can't splash the cash every now and then? From what I saw of him he didn't get much fun out of anything really.'

'Well, he did like his history though,' Paddy pointed out.

'That's true, I think I nearly saw him smile once when he was talking about the great art of ancient times, especially the statues,' Simon said. 'It didn't last long though as he'd then mutter something about how the world is going backwards.'

'Yes, he said that the world's going backwards and that he'd be glad to be leaving it before it goes to hell in a handcart altogether,' Paddy said.

'He said that he'd be glad to be leaving the world?' Mac asked.

Paddy nodded.

Mac made a mental note of this.

'I take it that you're ex-RAF Don?' Mac asked wanting to know something about the four of them.

'Yes, I used to be a pilot, flying tonkas out of Akrotiri,' Don replied.

'Tonkas?' Mac asked.

'Tornadoes,' Jim replied. 'Don wasn't just a pilot though he was a Squadron Leader. He did quite a few missions over Kuwait during the Gulf War then there was Iraq, Libya and God knows what else.'

'The one thing you can say about this part of the world is that there's always something going on,' Don said. 'Now, you wouldn't think it to look at him but Jim here used to be our Chief Technician. He'd gaffer tape the planes together after we'd touched bottom with them while the ever-talkative Paddy here was our avionics expert and Simon, who looks like butter wouldn't melt in his mouth, he was our head weapons man.'

'There used to be a few more in the gang but a couple have dropped off the twig fairly recently,' Simon explained.

Don and Jim nodded sombrely at this.

'Do you all live here permanently?' Mac asked.

'Jim does ever since he married the beautiful Ada,' Don replied. 'I'm here most of the year round running this place. We still have a house near Stroud, not that we spend that much time there except for around Christmas. It doesn't feel like Christmas without a bit of cold weather now, does it? Simon and Paddy here share a flat in London. They come over for a couple of months at a time then they go back home for a week, decide that they can't stand it and come back here again.'

'You said earlier that there aren't that many English bars around these days, so how's business?'

'We're just about keeping ourselves in the black,' Don replied. 'It's a bit quiet at times but some of the boys from Akrotiri pop down for a drink now and then. It's lovely to talk to them and see what they're getting up to these days. Quite a few of the old boys regularly come over on holiday and do their best to drink us dry and we even get the odd tourist darkening our door now and again. Remember that bunch of Manchester lads last month?'

Jim, Simon and Paddy smiled and nodded.

'I thought that they might have been a bit lairy at first but they turned out to be a really good laugh and boy could they drink,' Don said.

Mac made some more small talk before calling Michalis to pick him up. Before he left, he promised that he'd come back for a 'proper chat' with them when he had time.

'So, where to?' Michalis asked as he pulled away from the pub.

Mac looked at his watch. It was nearly seven. He needed to make a call and he'd need a little time to think afterwards. The square would be as good a place as any.

'Back to my apartment please, Michalis.'

'Did you learn anything at the bar?'

Mac smiled and glanced over at him. Even his taxi driver was getting interested in the case now.

'No, not a lot I suppose,' Mac replied. 'He used to go to the pub and moan a lot from what I've been told. I suppose that's why he wanted to go to an English bar.'

'Ah, so they'd understand him,' Michalis said.

'Perhaps,' Mac replied.

'He looked like a man who would moan a lot.'

As he was really beginning to like his taxi driver, he decided not to mention Harold Jones' views on modern Greek Cypriots to him.

As they pulled up outside his apartment block Mac decided that he'd have to lay the law down.

'Now Michalis, I'm about to pay you for the ride plus a tip and you'll accept it,' Mac said. 'Otherwise, I'll only get embarrassed and end up having to use another taxi driver which I would hate as I quite like talking to you.'

Michalis smiled and shrugged his shoulders before taking Mac's money.

'You're here for a while, aren't you?' Michalis asked. 'Before you go home, we'll go out for an evening and it will be on me. Would that be okay?'

'That would be fine,' Mac replied. 'In fact, I'll be looking forward to it.'

His offer being accepted, Michalis drove off a happier man.

Mac sat down and caught the waitress's attention. He ordered a beer and then got out his phone. He had a question to ask. He rang Kate Grimsson and asked his question. He wasn't surprised to find that she'd beaten him to it. She gave him an update that gave him even more food for thought. Indeed, he was so deep in thought that he didn't even notice that he was hungry.

Chapter Eleven

The birdsong outside her window woke Kate. She didn't mind, it was a sweet way to wake up.

She and Toni chatted about their cases over breakfast and this carried on until she reluctantly parted with Toni at the police station. DI Toni Woodgate was the head of the local detective team while, as Kate often said in teasing way, she was just a mere sergeant and therefore could be ordered to do anything.

She made her way to the Major Crime Unit's room and opened the door. Her boss, Dan Carter, was talking to Adil and Andy.

'Any idea who he is?' Dan was asking.

Kate had to look around Dan so she could see who he was talking about. It was Colin. He was at the same desk that she'd left him at the previous evening but now his head was on the desk and he was fast asleep.

'His name is DI Colin Furness,' Kate said. 'He turned up last night. He's the money laundering expert from the Met that Mac recommended.'

'Oh, hello Kate,' Dan said as he turned around. 'Couldn't he get himself into a hotel for the night?'

'Oh yes, he's booked into the hotel just down the road,' Kate replied. 'He said he was going to work for a few hours as he wanted to talk to someone in Australia.'

'Well, I like people to be keen on the job,' Dan said, 'but tell him not to take it too far.'

Andy and Adil followed Dan into his office. Kate gently shook Colin but he only murmured something and carried on sleeping.

'Someone's been burning the midnight oil,' Tommy said from behind her.

'I'm trying to wake him up,' Kate said. 'He needs to go to his hotel and get some sleep.'

97

'Here let me try,' Tommy said.

He gently shook Colin and then whispered something in his ear that Kate couldn't quite catch. Colin sat up and put a finger in his ear. He had a dazed expression on his face and it took him a while to get his eyes to focus. Once he did, he looked from Tommy to Kate and then to the window.

'Is it morning already? I'm sorry, I must have dozed off,' he said apologetically.

'Would you like a coffee?' Tommy asked.

'Oh, yes please,' Colin replied with deep gratitude.

He stood up and stretched as Tommy went out of the door.

'I was up quite late as I was waiting for one of my opposite numbers in the Australian police to get back to me,' he explained to Kate. 'I've managed to track down some of the missing money, around sixty million or so, to an up and coming logistics company in Bulgaria. It was used to buy a large stake in the company. Since then the company's done well and the shares have gone up in value. Then last week Mr. Jones sold the shares back to the company for about ten per cent less than he paid for them which is strange to say the least. The remaining fifty-four million then ended up somewhere in the Far East markets, Singapore and Hong Kong we think. The Australians are the experts on those markets so they're trying to discover where the money went to next.'

'It sounds complicated,' Kate said.

She was a banker's daughter yet she knew next to nothing about the world her father had lived in. That was by choice.

'It is but we'll get there,' Colin said optimistically. 'It'll mean another late night for me tonight but I must say that I'm finding it all quite intriguing.'

Tommy came back with the coffees.

'Oh, thanks Tommy, I really need this,' Colin said just before he took a sip.

'What was the name of the Bulgarian company?' Kate asked.

'It was Lefkhod Logistics.'

Colin spelt the name out loud for her.

'It's based in Burgas, a port on the Black Sea,' he continued. 'It started off in oil but it's been diversifying quite successfully lately into shipping, containers mostly, as well as haulage and supply chain management. It's on its way up and selling shares at well below their current price is very odd, very odd indeed. So, remind me, what are you doing today?'

'First we're going to see Harold Jones' grand-daughter. Her name is Chelsea Jaskolski and she lives in Stevenage,' Kate replied. 'Then we've got an appointment with his solicitor in Knebworth. I'm not sure what else after that. I'm hoping that we might get some leads we can follow up on but, if not, we'll come back here and see if anything new has turned up.'

'Okay then, I'm going to belatedly check into my hotel and finally get some proper sleep,' Colin said. 'I should be back here around four or five so I'll hopefully catch you before you finish for the day.'

They watched as Colin wearily packed his laptop away

'I know your hotel's only down the road but we'll drop you there. You look half-dead,' Tommy said.

'Thank you, Tommy. In this case I'm more than happy to accept your kind offer.'

After dropping Colin off they headed off for Stevenage.

'Not taking the motorway?' Kate asked as the car headed off towards Hitchin.

'No, Letchworth Gate can get really busy in the morning and, anyway, Symonds Green is easier to get to if we go through Wymondley.'

Kate looked out of the window with interest as she couldn't remember taking this way for quite a while. It was a nice morning and looking out over the lush green landscape on either side of the narrow country lanes brought a smile to her face.

They crossed over a small traffic island and up a hill before turning left. A sign said 'Titmore Green'.

'Is that for real?' Kate asked.

'What Titmore Green?' Tommy asked with a broad smile. 'Yes, it is but it sounds like it should be in a 'Carry On' film, doesn't it?'

A few seconds later and they were in Symond's Green.

'What was the road again?' Kate asked.

'Bude Crescent,' Tommy replied.

She noticed that they were on Clovelly Way and had just passed Scarborough Avenue.

'Are all the streets here named after seaside towns?' Kate asked.

'Yes, I think so, although I've no idea why,' Tommy replied. 'I'm glad that we've got the satnav, I'd get lost around here every time otherwise. All the streets look exactly the same.'

The home of Jan and Chelsea Jaskolski was a modest red-brick semi-detached hidden away at the very end of the road. The road was a dead end and finished in a large parking area. From there they had to walk a few yards down a path on either side of which stood two semi-detached houses.

'You'd never find these if you weren't actually looking for them, would you? It's this one, I think,' Tommy said as he pointed to the end house on the right.

Kate noticed that the little gardens in front of all four houses were all well-tended and glowing with colour and she couldn't help thinking that there was something quite snug and inviting about their situation.

Tommy rang the bell and the door was eventually opened by a woman in her early thirties. Her long dark hair was bundled up into a brightly coloured head scarf. She was wearing jeans and a red and green patterned top. She looked somewhat harassed and the bright yellow rubber gloves she wore and the rubber plunger she held in one hand gave Kate a clue as to why.

'Sorry, you did say that you were coming but the bloody toilet is playing up again. Please come in,' she said leaving the door open for them.

They walked down a short hallway the walls of which were covered with photos of children and their attempts at art. The living room had children's toys scattered across the floor but Kate liked it. She thought that it looked real, it was somewhere people lived. The woman came back into the room and flashed them a smile before she started picking up the toys and placing them into a big red box in the corner of the room.

'I keep telling them to put their toys away when they're finished playing...' she said to herself.

Kate sat down on the large sofa then stood up again. She picked up a block of Lego bricks, handed them to the woman and sat down again. The woman's eyes scanned the room for any overlooked playthings and, satisfied, she sat down.

'I'm sorry but I'm in a bit of a tizz this morning,' she explained.

Kate could see that. She took out her warrant card and introduced herself and Tommy.

'I take it that you're Chelsea Jaskolski?'

'Yes, that's me alright. I've been wondering what this is all about ever since you rang me yesterday evening.'

'I'm afraid that it's about your grandfather, Harold Jones,' Kate replied.

'Why what's happened to him?' Chelsea asked.

'He's dead. We think he was murdered.'

Kate watched Chelsea's reaction carefully and she was surprised. There was no reaction at all apart from a slight shrug of the shoulders.

'And what's that to me?' Chelsea asked.

'I take it that you and your grandfather weren't close?'

'Close? I've never even met him,' Chelsea replied with a bitter little smile.

Kate and Tommy looked at each other. It was an answer that neither of them had expected.

'What never?' Kate asked with a puzzled look. 'He only lived a few miles away.'

'No, never. I only ever contacted him once and that was when my mum died. He made it quite clear that he never cared about either of us and that he especially wanted nothing to do me,' Chelsea said.

Kate noticed that she smiled when she said this but it obviously still hurt.

'So, who killed him then?' Chelsea asked.

'That's what we're trying to find out,' Kate replied.

Chelsea thought for a moment and Kate could see the penny begin to drop.

'You don't think that I had anything to do with it, do you?'

'Not especially but we do have to cover every eventuality,' Kate said.

'Where was he killed?' Chelsea asked.

'Cyprus.'

'Cyprus?' Chelsea said with a surprised look. 'What was he doing there?'

'To be honest, we've no idea but why are you surprised that he was there?' Kate asked.

'I heard that he never left that house in Knebworth that he was holed up in.'

Kate made a mental note to check if Harold Jones had gone abroad before and, if so, where.

'I take it that you've not left the country over the last few days?' Kate asked.

'If only,' Chelsea replied, 'but as I've got three kids, a part-time job as a class assistant and a hungry husband to feed, I can only answer no.'

'I take it that you can confirm this?' Kate asked.

'When did he die, exactly?'

'Tuesday evening, around eight thirty Cyprus time,' Kate replied. 'That would be six thirty here.'

Chelsea thought for a moment before saying, 'Well you can rule me out then. At six-thirty last Tuesday I was with my Cub Scouts troop, I'm their Akela. It's the same as herding cats really, except these are in uniform.'

'Can anyone vouch for you?' Kate asked knowing that there would be.

Chelsea gave her the names of her assistant and two parents who had stayed for the whole session.

'Okay we'll check this out. So, if we assume that you weren't involved, who do you think might have killed your grandfather?' Kate asked.

'I've absolutely no idea,' Chelsea replied. 'As I said I've had nothing to do with him.'

'Your grandfather was quite rich...'

'Was he?' Chelsea interrupted. 'Much good it did him. Anyway, I know that I won't be seeing any of it.'

'How can you be so sure?' Kate asked.

'He said so after I wrote to him and told him that my mum, his only child, was dead. Here I'll show you.'

Chelsea got up and left the room. She returned a few minutes later with a single sheet of paper which she gave to Kate. The paper was embossed and it had

Harold Jones' name and address on the top. The note itself had handwritten. Kate read it.

'So, Rebecca is finally dead and you're her little bastard. I didn't want to have anything to do with your mother when she was alive and I certainly don't want to hear about her now she's dead. To be honest I'm surprised that she lasted this long, she was weak and useless and no better than a whore.

If you're hoping for any money from me, you can forget it. My will has been written and you will not be getting a single penny from

H. Jones'

Kate raised her eyebrows and passed it to Tommy. She asked Chelsea before she took a photograph of the letter.

'How old were you when she died?' Kate asked.

'Sixteen. It was really lucky for me that she lasted that long,' Chelsea replied.

'Why is that?'

'Well, she didn't exactly look after herself and, if I'd have been any younger, I might have been put in care. I did my best to help her but I couldn't, the damage had already been done.'

'In what way?' Kate asked.

She found that she was getting interested in Chelsea's story.

'They talk a lot about 'low self-esteem' nowadays, well my mum's self-esteem was rock bottom,' Chelsea said. 'My grandmother had the sense to leave her husband when mum was only two but, unfortunately, she forgot to take her daughter with her. Harold blamed her for his wife leaving him and he took it out on her daily right until the very day she left home for good. She was just seventeen. My mum had nothing but problems; drink, drugs, mental health issues, anorexia, bulimia, you name it she had it. Harold was right about one thing though;

104

it was a wonder that she lasted so long. She was just thirty-eight when she died.'

'How did she die?'

'It was a heroin overdose. It was ruled as 'Abuse of Drugs' by the Coroner but I think she did it on purpose. I think she'd just had enough,' Chelsea said with a sad shrug.

'What about your dad?' Kate asked.

'My dad?' she said with another bitter smile. 'My mum had absolutely no idea who he was. She was off her head so often that it could have been anyone.'

'So, what happened to you after your mother died?'

'Jan's family took me in. It was the best thing that ever happened to me,' Chelsea said with a warm smile.

'Jan's your husband?'

'Yes, we married when we were eighteen but I've known him since we were both eleven. I remember the first day I met him at school, I knew then that he was someone special. I don't think that his mum was all that keen on me though. I think she wanted Jan to marry a nice Polish Catholic girl.'

'What was that like?'

Kate knew this question probably had nothing to do with the case but she still wanted to know.

'It was awkward at first,' Chelsea replied. 'His dad was okay with it, as anything that made Jan happy was okay with him, but his mother, Hanna, was suspicious to say the least. She made me sleep on the sofa downstairs and she used to put talcum powder on the stairs in case I tried to sneak up to Jan's room in the night. I used to watch her all the time, which I suppose didn't make her feel any better about me, but I had no idea what a real mother was like and I really wanted to know. So, I started helping with the cleaning and I used to watch her cook. She eventually let me have a go. I think she finally accepted me when I did a plate of Golabki all by myself and it was actually edible. The talcum powder disappeared and I became part of the family. I honestly don't think I'd have had any kids if it hadn't been for her and, in the end, Hanna got her wish. I became a Catholic and she tells me that I'm now even more Polish than she is.'

'You sound as if you're happy,' Kate said.

'I suppose I am, except for when the bloody toilet goes on the fritz that is. My husband's business is doing well, he's a plumber.' She stopped and pulled a face. 'I know it's a bit of a stereotype but Jan's made it work in his favour. I have three wonderful kids, well wonderful some of the time. I love my house and my little job and we have some really good friends. What more could I need?'

Kate gave Chelsea a card and asked her to contact her if she thought of anything.

As she walked back to the car Kate stopped and looked back at the little house. She'd only spoken to Chelsea Jaskolski for a half an hour or so but she found that she had some admiration for her.

'She seems to be really well-grounded considering the life she must have had as a kid,' Kate said.

'Yes, I guess that she was lucky that she met Jan at such as early age,' Tommy replied. 'Too many kids in her position would have gone down the same road as her mother. The solicitor's next, isn't it?'

'Yes,' Kate said as she looked at her watch. 'We're supposed to be seeing them in twenty minutes.'

'We should easily make it,' Tommy said as he drove off. 'Knebworth is just down the road.'

Just down the road, Kate thought. Yet a grandfather couldn't have been bothered to make that short trip to see his only grandchild, not even out of curiosity. She was rapidly coming to the conclusion that Harold Jones had been a miserable excuse for a human being.

Chapter Twelve

As they drove to Knebworth Kate asked the question that had been on her mind for a while.

'What did you say to him?'

'To who?' Tommy asked.

'To Colin,' she replied. 'What did you say to make him wake up so quickly?'

'It's something we used to say in the Scouts when we were out camping and couldn't get someone out of bed,' Tommy said with a smile. 'I told him that he had an earwig in his ear.'

Kate laughed out loud as she remembered Colin's dazed expression as he sat up and put his finger in his ear.

'It's crude but it works surprisingly well,' Tommy said.

They were soon in Knebworth. The solicitor's office consisted of a large detached house situated just before a row of shops on the way into the town centre. The lobby was quite full and Kate and Tommy had to join a short queue and then wait until the receptionist had finished a phone call.

'I've an appointment with Stephen Harris,' Kate said as she showed the young blonde receptionist her warrant card.

'Oh yes of course,' the receptionist said. 'Mr. Harris told me to bring you straight up to his office. Please follow me.'

They followed her up a flight of stairs and then down a surprisingly long hallway to the door at the very end. She knocked lightly and went in closing the door behind her. The door opened a few seconds later.

'You can go in now,' the receptionist said holding the door open for them.

Stephen Harris was a small man with a completely bald head. He sat behind a very large desk that made him look even smaller. He wore thick glasses with rims that matched his jet-black suit and tie. Kate guessed that he was in his early sixties.

'So, how can I help the police?' he asked. 'I know this is about Mr. Harold Jones but you must be aware that I can't tell you anything without his permission.'

He smiled an emollient smile.

'We don't need his permission,' Kate said. Mr. Harris gave her a somewhat sceptical look. She continued, 'He's dead, we think that he might have been murdered.'

The solicitor's face dropped.

'He's been murdered? Really?' he exclaimed in total surprise.

'Yes, really,' Kate confirmed. 'He was pushed off a balcony in Cyprus.'

'Cyprus? What on earth was he doing there? I thought that he never went abroad or at least that's what he told me. Are you sure that you've got the right Harold Jones?'

Kate showed him a photo on her phone.

'Yes, that's him alright,' the solicitor confirmed.

'So, I take it that you've no idea as to what he might have doing in Cyprus then?' Kate asked.

'None at all. We only met two or three times a year when he had something for us to do. Our work for him was centred around the various properties he owned; contracts, conveyancing, tenancy agreements and so on.'

'When was the last time that you saw him?'

'It must have been about four months ago. He informed me that he was liquidating all his property assets, including his own house, and that he would no longer need our services,' Mr. Harris said with something of a scowl. 'Oh yes, and he updated his will.'

'What do you mean updated?' Kate asked. 'Can we see a copy?'

'I'm not sure. I know Mr. Jones is dead and you're conducting a murder enquiry but...'

'If I get someone to send you a formal request would that help?' Kate asked.

'Yes, that would be good,' he said as he handed her a card with his email address on.

Kate phoned Martin Selby and asked him to send a formal request by email as soon as he could.

'Do you have any idea how much Mr. Jones was worth?' Kate asked.

'Not really,' the solicitor replied. 'I know that he had some shares and other holdings but we never discussed those. We only dealt with his property portfolio and in total that was worth around sixty-eight million pounds. I've no idea how much he sold it for. If he sold it as a package, then I guess that he'd be bound to make quite a loss.'

It was all part of pattern, Kate thought. Selling everything off at well below its current value. What was it that had been driving him to do something so out of character? An idea popped into her head.

'Are you aware of any health problems that Mr. Jones might have had?' Kate asked.

'No but, then again, I dare say that he wouldn't tell me. You should ask his doctor.'

'And do you know who his doctor is?'

'Oh sure, his office is just down the road. He rents one of Mr. Jones' properties or rented I should say. God knows who owns it now,' the solicitor said as he leaned forward to look at his computer screen. 'Your email has just come in.'

He printed it off and then read it in minute detail.

He finally said, 'Well that seems to be all in order. I'll get you a photocopy of the will.'

'Can you also get me a copy of the previous version of the will too?' Kate asked. 'While we're waiting, perhaps you can you tell us what the major changes to the will were.'

'Well, that won't take long,' the solicitor replied. 'In the previous version of the will he left the whole of his estate to various universities, including his own alma mater. The bequest stipulated that the monies had to be put towards a new building project and that the building must then be named after him. It's not an unusual request I believe.'

'He was looking for a little immortality then,' Kate said.

'Possibly. However, in the latest version of his will he had all those bequests deleted. Now all his estate goes to a single recipient. His granddaughter.'

Kate and Tommy gave each other a surprised look.

'Are you sure? We have it in writing from Mr. Jones himself that he wouldn't be leaving her a penny,' Kate said.

'He obviously had a change of mind then,' the solicitor observed.

After they'd finished quizzing the solicitor Kate and Tommy sat in the car reading both wills in detail.

'What's going on here?' Tommy asked. 'He doesn't want anything to do with his own granddaughter and then he leaves her everything. Is it some sort of joke, do you think?'

Kate looked at Tommy as a thought struck her.

'I think you might be spot on there, perhaps it is just a joke after all.'

'What do you mean?'

'Well, in his letter he said that Chelsea would never get a penny from him. Perhaps that's the truth after all,' Kate said. 'All his money has disappeared so perhaps his estate is now worth exactly nothing.'

'That would be an incredibly mean thing to do,' Tommy said.

'From what we've heard I think that he might have been an incredibly mean man,' Kate said. 'Come on, let's go and see his doctor.'

Doctor Samuel Preston was a partner in a swish looking private practice. The few people waiting to be seen were all elegantly dressed and obviously well off as was the doctor himself. Once Kate had explained the situation, Doctor Preston told them what he knew without waiting for any formal request.

'So, he's dead then. He wouldn't have lasted too much longer anyway,' the doctor said with a shrug. 'You see, Mr. Jones came to see me just before Christmas complaining of trouble with his waterworks. He'd waited until it had gotten quite bad before he'd bothered telling me about it. I had all the tests done and it turned out that he had a cancer of the prostate, quite an aggressive one too, and it had spread. His age and state of health were against him so we could only do so much.'

'Did he ask you how long he had to live?' Kate asked.

'Yes, he did and that's a question that we don't normally like answering. Cancer is unpredictable at the best of times and it can affect each person quite differently so we try not to make predictions,' the doctor said.

'But you made one in this case?' Kate persisted.

'Well, he pushed me so in the end I told him. It was two weeks into January and I told him that, even if the treatment that I was proposing worked, it was highly unlikely that he'd see out the year.'

'How did he react to that?' Kate asked.

'He didn't really, he just started asking me about the treatment and how long he'd be able to be active for. I

111

told him that, with the treatment, he'd probably be okay for six or seven months and he seemed quite happy with that.'

As Tommy drove them back to the station Kate said, 'We're building up a narrative now, aren't we? Harold Jones finds out he's dying and it looks as if he decided to play a particularly nasty joke on his only relative. In his former will it seemed that he wanted to be remembered in some way, so what changed that?'

'Well, I'd guess that, if we could find where all the money went, then we might be able to answer that one,' Tommy said.

'You're right, I suppose the ball's now in Colin's court,' Kate said.

Tommy parked up and suggested that they walk around to the Magnets to get a little late lunch. It was only then that Kate realised that she was hungry. As they walked towards the pub, they could see Colin sitting at a table by the window eating a Full English breakfast. He had his laptop open next to him and he was tapping away in between eating forkfuls of food.

'Did you sleep okay?' Kate asked as she sat down next to him.

'Oh, hello Kate, Tommy,' Colin said as he looked up. 'I slept wonderfully well, I only got up half an hour or so ago. Breakfast seemed to be the thing to do.'

Kate and Tommy decided on a panini and coffee each.

When Tommy came back with the coffees Kate asked, 'Have you found anything yet?'

'No, we've found nothing new so far,' Colin replied as he chewed on his last piece of toast, 'but I'm hopeful that something might come to light later when I speak to Bob Barker of the Australian

Federal Police. He's one of the bright sparks in their Fraud Unit in Sydney.'

Kate told him what they'd just discovered.

'Well, it certainly seems that the prognosis he received from his doctor might have sparked whatever it is he was up·to,' Colin said. 'All we can do is follow the money, if that's possible that is.'

Kate looked at Colin thoughtfully.

'Your job is pretty specialised, isn't it? So, how you get into fraud investigation?' Kate asked.

'I started out on the other side as it were,' Colin replied. 'I was a trader in the city for just over six years, I was good at it too.'

'A trader?' Tommy said. 'I've heard that they can make good money.'

'In my best year I made well over a million pounds,' Colin said.

'Really? What made you give it all up then?' Kate asked.

It was Colin's turn to be thoughtful.

'Three things really. The first was when my best friend quit the job. We'd met and became friends at university and then we were both headhunted by the same firm. He was good at the job, even better than me, but then one day he told me that he was giving it all up. He was joining an ethical finance company at about a twentieth of what he'd been earning. I asked him why and he told me that he wanted to be able to sleep at night.'

Colin stopped and took a sip from his coffee.

'That really stuck in my head especially when I had a sleepless night which, at the time, were becoming much more common. The work was so full on and draining that I was only just about stumbling over the finishing line at the end of the day. Then it was straight to some bar, drinking too much and sniffing lines in the toilet. Yet, even though I was dog tired, there were

113

times when I just couldn't sleep. It was like my brain was on fire and I couldn't slow it down. Then the second thing happened. One night I had a sort of epiphany. I realised that money, as most people know it, doesn't exist.'

He paused while he wiped his lips with a paper napkin and then pushed his plate away.

'What is money after all?' Colin continued. 'It's just a shared delusion that's all.'

'So, what do I have in my wallet then?' Tommy asked looking a little puzzled.

'That's not money. Money used to be a certain amount of a precious metal. It was precious because it was scarce and also very beautiful when worked up into jewellery and so forth. Gold will always have value because of what it is and what you can do with it. Banknotes started because people didn't want to carry large ingots of gold or silver around with them. So, you'd deposit your gold at one bank and get a note for it. Then you'd travel somewhere else, hand your note in and get your gold back. The note itself is worthless, it's just a receipt really, it's the gold that was worth something. Paper money used to be just that, a receipt for a certain amount of gold or silver, but the Great Depression saw to that. So now a currency is supposedly linked to a country's GDP, what a country's worth. In reality it's a very loose linkage at best. A dollar is worth what it's worth because we all believe it to be worth that. When we believe it to be worth less, then it is. It's all about belief, a shared delusion. Beliefs and delusions can be gamed and that's what I did for a living as a trader.'

Colin stopped and downed the remainder of his coffee.

'I killed myself daily and for what?' he continued. 'In reality it was so that some ones and zeros held in one computer server could be transferred to another server somewhere else. That's all money is nowadays, it's just bits of computer code. If all the servers in the world crashed there would suddenly be a lot fewer rich people. Unless you've got land or a couple of gold ingots in the cellar then wealth is just a mirage, a ghost in the machine. Well, that was my epiphany and it was a thought that I just couldn't get out of my head. Then, a week later, the third thing happened. After another sleepless night I took my morning double espresso out onto my balcony. I had a beautiful view over the Thames but it was my next-door neighbour's balcony that I found myself looking at. It had a piece of rope tied to it and it was hanging down out of my sight. I stood up and looked over my balcony so that I could see the end of the rope. I discovered that it was tied around my neighbour's neck.'

Colin paused for effect.

'He was a trader just like me except that he'd been in the business a bit longer than I had. He had a good reputation for being a closer, for getting the job done. While I waited for the police to come, I couldn't help but watch his body twisting in the breeze coming in from the river and wonder why he did it. It was as if he wanted to tell me something. I listened to him. I quit my job that day and never went back.'

'That's some story,' Tommy said.

'So, what made you want to join the police?' Kate asked wanting to know more.

'Pure luck really,' Colin replied. 'I put a job search into the internet and the City of London Police Economic Crime Department, AKA the Fraud Squad, popped up. I dismissed it at first as it paid peanuts and, well, it was the police. However, the more I thought about it the more it grew on me. I'd be able to use all the financial skills I'd learned but I'd be putting it to good use this time. They seemed to be more than glad

115

to have me and even kept me on after I'd had a few sticky patches.'

'What do you mean by sticky patches?' Kate asked.

'Well, as a trader I'd been taught to be competitive and to trust no-one. It took me quite a while to get used to being open and working cooperatively within a team. In some ways it was the biggest learning curve that I've ever had to negotiate. But, eventually, I learned and it changed me in a lot of ways that I never envisaged. I could now see that every member of the team was a vital cog in the machine and that they all did their bit as did the office staff, the tech guys, the canteen workers and so on. Take the office cleaners for instance, I must have worked late more often than not as a trader yet I don't ever remember actually seeing a cleaner. They must have been there but they were invisible to me because they just weren't relevant.'

Colin smiled to himself before he continued.

'There are times when we have to work a different shift pattern to everyone else if we're dealing with a major case abroad so that we can liaise in real time with teams in other countries. On this one occasion I was on New York time and, as they're five hours behind us, I worked from two in the afternoon until ten in the evening. The cleaners usually came in around eight or so and I actually started to notice them. Then I found that I started noticing this one cleaner in particular. She was young and quite pretty, at least I thought so. She was obviously originally from the Mediterranean some-where and she had these gorgeous dark eyes. I just couldn't stop looking at her. I watched out for her each evening and we started talking, just small talk really. This carried on until I finished the case. After that I started staying late anyway, just to speak to her. I discovered that her name was Sarah and that she was a design student. She was working as a cleaner to make some money while she studied. She'd come over to the UK with her mother from Libya as an asylum seeker a couple of years before. Her father had been a translator for the British Army there until he'd been murdered.'

The paninis arrived but Kate wanted to know the end of the story.

'So, what happened?' she asked.

'Well, she asked how the case was going and I told her the truth. I told her that the case was over and that I was only staying late so that I could see her. She just laughed and suggested that we could try meeting somewhere where the ambience was a little better. That was just over eleven years ago now.'

Colin stopped. He could see that Kate wanted to know how the story ended and he decided to tease her a little.

'And? And?' Kate demanded.

'And so, we met up and, well, it didn't quite work out as I thought it would,' Colin said as he gave her a sad look.

'Something went wrong?' Kate asked with some sympathy.

'No, for once in my life things went spectacularly right. Sarah and I got married three months later and, after eleven years together, we still get on surprisingly well. She's a freelance designer these days and we've got two great kids, well great some of the time that is.'

Kate laughed out loud as she realised that she'd been had.

'Anyway, Sarah and her mother have taken the kids to see some relatives in Leicester for a few days and that's why I've been able to come to sunny Letchworth and help you guys out.'

'I'm glad you came,' Kate said with real sincerity.

117

Colin was starting to grow on her.

'Anyway, I'd better be getting back to the station,' he said. 'My friend Bob in Sydney will be coming online soon and I've got a bit of work to do first.'

They walked back to the police station together and then they had a short debrief. Dan Carter joined them.

'So, have you any idea of what you'll be doing next?' Dan asked.

'Not really,' Kate shrugged and looked at the other two for inspiration. 'We'll need to speak to Chelsea Jaskolski again at some point and tell her about the will but apart from that...'

'There's a chance that we might get a few leads from the Australian Police tonight,' Colin said. 'My contact there thinks that he might be onto something.'

Dan looked at his watch. It was four thirty.

'You might as well finish for the day and try again tomorrow,' he said. 'Make sure you update Mac before you go. You never know but he might have come up with something at his end. He usually does.'

Kate sincerely hoped that Dan was right.

Chapter Thirteen

Mac sat in the square nursing his pint. For once he was oblivious to the scene around him and didn't even notice the white cat that sat near his foot, looking up at him beseechingly for food. He was thinking about what Kate had just told him and wondering what kind of man Harold Jones had been.

A particularly nasty one it would seem. Having ignored his own granddaughter for her entire life he was now going to leave her everything. However, 'everything' equalled exactly nothing as all his shares and properties appeared to have been sold and all the money generated by this had mysteriously vanished. Harold Jones was on his last legs and, from his previous will, it seemed that he wanted to leave some sort of monument behind so that his name would live on. Mac wondered if this still might be the case. The idea occurred to him that Harold Jones might have found another way of ensuring some immortality for himself. But what could it be?

Whatever it was the money had to be the key.

He was glad that Colin had joined the cause. If anyone could discover where the money had gone then he could. However, he was beginning to get the idea that Harold Jones had been devious in the extreme and that there might be quite a few detours yet before they finally got to the truth. If they ever did that is.

'Any news from England?' Dave asked as he sat down.

The unnoticed cat ran a couple of yards away and observed the two policemen from a distance.

Mac had been miles away and looked up with some surprise. He noticed that Dave looked a little tired. He told him what he'd learned from Kate.

'So, he was dying anyway. It makes you wonder why anyone would want to speed the process up and kill him now, doesn't it?' Dave said. 'Why not just wait a few months?'

'Yes, that's a good point. There must have been some pressing reason to kill him now but what? Did you have any luck with the press conference?' Mac asked.

'I had a whole team of people waiting for the flood of calls and we took ten all night,' Dave replied with a grim shake of his head. 'I could have saved a lot of overtime being booked and took them all myself.'

'Did you learn anything from the calls?'

'Not much really. Three callers said they'd seen him in the Tornado Pub, which we already knew about of course, and we also had calls from Nicosia, Paphos and from Poli Crysochous which is right at the other end of the island. I'll get the local police to check those out but I'm not holding my breath. Most interestingly we also had two calls from Limassol, both dock workers who said that they'd seen him in a place called Chloe's Canteen. I've been there before, it's a little café that's situated inside the port and it's mostly used by the people who work there. It's a strange place to be seen in and, as we had two callers who seemed certain that it was him, we'll be checking it out first thing tomorrow. Fancy coming? Unlike our little trip today the road to Limassol is really good and it should only take us around an hour to get there.'

Mac didn't need to think too hard about this.

'Yes, I'd love to go with you. I take it that you didn't find anything at Pano...' Mac couldn't quite remember the full name of the town.

'Pano Lefkara? Just a lot of rocks unfortunately,' Dave replied. 'The land that Harold Jones bought is a good stretch from the town but the roads weren't too bad, apart from the last mile or so that is. That last bit was so bumpy that I felt as if I was in a washing machine. It's right up in the foothills of the mountains and it's not even that great for sheep. We learned that from the former owner, Mr. Pitsillides. He said that he had no idea why Mr. Jones wanted to buy the land or what he was going to do with it. It's my guess that he didn't care all that much, he just wanted to get his hands on the money. Twenty five thousand euros for a pile of rocks isn't bad.'

'So, you learned nothing at all?' Mac asked.

'No, I wouldn't say that. Mr. Pitsillides lives at the other end of his property which is a good bit away from the parcel of land that Harold Jones bought. Even so, he said that he heard some strange noises three or four weeks back, heavy machinery of some sort he thought. He checked it out the morning afterwards but there was nothing there. He heard similar noises again about a week later. He was curious but he said that he had to visit his sister in Kato Lefkara who was ill so he wasn't able to have a look until a couple of days later. Again, he found nothing, apart from a few tracks that he thought could have been made by heavy truck tyres.'

'So, what do you think was going on?' Mac asked.

Dave shrugged, 'I've no idea. Noises in the night? It's all very non-specific, isn't it? However, Mr. Pitsillides didn't strike me as being the type who'd make things up so I'm going to get a few men up there to have a look around. Have you eaten yet?'

'No, you're not going to the taverna again tonight by any chance, are you?' Mac asked hopefully.

Dave laughed, 'Yes, the family have already eaten but they said that they'd join me there, if that's okay?'

It was better than okay. After the story he told him about how he and his wife met, Mac was quite curious to meet Eleni.

'Would you mind if we stopped at the Tornado Pub for a few minutes on the way there?' Mac asked. 'There's a question that I need to ask someone.'

Dave waited in the car for Mac while he went inside the bar. He didn't take long.

'Well?' Dave asked as he drove off.

'Paddy McGuinness is absolutely certain that the man who visited Harold Jones in the pub was from Lefkhod Logistics. The man had a logo on his work clothes and, when I told him the company's name, Paddy remembered that the word had reminded him of 'lunokhod' which apparently was a Russian space-craft which landed on the moon. He's a bit of a space nut apparently.'

'Yet another mystery then. Why would a Bulgarian logistics worker be speaking to Harold Jones?' Dave stopped speaking and was thoughtful for a moment. 'Mind you a logistics company would have lots of heavy machinery and trucks, wouldn't they?'

Mac thought that this was an excellent point.

'Yes, they would. It's certainly worth exploring,' he replied.

'I'll get my men to check Lefkhod Logistics out tomorrow. We'll see if they're active on the island and, if so, what they've been involved in.'

As before Dave parked his car outside his house. An upstairs light was on and music could be heard playing.

'I guess that my oldest, Christina, won't be joining us. She's fifteen now and she prefers the company of her friends these days,' Dave said a little ruefully.

'I know the feeling well,' Mac said. 'My daughter's nearly twenty-eight now, she lives with her boyfriend and she works long hours at a hospital but I still see more of her nowadays that I did when she was a teenager.'

This made Dave smile.

'I doubt that you'll see much of the other two either. The owner of the taverna also has two sons and my sons Nikos and Theo go to school with them. They're good friends too so, like most young boys, they'll be upstairs blowing up planets or whatever it is they do on their games consoles these days.'

Dave appeared to be right as he steered Mac towards a woman who was sitting at a table by herself. She was slim, dark-haired and dark-eyed and, although Mac guessed that she must be nearly forty, she looked much younger. Dave bent over and gave her a kiss before he introduced her to Mac.

'Panni's been telling me all about you,' she said with a wide smile. 'Two Brummie detectives working on the case together.'

She said the last sentence in such a creditable version of a Birmingham accent that Mac couldn't help laughing out loud.

'I take it that you've been to Birmingham then?' Mac asked.

'Yes, we've been there quite recently as a lot of Panni's younger relatives seem to be getting married one after the other lately,' she replied.

'Do you like going to Birmingham?' Mac asked wondering what someone who came from such a fabulous Mediterranean island might make of his hometown.

'Oh, I love it,' she said with a smile.

Mac knew that she meant it too. She had one of those animated faces that were easy to read.

'Eleni loves the shops anyway,' Dave said. 'The last time we were there I dropped her and Christina off at the Selfridges store early in the morning and twelve hours later they had to be escorted off the premises by the security guards.'

'No, that's not true,' Eleni said with an embarr-assed laugh as she playfully smacked her husband's forearm. 'We didn't spend all day in Selfridges, we went to a few other places as well.'

'But they did have to escort you out though, didn't they?' Dave persisted.

'Well, you're wrong there. They were just being very nice when they walked us to the door, that's all.'

Mac couldn't help notice that Eleni looked a little shame-faced as she said this.

'It's such a nice store though,' she said with a smile as she turned to Mac. 'We've got nothing like it here in Larnaka.'

Mac had been watching Eleni's mobile face and the way it reflected her thoughts. It somehow made everything she said more interesting. Although she looked nothing like her, he realised that she was a lot like someone else in that respect. His Nora.

He had a sad moment but, luckily, the food arrived which meant he could disguise it until it passed.

He knew that he wouldn't be up to eating the feast he'd had the night before so he'd asked Dave to just order him some souvlaki. What he got was a large plate half filled with chips and the other half with salad on top of which perched five long wooden skewers of grilled meat. The aroma was fantastic and Mac dug in. He surprised himself by only leaving a single lettuce leaf on the plate. He'd been hungrier than he'd thought.

Dave had ordered the same. Eleni had already eaten so she watched them eat until Dave handed her a skewer and then gave her a fork so she could help him out with the chips and salad. It was a simple thing, sharing one's food like that, but it also showed how close they were. Mac was almost jealous for a moment.

'So how are Birmingham's best doing with the case?' Eleni asked as Mac pushed his plate away.

Mac let Dave answer.

'Great, we'll have it cracked within the hour,' he said confidently.

Eleni was clearly surprised by this answer, as indeed was Mac, although he tried not to show it.

'Really?' she asked.

'No, not really. I just said that because you looked so sure of yourself. We're finding out a little more about the man who died but we've still got a way to go...'

Dave was interrupted by his phone going off.

'It's Andy,' he said before he stood up and walked a few steps away.

'How's it going really?' Eleni asked with a more serious expression.

'It's early days and we're still digging,' Mac said with a shrug.

'Do you think you'll find whoever it was that killed that old man?' she asked.

He looked over at Dave who was still in deep conversation with his partner. He decided to answer her question as best he could.

'If I'm being honest, I've no idea. My old boss used to say that an investigation is like peeling an onion, you take one layer off and there's another below. You can never tell how many layers you'll have to peel before you get to the truth and, even though it'll make you cry at times, you just have to keep on going. Unfortunately, sometimes it's just onion all the way down and you never get anywhere.'

'That's not a bad way of explaining it,' Eleni replied. She glanced over at Dave and said, 'He really wants to solve this case.'

'I'd guess that there's a lot of pressure on him from his bosses to get the case solved quickly,' Mac said.

'Yes, a murder is never good news in a town that relies on tourism but it's not that, it's the pressure he puts on himself.'

'He's a good policeman and that's what good policemen do,' Mac replied.

'Thanks,' she said with a smile.

'He told me how you two met,' Mac said. 'That was quite a story. You must have been surprised when he stopped you like that.'

Eleni glanced over at Dave to make sure he was still speaking before she spoke herself.

'Well not really,' she replied with a mischievous smile. 'Did he tell you that I never turned around? Well, I've never told him but we women always carry a rear-view mirror. I checked him out in my compact mirror and I thought he was cute. I could see that he was looking at me so I left in the hope that he'd follow. I had to slow right down so he could catch me up.'

Mac laughed out loud and remembered an old saying about how a man chases after a woman until she catches up with him.

Dave came back and sat down. He had a puzzled look on his face.

'That was Andy,' he said. 'Forensics did an initial sweep of the room and found quite a few sets of fingerprints. Harold Jones and those belonging to the cleaners were the most common. They also found several sets that we're presuming belonged to people who previously stayed there. We're contacting them and asking them to give their fingerprints to the local police so that we can rule them out. It was only when they got around to moving the safe and dusted the sides for prints that they found something interesting.'

Dave paused for effect and looked at Mac and his wife.

She picked up a spoon and rapped the back of his hand with it.

'Go on,' she said.

'That hurt,' Dave said with a pained expression, one that was completely put on of course. 'Anyway, the prints belong to someone who's known to us. His name is Loukas Liourdis and, although he's got a Greek name, he's not a local. He's from Athens and he's well known to the police there too. He's an opportunist thief who specialises in stealing from tourists. He usually works the top end hotels so it's a bit of a surprise to find his prints at somewhere like the Libretta.'

'What's his MO?' Mac asked.

'He likes to think of himself as a 'cat burglar' but, in reality, he gained access to his victims' rooms via the female hotel staff. He's quite good-looking and a bit a charmer too. He's clever and, while some of the women he was involved with knowingly helped him rob their clients, quite often the cleaner or recep-tionist or whoever it is that he'd targeted, didn't realise what he was up to until it was too late.'

'How did you catch him?'

'Well, as much as I'd like to take the credit, he just picked the wrong person to rob,' Dave replied. 'He was discovered trying to open the safe in the room of a foreign government official. This official had his own minders and, although they said that they never touched him, Mr. Liourdis somehow found himself flying out of a third storey window.'

'How did he survive that?' Mac asked.

'Unlike Mr. Jones something broke his fall,' Dave replied. 'He fell onto a café awning which collapsed. He had a broken leg, arm, ribs and God knows what else but he wasn't even listed as critical when he got to hospital. He was in hospital for six weeks and now he's in jail in Nicosia serving an eleven year sentence.'

'Eleven years? That sounds a bit steep.'

'He asked for one hundred and eighteen other offences to be taken into account,' Dave replied with a wry expression.

'Well, that might account for it then,' Mac said with a laugh.

'Would you be up for a trip to Nicosia as well?' Dave asked. 'I'd like to see Mr. Liourdis for myself.'

'Absolutely, so long as there are no 'washing machine' roads.'

'I can promise you that and just think, you'll be getting a free guided tour of the island as well,' Dave said with a smile.

Chapter Fourteen

As promised the road was smooth and they made good time. Mac had enjoyed a leisurely breakfast in the square before Dave and Andy had picked him up and he was now sitting back and enjoying the ride. He even managed to get a few glimpses of the sea before they found themselves in the busy streets of Limassol.

It looked a lot like Larnaka to Mac except that there was perhaps a little more hustle and bustle about the place. They pulled in at a check point at the entrance to the port and Dave got out and spoke to a security guard. He disappeared inside the little office and didn't come out for nearly ten minutes. While they waited Mac and Andy got out of the car and found some shade. There was a lovely breeze coming in off the sea.

Mac was glad that Dave was taking his time. He'd been waiting for an opportunity to ask a certain question.

'So, tell me, how did a boy from Croydon end up working for the Larnaka police then?' Mac asked.

'Well, I liked living in Croydon and I had a lot of friends there but I loved coming over here in the holidays,' Andy replied. 'Ever since I was fourteen, I used to come over in the school holidays every summer and work at my uncle's restaurant. I always had the feeling that I might end up living here eventually. I took all my exams in England but I also spent a lot of time researching about how I might be able to get a job with the police here. When I was eighteen, I made my decision. I applied for and got a Cyprus passport, then I flew over and immediately volunteered to do my military service. Everyone here has to do a stint in the army so I thought I might as well get it out of the way. My parents weren't so happy about that though, especially my mum. She was a kid when the war in 1974 broke out and I think that it really scared her. I think that was one of the reasons why she came over to England, she was always worried that it might start up all over again. However, I had a great time and made some very good friends too. After I left the army, I applied for a job with the police and they took me up straight away. I'd guess that, after spending fourteen months doing national service, they knew that I was serious about it.'

'And how are you finding it now?' Mac asked.

'I love it even more. It's nice working with Dave's team, I don't get any of the snide remarks I used to get from some of the others. The younger coppers are generally okay but some of the older ones...they sometimes call us The Two Charlies or The Sweeney.'

Mac gave Andy a puzzled look.

'I take it that 'The Sweeney' is after the old TV series.'

'That's right, it's still shown over here from time to time and, as it features an older and a younger detective, I suppose that you might be able to understand that one,' Andy said.

'The 'Two Charlies' though? Why do they call you that?' Mac asked.

'Well, a 'Charlie' is what some people of my dad's generation used to call people of Cypriot descent who were born in England or Cypriots who had worked there for some time. Let's just say it's not exactly a nice name. Of course, they never call us that to our faces.'

'And is there much prejudice against English Cypriots here?' Mac asked. 'I'm interested because I think that I'd get a similar response from the locals if I ever moved back to Ireland. Even if I'd lived there for decades, they'd still call me a 'blow-in'.'

'No, it's not too bad really. A lot of the remarks are quite humorous anyway and I don't mind those. As for those that aren't, well, I've got quite a thick skin. I think a lot of it is just jealousy anyway. Dave's team have been consistently the best performers for some years now and that doesn't sit well with some of the others.'

'Yes, I've come across that before as well,' Mac said.

He was about to say something else when Dave emerged and walked towards them. He was smiling. Mac took this a good sign.

'He was here alright,' Dave said. 'He used a card issued in his name by the Port Authority. It was requested by someone working at Lefkhod Logistics.'

'Do they operate from the port?' Mac asked.

'They're not one of the biggest companies but their business at the port has been growing or so I was told by one of the port managers,' Dave said. 'They had around eight per cent of the container traffic last year.'

'And what's that in containers?' Mac asked.

'Around eighteen to twenty thousand, I think.'

'Okay, so it's not inconsiderable then. What do they ship in these containers?'

'I asked that question too,' Dave said. 'The manager said that Lefkhod was much like the other logistics companies in that they exported mostly food and pharmaceutical products while they imported just about everything else. He said that they're growing quickly because of their geographical position. Goods from Eastern Europe, the Baltic and Scandinavia can be taken overland and then shipped out all over the Middle East and North Africa. And the other way around, of course, but I wonder what Harold Jones wanted from them? Anyway, they've got a small office over the other side of the port, so we'll go and see them once we've interviewed the two men who said that they saw Harold Jones. I've been told that we're to wait in the canteen for them.'

131

They got back into the car which was now as hot as an oven inside. Andy turned the air conditioning on full and drove the short distance to the canteen.

The canteen was a small building that was dwarfed by the two huge warehouses that stood on either side of it. Opposite the canteen Mac could see stacks of multi-coloured containers that were waiting to be loaded onto the ships that were moored nearby. Two giant cranes were in the process of picking up some of the containers and stacking them delicately on one of the ship's decks as if they were giant Lego bricks. It all looked quite busy but in a very controlled way.

Beyond the ships the azure sea rolled off into the hazy blue distance.

The canteen itself was larger than it had first looked. It was all under cover but one side was open so that the sea breeze could act as a natural air conditioner. The interior seemed quite dark until they stepped inside out of the sun and their eyes adjusted. Tables and chairs were scattered around and most of them were occupied by men in yellow and orange hi-viz jackets. A number of people were waiting to be served at a counter to their right.

'Do you want something to drink?' Andy asked.

Mac did, he'd only been out for an hour or so but he was already feeling a little dehydrated. The cold fizzy water that Andy came back with was more than gratefully received. Dave quickly drank his coke while looking around the canteen.

'They said that the two men would be accompanied by a security guard,' he said.

'Behind you,' Andy said.

Dave turned around and, walking towards them, he saw a uniformed guard walking behind two middle-aged men who were wearing denim overalls and yellow hi-viz jackets. They didn't look at all happy. Dave found two tables in the corner that were a good distance away from the rest of the customers. He waved at the security guard who waved back and then turned in their direction.

'Andy you take one and I'll take the other,' Dave said as he pulled the tables further apart. 'Concentrate on finding whoever it was that Harold Jones might have been seeing when he was here.'

Mac could only sit and watch. He tried to learn as much as he could from the men's body language. They had their arms crossed and sat back in a defensive pose. They seemed to be responding with only single word answers and sometimes just a shrug. Andy asked his man something and then stood up and asked a question of the man that Dave was interviewing. He nodded as did the guard. Andy went to the counter and came back with three cold drinks which he handed out to the men and the guard.

After that the men smiled and their body language changed too. They sat forward and spoke more freely.

Well done Andy, Mac thought. A little bit of thought can sometimes make all the difference.

When they'd finished, Dave and Andy came and sat down next to Mac.

'So, did you find anything?' he asked.

'They were both definite that it was Harold Jones they saw but only one of them saw him with some-one else,' Dave said. 'He said that it was a man in his late thirties. He was certain that he wasn't a Cypriot as he had blond hair and his skin was too light. He couldn't tell us much more other than the fact that he had an orange hi-viz jacket on. The jacket had the Lefkhod logo on it.'

'So, I take it that we're definitely visiting their offices next then?' Mac asked.

'You bet,' Dave said as he stood up.

The offices were on the other side of the port near the Harbour Road. They had some trouble locating it as it turned out to be just a large single room in a small office block. The room was divided into two. A middle-aged man sat in an office behind a glass partition at the back while, in front of them, two young women were busy tapping away at their keyboards. One of them looked up.

Dave asked her a question. She got up and tapped on the door to the private office. The man looked up, listened to what she had to say and then waved at them to come in.

He said something in Greek to Dave. Dave said something back and, thankfully for Mac, the rest of the conversation was carried out in English.

'So, how can I help the police?' the man asked.

He seemed relatively unperturbed by their visit. Dave asked him for his name.

'Grigoris Stassinos, I'm the general manager here. I'm basically in charge of all of Lefkhod's dealings with the port.'

Dave showed him a photo of Harold Jones and explained the situation.

'You say that the man who died was a major shareholder in the company?' Mr. Stassinos said. 'He never made himself known to me.'

'Did he meet any other Lefkhod employees as far as you know?' Dave asked.

'Well, I certainly didn't meet with him and there's only myself, Maria and Anna who work here.'

'You don't have any people working in the dock?' Dave asked thinking about the man that Harold Jones had met in the Tornado pub.

'No, all that's run by the port authority. We just handle the paperwork and do an inspection every now and then.'

'We have witnesses who said that they saw Mr. Jones meet someone in Larnaka who was wearing work clothes with the Lefkhod logo on. He was of medium height, stocky with dark hair and possibly Russian or Eastern European they said.'

Mr. Stassinos shrugged, 'Dark hair, you say? I've no idea who that could be. Anyway, it's quite possible that the company has other interests in Cyprus. They wouldn't necessarily tell me unless it impacted on the port here.'

Mac thought that this was a good point.

'Mr. Jones was also seen with someone who was wearing a Lefkhod hi-viz jacket in the canteen here in the port,' Dave said. 'Have you any idea who that might have been?'

Mr. Stassinos sat back in his chair and scowled.

'Did he have fair hair by any chance?'

'Yes, he did. Do you know who he was?' Dave asked.

'I was told some weeks ago that I'd be getting a visit from head office. I wasn't surprised, we'll be more than doubling our traffic in the coming year and I've been working on some development plans that head office had requested. However, he wasn't at all what I was expecting.'

'In what way?' Dave asked.

'Well, he wasn't the slightest bit interested in my development plans that's for sure,' Mr. Stassinos replied. 'He was only interested in knowing how our container shipping system worked. So, I told him as best I could and then I showed him around the port. He seemed especially interested in where all our containers are stored prior to shipping. I thought he was trying to catch me out as some of the questions he asked were quite basic. So basic in fact that anyone who'd worked in shipping for five minutes would know the answers.'

'So, would it be fair to say that he didn't know that much about Lefkhod's business here?' Dave asked.

'I quickly came to the conclusion that he knew next to nothing about it,' Mr. Stassinos said. 'It worried me so much that I rang head office to confirm that he was for real.'

'And was he?'

'As it turned out, yes. They said he was on some sort of fact-finding mission but they wouldn't say what. At first, I thought that he was might have been one of the top boss's stupid relatives who they were finding work for. It's happened before,' he said with a shrug. 'However, I don't think that was the case with him now I've thought about it. He was quite sharp, I never had to tell him anything twice.'

'Is he still around?' Dave asked.

'I've no idea. I haven't seen him for a few weeks but he hasn't returned the pass I gave him or the hi-viz jacket.'

'So, he'd still be able to access the port?'

'That's right, the pass is valid for six months.'

'What's his name?' Dave asked.

'Richard Gatling, he was English he said but he had a strange accent. However, he definitely wasn't Russian.'

They didn't get any more from Mr. Stassinos so they made their way out. Only one of the girls was working, she turned out to be Anna. Dave asked her a few questions. Unfortunately, she said that she'd only been working for Lefkhod for a few weeks and, as far as she knew, she'd never met Mr. Gatling. They found Maria outside having a cigarette. She was in her late twenties and she had a sceptical streetwise look that couldn't be mistaken.

Even so Mac thought that she was quite attractive.

Dave explained why they were there.

'Did you ever meet this Mr. Gatling?' Dave asked.

136

'Unfortunately,' she replied.

'Why do you say that? Did he ever try anything on with you?'

'No, nothing like that. He was too much of a cold fish for that,' she replied. 'He was a bit creepy and he had these eyes, they were like a dead man's eyes. There was no expression in them. I've met men like him before ...well, one anyway.'

She gave the policemen a sad look.

'Anyway, I found myself being really careful not to upset him, I had the feeling that I might not like it if I did.'

'Your boss thought that Mr. Gatling might have been English. What did you think?' Dave asked.

'He was English alright, from the North East. I worked in London for a time and one of the girls I worked with had that accent.'

'So, you think that he might have been from the Newcastle area?'

'I'd guess,' she said with a shrug as she ground out her cigarette end with the sole of her shoe. She turned to go inside but then stopped. 'Another thing, I don't think that Richard Gatling is his real name.'

'Why do you think that?' Dave asked getting really interested in what she had to say.

'Well, he was in the office one day waiting for Mr. Stassinos when I tried to get his attention. I said his name several times before he realised that I was talking to him. He tried to cover it up saying that he was miles away but I didn't believe him. I mean if someone mentions my name in a crowded room, I pick it up immediately.'

Mac knew exactly what she meant. They stood there for a while thinking after she'd gone back inside.

'I take it that his pass would have his photo on?' Andy said.

'Yes, of course,' Dave said with a smile. 'Well done, Andy!'

'And I know someone who's a bit of a genius at finding people by their faces alone,' Mac said.

'Good, we'll stop by the security office on our way out then,' Dave said with a wide smile.

Chapter Fifteen

Kate and Toni once again walked to work together. The sun was out and the birds were singing. The trees swayed in a warm breeze and the grass was greener than green. The air was light and felt full of possibilities.

'Do you think that we could play hookey from work and go for a picnic instead?' Kate suggested as they neared the police station.

'I wish,' Toni said with real regret, 'but I do have a case on. Anyway, don't you think they'd twig if both of us went missing?'

'I suppose you're right,' Kate said making a sad face. 'Well, it was a nice thought while it lasted.'

She regretfully parted with Toni and made her way to the Major Crime Unit's room. Tommy was already at his desk, in fact, he was the only one in the room.

'Where is everyone?' she asked.

'Well, there was a burglary over in Buntingford last night in which an old lady was seriously injured and a suspected murder in Stevenage. Someone got run over outside a night club in the Leisure Park. I asked Dan if he needed any help but he said that he wanted us to plough on with the case,' Tommy replied. 'Not that ploughing is the word I'd use for this case, more like a gentle amble really. By the way, Colin left us a note.'

She read it and then said, 'So, he's still chasing the money down then. He sounds quite hopeful though.'

'Well, as we don't seem to be making much progress, it would be nice if he could come up with something,' Tommy said.

'You're dead right about that,' Kate said with a sigh. 'In the meantime, we've still got a lot of stuff to go through, all of those card indexes for instance,' Kate said. 'Did they take absolutely everything out of his house that might be useful?'

'As far as I know but it might be worth checking again just in case,' Tommy said.

'Okay then, let's get stuck in and we'll take a break around midday and check the house again just to be on the safe side,' Kate said.

She wasn't sure that it would really push the case on that much further but it was such a nice morning and she didn't want to spend the whole day indoors. She sighed as she looked at the boxes stacked up in the corner by her desk. She picked up the first set of cards and started off. There were around a hundred or so of them squeezed tightly into a cardboard box. She picked out a few at random, they were all handwritten. She recognized the letters and the numbers but, taken together, they made no sense whatsoever to her. She tried another box and then another but she got no further. Over two hours had gone by.

'Are you having any luck?' Kate asked in desperation.

Tommy shook his head.

'He might as well have written these in Egyptian hieroglyphs for all the sense they make to me.'

'I'd guess that they're related to his financial activities but I've no idea how,' Kate said. 'Come on, let's go and check his house out and, when we come back, we'll have a look at the rest of the documents. Hopefully they might make a little more sense to us.'

Martin Selby came into the room just as they were about to leave.

'Martin, did you manage to have a look at any of the stuff they brought over from the Jones house?' Kate asked hopefully.

'Yes, I did. I was curious about the card indexes but I couldn't make much sense of the ones I looked at. Oh, apart from a few where I was fairly sure that he might have been looking at share prices,' Martin replied.

Kate had been thinking of handing over the card files to Colin to see what he could make of them. Martin had just confirmed that this might be the way to go.

'Oh, by the way Mac's sent me over the photo of a man,' Martin continued. 'He wants me to try and trace him if I can. It's someone who he said met your murder victim in Cyprus fairly recently.'

'Well, it sounds like he's doing better than we are,' Kate said. 'Let us know if you come up with anything.'

'Will do,' Martin replied as he opened up his laptop.

They passed by the lido on their way to Knebworth. Kate was quite envious of the families queuing outside to get in. Floating about in a cool swimming pool would be the perfect thing to be doing right at that moment. She kept her window open as they drove the twelve miles or so to Knebworth. She enjoyed feeling the cool air rush by and the warmth of the sun's rays on her arm.

By contrast the house was dark and gloomy inside, even the air felt as dead as its owner. They checked all the empty rooms and the downstairs bedroom just to be sure before they started on the living room.

More of an office really, Kate thought, as it had no sofa, no coffee table and no television.

There was an old transistor radio in the corner. She turned it on. It took a few seconds to warm up. She eventually heard the voice of a BBC Radio announcer. It was Radio 4, a speech only channel. She looked closely at the radio tuner, from the dust around the dial she could see that it hadn't been moved for some time. It seemed that Harold Jones didn't have much time for music. She turned it off again.

They searched all the nooks and crannies in the room but found nothing of interest.

'Are we going to look through those?' Tommy asked pointing towards the eight stacks of pink financial newspapers lining one wall.

'I suppose we should,' Kate replied with a sigh.

There was nothing hidden in the stacks, they were just newspapers. There was the odd annotation next to a share price but that was it. The only interesting thing was that they'd been kept in strict date order with each stack containing exactly three months of newspapers.

'Just those to go and we'll call it a day,' Kate said pointing to the books. 'I think they've been checked for anything that might have been hidden in there but that's all. You never know, it might be well worth our while having another look.'

One complete wall was filled from the top to the bottom by shelves of books. A ladder on wheels enabled access to the top shelves.

'There's a lot of them, aren't there?' Tommy said with no enthusiasm whatsoever.

'Tell you what, I'll let you take the top four shelves and I'll take the lower ones.'

'Scared of heights?' Tommy said teasingly.

'No, scared of that ladder more likely,' Kate replied. 'It doesn't look all that strong to me.'

Tommy could see her point. However, it proved strong enough to take his weight for the time it took him to look through the four shelves. Kate counted the books that they had put to one side.

'So, we've got forty-two books that Harold Jones has annotated or put sticky notes in,' Kate said. 'Do you think we can whittle them down a bit more? Some of these are quite big. We might do ourselves some damage trying to get them back to the car.'

They spent the next hour or so examining the books more carefully. They managed to whittle it down to just six.

'This looks the most interesting so far,' Tommy said holding up an old embossed leather-bound book.

'What is it?' Kate asked.

'The Collected Letters of Robert FitzWarren, 6th Viscount FitzWarren of Holles, Volume Three.'

'Well, that sounds like a real bundle of laughs,' Kate said.

'It does look a bit dry but he's got lots of notes in there and they all seem to be in the same section,' Tommy said.

'Let's see.'

She found that Tommy was right. The notes were only in a section entitled 'Letters from Antiquaries 1800-1815'. It looked like every other page had a note stuck to it or had scribbles in the margins.

'Well, I can't see what it could possibly have to do with the case but we'll take it along with the other five anyway,' Kate said. 'They might at least be able to tell us something about the kind of man Harold Jones was but, from what I've learned about him so far, I'm not sure if I want to know much more.'

They bought a sandwich on the way back and arrived at the station just after four thirty. Colin was already there. On his desk, in front of an empty cardboard box, there stood three neat stacks of index cards. Colin was looking at them thoughtfully.

'Oh hi,' he said finally noticing that Kate and Tommy had arrived. 'I hope that you don't mind but Martin mentioned the cards to me and I thought that I'd take a peek.'

'Not at all, in fact I was going to ask you to have a look as we couldn't make much of them,' Kate replied. 'Why are there three stacks?'

'Well, this first stack are cards that I'm fairly certain relate to particular share price movements while the second stack here might be something to do with information on various companies, balance sheets, cash flows, that type of thing. This third stack I haven't got a clue about if I'm being honest.'

'So, what's the point of it all? Any ideas?' Kate asked.

'Well, I think that it might be a sort of paper computer relating to company information,' Colin said. 'A lot of the cards are quite well thumbed so it's obviously something that he used a lot. Anyway, I'll have some free time tonight while I wait for Bob Barker in Oz to come up with the goods so I'll see if I can puzzle it out a little more.'

'Thanks Colin, that would be a great help,' said Kate with some relief.

'Some light reading?' Colin said looking at the books that Kate and Tommy had placed on the table.

'Hardly, we've just had another look through Harold Jones' house and this is all we came up with,' Kate replied. 'I don't get it though. How could he have possibly managed all his business interests when he didn't even have a computer?'

'Well, people managed perfectly well for decades with just a copy of the Financial Times and the odd phone call to their broker. Even with all this,' Colin said waving at the boxes of cards, 'I'd guess that he kept most of the information in his head which, of course, doesn't help us much.'

Their conversation was interrupted by the sound of cursing coming from the corner of the room. Kate was surprised, it was the first time that she'd ever heard Martin swear.

'Are you alright?' she asked as she went over to him.

'Oh, I'm sorry,' he said looking more than a little embarrassed. 'It's this stupid system. I've been having problems with it all day. Even though my password is right it keeps kicking me out.'

'What system are you trying to use?' Kate asked.

'It's the Police National Database,' Martin replied. 'I'm trying to do an image search and it's clunky at the best of times but it's driving me up the wall today. While I've been waiting, I've checked most of the main social media sites but it seems that Mac's mystery man has been keeping a very low profile.'

'Have you tried the helpdesk?' Kate suggested.

'Yes, and unfortunately it seems that I'm not the only one having problems. They'll have it fixed by tomorrow for sure, or so they said. I suppose I'll just have to wait. But it's just really, really annoying.'

Kate had to admit that Martin did look really annoyed.

'We'll be knocking off for the day soon. I'll buy you a pint if you like,' Kate offered.

'Now that's the nicest thing anyone's said to me all day,' Martin replied with a smile. 'You're on.'

'Can I come too?' Colin asked.

'As you've been so kind to volunteer to help with the card indexes, I'll buy you one too,' Kate said with a smile.

She texted Toni to meet her in the Magnets. It was still sunny and with some luck they'd be able to get a table outside. Perhaps she'd get her picnic after all.

Chapter Sixteen

They went back towards Larnaka for quite a way before eventually turning left and heading inland. A sign told them that it was only forty kilometres to Nicosia. Mac was getting an idea of just how small the island really was.

'So, what's Nicosia like?' he asked.

'It's big, well bigger than Larnaka anyway,' Dave replied. 'But it's nothing like Birmingham. It's not that big, nothing in Cyprus is.'

'Anyway, we're not going to Nicosia itself,' Andy said. 'The Central Prison is in a suburb called Agios Dometios and its walls are just a few yards away from the border with Northern Cyprus.'

'That's the Turkish part of Cyprus then?' Mac asked.

'That's right,' Dave replied. 'The border goes right through the city and more or less cuts it in half.'

'And how does that work?' Mac asked. 'I was in Ireland not that long ago and they were worried that there might be a hard border running right across the country after the UK leaves the European Union and that it would cause chaos.'

'They're right to be worried. It's certainly caused enough chaos here,' Dave said. 'The border, or the Green Line as it's sometimes called, is actually two borders with a 'no man's land' in between. It still isn't an internationally recognized border but that doesn't stop it from being hard all the same. It was only opened in 2003 and that was the first time that Greek Cypriots could go to the North and Turkish Cypriots could go south in nearly thirty years. Even today there are still only seven points at which you can cross over the border and two of those are in Nicosia.'

'So, after forty-five years a hard border's still there?' Mac asked with some surprise.

'It's a mess really,' Andy said. 'I think it was originally drawn up by the British as a temporary measure to keep the two communities apart but now it's set in stone. The border makes absolutely no sense and it's really been holding the island's economy back. Then, just when you think cross-border relations are getting better, Turkey feels that it has to show some muscle and starts drilling for oil just off the coast and that's pissed just about everyone off, including the EU. Not only that but, when I was in the Army, I found that some of my fellow soldiers were very anti-Turkish which I found a little puzzling. They were mostly young and had probably never met a Turk, Cypriot or other-wise. I find the same sentiments being expressed by some of my police colleagues as well. As peaceful as it all looks, I still get the feeling that it wouldn't take too much for it to all kick off again.'

Dave nodded in agreement, 'I think that just about everyone's worried about that and, with the Turkish government being so right-wing these days, it's becoming more and more of a possibility. The two communities on the island had rubbed along together for centuries but now they seem to be moving further and further apart. I'm sorry Mac but, if Brexit happens and Ireland gets a hard border, then I can't see it turning out any better than it did for us.'

Mac looked out at the countryside whizzing by and came to the conclusion that, while you could sometimes marvel at the human race's creativity and intelligence, you equally had to wonder at its stupidity. To arbitrarily cut a small island in two and to then keep it going for nearly fifty years seemed like a sin to him. He thought of his family and the people he knew in Donegal and said a little prayer that a solution might be found for Ireland.

147

He was still deep in thought when he suddenly realised that he was in a town. Well-kept villas were passing him by as did a beautiful domed white and blue church.

'Agios Dometios,' Andy said.

They turned around a corner and were forced to stop at a checkpoint. Dave showed his warrant card. They were then let through into the prison itself. Mac noticed that they passed by a couple of tourist buses that were parked up. Just beyond these he noticed that a large group of people were being ushered into a building. Nearby there was a small cemetery with several graves that had white crosses on them. Each grave had fresh flowers on them.

'What's going on over there?' Mac asked.

'In English they're called the 'Imprisoned Graves'. It's a graveyard where thirteen EOKA fighters are buried, nine of them after they were hanged by the British in the 1950s,' Andy said.

'EOKA? So, I take it that they were fighting against the British?' Mac asked.

'Yes, they wanted 'Enosis', a union with Greece,' Andy replied.

'Of course, they never bothered asking the Turks who lived here if they wanted to go along with their plan,' Dave said. 'And there lay the problem. Anyway, they've got a museum in there and you can also see the room that they were all hanged in.'

'I've already seen one of those and once is enough as far as I'm concerned,' Mac said with conviction.

'Strangely enough the man they brought over from England to hang all those men was called Harry Jones too,' Andy said as they pulled up at another checkpoint.

Dave got out, showed the guard his warrant card and had a word with him.

148

'He wants us to park the car here and walk through,' Dave said. 'He says that they'll bring Loukas Liourdis to one of the visitor's rooms. It's not far to walk from here. Oh, you'll need to leave your phones with the guard, they're not allowed inside the prison itself. Andy I'll need your gun too.'

Andy pulled out a nine-millimetre pistol from the holster on his belt and handed it over. The guard reappeared and Dave handed over the phones and guns and had another quick word. From the guard's response it looked like he was giving Dave directions. The barrier was lifted and they walked through. About sixty or seventy yards down the street Dave opened a door and ushered Mac and Andy inside. Two guards greeted them, patted them down and checked their warrant cards before taking them to the visitor's room. Inside two armed guards stood against the far wall behind a man who sat at a table.

He sat quite still with both hands on the table, palms down. He was around six feet tall and slim built. His black hair was going grey in places and he had a three-day stubble on his chin yet he was still quite handsome. Mac could see why women might be attracted to him. He smiled as they all sat down. Dave said something to him in Greek. He looked up at Mac.

'Of course, Chief Inspector Christodoulou,' he said in perfect English. 'Anyway, what a pleasure it is to see you, to see anyone to be honest. All those women who swore that they loved me, not one of them has visited me in prison.'

'Well a few of them are still in prison themselves for being your accessories if I remember right,' Dave pointed out.

'There is that, I suppose,' he replied with a rueful smile. 'So, what do you need from me?'

'Libretta House, what you were doing there?' Dave asked.

The prisoner looked puzzled by Dave's question.

Dave went on, 'You left a fingerprint on the safe in a room on the third floor.'

Mr. Liourdis thought some more and then nodded.

'I remember now. It wasn't exactly one of my more successful projects, in fact, it was a total waste of time.'

He stopped and looked intently at Dave.

'If I tell you what I know, will that help me with getting an early release?'

'I'll make sure that your cooperation is entered into your record,' Dave replied not committing himself.

'That's better than nothing I suppose. Okay, I was seeing a chambermaid at the time who worked in one of the fancy apartment blocks. As she's still enjoying the luxury of having doors that open when you want them to, I won't be giving you any names. Besides her normal work, she sometimes covered at Libretta House when they were short staffed. One day she came to see me and she was almost breathless. She said that she'd overheard one of the guests at Libretta House say that they had lots of cash in their room safe. 'Hundreds and thousands,' she said, so I thought I'd check it out. You don't have a cigarette on you, do you?' he asked with a hopeful look.

Dave pulled a full pack from his pocket and passed them over to him.

'You're a gentleman,' he said with a genuine smile.

They waited while he lit up and then took his first drag. He smiled a satisfied smile.

'So, I got into the apartment block, picked the lock of the room and opened the safe. People are so lazy, I only had to use the standard PIN to open it. Inside the safe I found sixty euros in cash, some trashy jewellery and a small cardboard box. I looked inside the box and found that it contained twelve plastic tubes. I thought that they might be drugs until I pulled one out and had a look.'

He stopped and took another long drag from his cigarette.

'They were full of these multi-coloured sprinkles that you put on cakes...'

Mac laughed out loud.

'We call them 'hundreds and thousands' in England.'

'That's right,' Mr. Liourdis said with a broad smile. 'So, I closed the safe and left as quietly as I could. It was only when I got outside that I realised that one of my latex gloves had a rip in it and that I might have left some prints. It didn't bother me though, after all I hadn't actually taken anything.'

'How did you get into the apartment block?' Dave asked. 'I take it that you didn't go through the lobby?'

'No, they have cameras in the lobby and, anyway, someone might have seen me. I came in through the fire escape using the door on the third floor. My friendly chambermaid had left it open for me.'

'I thought that all the fire escape doors were alarmed?'

'Yes, they are but the alarm system is old and there's a glitch,' Mr. Liourdis replied. 'I don't know how they found out about it but, if you trip a certain switch on the main breaker box and then open the fire escape door, the alarm won't go off. You can then leave the door open and trip the switch back on and the system still won't pick it up. Only once the door is shut will the alarm become operational again.'

The three policemen looked at each other. This new information opened up a host of new possibilities.

'You said that 'they found it out'. Who are 'they'?' Dave asked.

'The cleaners,' he replied. 'If you're working on the third floor and you want a cigarette it's easier to trip the switch and sit on the fire escape than to go all the way down to the street. I was told that the girls used to have their breaks out on the fire escape landing too.'

'I take it that the people who own the apartments know nothing about this?'

'I'd guess not or they'd have probably done something about it,' he replied.

As soon as Dave got outside, he took out his phone. He talked all the way back to the car.

'I've just told the team to bring all the cleaners in,' Dave said as he put his phone away. 'There are nine of them in all, seven are currently working shifts while the other two are there for cover in case of illness.'

'What about previous employees?' Mac asked.

'The hotel owner should be putting a list together for us right now,' Dave replied as he started the car up.

'So, now we've got nine cleaners in the frame plus anyone else who worked in the apartment block,' Andy said.

'Not forgetting the cleaner's husbands and boy-friends and anyone else they might have mentioned the fire alarm glitch to,' Dave said. 'Let's double check the hotel staff too, someone there must have known about it.'

'You've got plenty to do then,' Mac said knowing that this was something that he couldn't help them with.

'Shall I drop you back at your apartment?' Dave asked.

'Yes please.'

It had now gone three o'clock and Mac was feeling a bit tired.

'I'll try and catch up with you later,' Dave said. 'Around eight at the little bar that we met at before?'

'Yes, that would be good,' Mac said. 'I'll give the police team in the UK a call and see if they've come up with anything. I'll update you when we meet up.'

Dave dropped him in the square. He walked around the corner and saw a van pull up outside the entrance to the apartments. A man in a white all-in-one suit got out and retrieved a big black case from the back of the van. Mac held the lift for him and, of course, he was going to the third floor.

Forensics, Mac thought. He's going to dust the breaker box for prints. The team had moved quickly.

He was grateful to be walking back down the hall towards his little apartment. His back was hurting and he suddenly felt dog tired.

Once in his room he pulled the curtains across and turned the air conditioning on. He undressed and gingerly lay down on the bed. A spike of pain made him grunt. Once that was out of the way he knew the pain should ease off a little.

It did. Within five minutes he was fast asleep.

He woke and, for a few seconds, he didn't know where he was. Then his trip to Limassol and the prison in Nicosia flashed into his mind and he remembered. He looked over at the clock. It was nearly six, he'd slept for almost three hours and he felt all the better for it. After a shower and a shave, and with some brand-new clothes on, he felt ready to face the world.

The cafes in the square were doing good business. He found a table and decided that he wasn't all that hungry. He ordered a tuna sandwich and a sparkling water. He sat and happily watched the people around him while he ate.

After he'd finished, he rang Kate and got the latest from the investigation in the UK. She too was sitting outside and she seemed to be enjoying herself from what he could hear. The call didn't take very long as there wasn't all that much to report. He thought that what she'd told him about the wills was interesting though. At seven thirty he started to make his way towards the bar for his meeting with Dave.

He walked around the back of the fort and past a little restaurant. He turned the corner and saw a large group of cats queuing near the kitchen window. He stopped for a moment as a piece of meat flew out of the window and was pounced on by several cats. A lot of the cats he'd seen so far looked thin and mangy but all of these were fat and sleek.

He then turned left towards the glimmering sea. He stood for a while, arms resting on the glass wall, as he looked out over the water. It was still light out but it looked as if it wouldn't be long before the sun disappeared. Even in the short time he'd stood there it had gotten a little darker. He turned and walked past the group of backgammon players as he made his way back across the street. He noticed that the back-gammon board had been positioned right underneath a streetlamp and he thought that it would be just like a football game being played under floodlights.

The white-haired man was sitting outside watching the backgammon players and the cars going by. He went inside when Mac did. He seemed to have remembered Mac as he smiled and gestured towards the fridges. Mac helped himself to a large bottle of beer and once again paid a very small amount for it. He took it outside and sat down. The beer was crisp and refreshing and he was quite happy as he sat and watched the sea change colour as the sky gradually darkened overhead.

He was woken from his reverie by shouts and the noise of backgammon counters being slammed down. An old man with a stick walked off with a scowl on his face. He turned and aimed some

154

invective back at the small group of players who were left. They just laughed and waved at him to go away.

Probably a bad loser, Mac thought.

He watched as a small electric three-wheeler came to a stop and parked just a few yards away from him. An old man slowly got out of the one-seater vehicle and hobbled towards an empty chair. He and the white-haired man exchanged a few words. The white-haired man disappeared into the bar before returning with a can of beer. A conversation then started up between the two of them.

The road was narrow enough and, with the three-wheeler parked on the kerb, the stream of cars had to slow right down as they passed it by. He also noticed that the little vehicle had a panier in the front and sitting in it was a cute little bright-eyed dog who seemed to take great interest in everything around him. He was so cute that tourists passing by stopped to take selfies with him. Mac thought about Terry and somewhat guiltily hoped that he was okay.

As he returned to looking at the sea the fort caught his eye and the name Harry Jones popped back into his head. He didn't have to think hard to get the connection as his visit to the execution room had never really left his mind. Andy had said that he was the hangman that had despatched all those EOKA fighters. The name was familiar to him for some reason but it took him a while to locate the memory. He remembered that it had been a few months after he'd joined the police and he'd been having a drink with one of his sergeants who was about to retire. They were talking about capital punishment and hanging and this sergeant mentioned Harry Jones.

'Jones and Pierrepoint, they were the two who did most of the hangings,' the sergeant had said. 'I never met Pierrepoint but I did meet Jones. He was a little man and he always wore a bow tie during the hanging itself, for respect he said. You'd think nothing of him otherwise. He was incredibly professional though and checked everything twice. He never ever had a thing go wrong at any of his hangings or so they said.'

Mac took his phone out and looked up Harry Jones on the internet. He found him on Wikipedia as 'Harry Jones Executioner'. He was surprised at how many hangings he'd carried out and how famous some of the cases had been. Apparently, Harold Jones had outlived his namesake as the executioner had died in the nineties. The article was quite long and Mac had only read part of it when Dave turned up.

'Anything?' Mac asked.

Dave shook his head, 'Not yet anyway. Anything from the UK?'

'I'm sorry but there's not much to report on that front either,' Mac said.

Dave sighed and stood there for a moment.

'Another beer?' he asked.

Mac didn't say no.

He could hear Dave and the white-haired man having a conversation in Greek. Once again there was laughter and, from the tone of their voices, Mac reckoned that they must know each other quite well. Dave eventually returned and placed a large bottle of beer in front of Mac and sat down holding a can of coke.

'What did the cleaners say about the alarm?' Mac asked.

'Well, out of the nine we interviewed, six admitted to knowing about the alarm but claimed that they'd forgotten about it. I'd guess that the real reason that they hadn't mentioned it before had more to do with their being afraid of losing their jobs. Three claimed that they knew nothing about it at all.'

'And you believed them?'

'Well, all three hadn't been working there that long and they're all non-smokers, so it's possible.'

'Had any of the cleaners told their husbands or boyfriends?' Mac asked.

'No, or so they claimed, but then they would say that, wouldn't they?' Dave said before taking a big gulp from his drink. 'Oh well, I'm sure that something will happen before long.'

As he said this the world suddenly moved into slow motion.

A motorcycle came flying around the corner and screeched to a halt some five or six yards past where they were sitting. A black helmeted figure turned and looked back at them as his right hand went inside his leather jacket.

'Get down!' he heard Dave shout as he saw a gun pointed directly at them.

Mac was pulled to the ground with some force as he heard the sound of one, two, three, four gunshots and a split second later the sound of each bullet ricocheting against the wall just over his head.

Then he heard more gunshots but this time they were coming from his left, in fact from just inside the bar! Mac could see the bullets rip through the motorcyclist's leather jacket. His body jerked as each shot impacted. There were four holes in his jacket, one in the centre of his back and the other three grouped to the left, around his heart. The gun slowly dropped from his hand and he teetered for a split second before he fell to the ground with the motorbike, engine still running, pinning down his right leg.

From under the table Mac saw the white-haired man walk out of the bar with a pistol held in front of him with both hands. He looked from left to right in

157

case there might be more shooters. All he saw was a group of white-faced holidaymakers who were standing frozen on the pavement opposite. They looked dazed and unsure of what to do next. As though moving past statues, a young couple who only had eyes for each other walked through them as though nothing had happened.

The barman ran over to the motorcyclist, knelt down and felt for a pulse. He then turned the engine off. A trickle of blood had started flowing from the shooter's back. Mac watched it as it slowly flowed towards them following the cracks around each of the cobblestones.

In the silence that ensued Mac heard the roll of the dice and the rattle of the backgammon counters. He looked to his left. One of the game's observers was standing up and seemed to be telling the others what had happened but the game itself never stopped.

Dave stood up, put the table back in place and then helped Mac to his feet. The white-haired man stood up too. He turned to Dave and shook his head.

The man who had tried to kill them was dead.

Chapter Seventeen

Mac sat nursing a cup of coffee while he waited for someone to turn up. He'd already given his statement to a young woman police officer and he'd been told to wait in the interview room until someone came to get him. That someone turned out to be Andy.

'Dave's got the whole team in and we're having a briefing,' Andy said. 'Are you okay Mac?'

'Well, yes, I mean the bullets missed me...'

'Only just from what I've heard. No, I meant your back. Dave was worried that he might have hurt you when he pulled you to the ground.'

In all the fuss since the shooting he hadn't given a thought to his back. He also reminded himself to thank Dave for his quick thinking. It had saved his life.

'No, my back's not too bad. Have you identified the shooter yet?'

'Well, we haven't had a formal identification but Dave knew who he was anyway,' Andy said. 'You'll hear all about it in a couple of minutes.'

The briefing room was quite full. On the other side of the room the white-haired man who had killed the would-be assassin was leaning against the wall. He waved a hand at Mac. He waved back.

'Who is he?' Mac asked. 'I thought that he was just a friendly neighbourhood bar owner.'

'Well, that's what he does now,' Andy replied, 'but he also happens to be Dave's old sergeant. His name is Ioannis Kyriakou and he retired from the police a year or so ago. He bought the bar for something to do.'

Now things made sense to him.

'He's certainly good with a gun,' Mac said.

'He is that,' Andy said. 'I think he still holds the record for the best ever score on the police firing range.'

Dave started speaking and the room fell silent. Mac looked around. The intent looks of concentration on the policemen's faces reflected how seriously they were all taking it. As before, Andy translated for him.

Dave told them that the dead shooter had been identified as Antonis Komodromos. He described him as a wannabee gangster who sometimes went under the name of Tony Smith. He had previous for robbery, car theft, assault and demanding money with menaces. The last count was related to a recent attempt to set up a protection racket. However, that hadn't turn out too well for him when he'd picked on the wrong restaurant owner. This particular restauranteur had a very large family and he hadn't hesitated to invite a dozen of his burliest male relatives to help him out. He'd armed them with pick-axe handles and they had literally chased Antonis and his crew out of town. The police hadn't heard from him since and they'd assumed that he'd been lying low.

They'd learned that he had a flat in Perivolia which Andy told him was a small town about ten kilometres from Larnaka. A squad was searching it now.

Dave said that, although Antonis Komodromos acted big and made out that he had friends in the Mafia, he had always been strictly small-time. Until now that is. Something or someone had persuaded Antonis to step up several leagues, to attempt not just a murder but the murder of two police officers. Most of Antonis' associates were also known to the police. They were to be all brought in and interrogated tonight. If they mentioned anyone else that Antonis knew, or had been seen with, then they too were to be picked up.

The teams were each given a list and were warned that it was going to be a long night. The room emptied quickly as the teams went about their business. Dave came over.

'Are you okay, Mac? I'm sorry if I was a bit rough.'

'No, don't be. Your quick thinking saved my life. Thanks, Dave,' Mac said with real sincerity.

'Well, if it wasn't for me getting you involved in the case you might not have been shot at in the first place.'

'No, please don't go there,' Mac protested. 'Getting involved in the case was all my own decision. I wanted to be involved, I still do.'

'I really wasn't expecting that to happen,' Dave said as he shook his head in wonder.

'We must be getting close if someone wants us out of the way. But close to what? Now that's what I'd like to know,' Mac said. 'I believe that you knew the shooter.'

'Yes, yes I did,' Dave replied with a sad look. 'I knew who he was straight away. He had tattoos across his knuckles on both hands, 'love' on the right hand and 'hate' on the left. Just to make sure I asked the forensics team to check for a certain tattoo on his right upper arm. That confirmed that it was him.'

'What was the tattoo of?' Mac asked.

'Robert De Niro, believe it or not.'

'You sound quite upset about it being him,' Mac said.

'Well, I suppose I am, more shocked really,' Dave said. 'While I knew the shooter, only professionally of course, I'd never have thought him capable of this. I first arrested Antonis some ten years or so ago when he was caught stealing TVs from a warehouse. He was a strange kid. He was both incredibly stupid about some things and quite bright about others. His family were good people and they had no idea why he'd turned out as he did. He had this thing in his head about the Mafia and he must have watched Goodfellas

161

a million times, he knew every scene and every word. If he hadn't had this weird fascination with gangsters then I think he could have done anything, you know?'

'Do you think that someone put him up to it?' Mac asked.

'I'm fairly certain of it. I can't see this being something that he'd dream up himself,' Dave said. 'If that is the case then I'm hoping that one of Antonis' friends might be able to tell us who that person might be. However, we need to go and see his parents first and I'm not looking forward to it.'

'The best of luck with that,' Mac said with some sympathy.

He'd been in Dave's position many times before and telling relatives about a tragic death was a part of the job that he'd always hated.

'Shall I organise a lift back for you?' Dave asked.

'No, you get on, you've got a lot to do tonight. I'll phone Michalis in a bit,' Mac replied.

He was envious as he watched them go. Now there was just him and the man who'd saved his life left in the room. He was still leaning against the wall with an impassive look on his face. He smiled as Mac came over.

'Thank you, Ioannis,' Mac said as he held out his hand.

'You're welcome,' he said in a gravelly voice as he shook Mac's hand. 'Everyone calls me Yanni.'

'Do you miss it?' Mac asked as he looked around the empty room.

'Like hell. Fancy a drink?'

Mac's wide smile was answer enough.

Yanni's beaten up little Peugeot was parked outside. They drove up the beach road towards the square. It was still only ten o'clock and the pavements and cafes were full.

'Unfortunately, we can't use the best bar in town as it will be crawling with forensics but there's one up the road that isn't bad,' Yanni said.

They turned right just before the fort and then left down the back streets. It was one of the older residential areas of the town and, while most of the houses were in good repair, several that they passed by were well on their way to falling down. They looked as though their owners had just shut the doors forty-five years ago and never came back which Mac surmised was probably the truth.

He wondered what the neighbours of these houses felt about it. It must be like living next door to ghosts.

They soon turned left again and Mac could see the dark sky at the end of the street. Yanni turned left again back onto the Piale Pasa and pulled up outside a white building. It had 'Kyrene Café and Snack Bar' painted in big letters on the side of the building. He followed Yanni towards one of the tables on the pavement at the front of the café. He was glad that Yanni had chosen to sit there as it had the most wonderful sea view. He could see the lights from as far as Finikoudes Beach to his left right up to Psarolimano marina to his right. Lonely lights out at sea told of ships passing in the night.

A waitress came and Yanni spoke a few sentences to her in Greek after which they both spoke English.

'What would you like?' she asked in a London accent.

Mac smiled. He was still getting used to the way people could so easily switch from one language to another.

'A beer would be good,' Mac replied.

'And something stronger too perhaps?' Yanni asked.

Mac nodded. His nerves were still jangling.

'Two zivanias as well, large ones,' Yanni said.

Mac didn't ask what zivania was. He guessed that he'd find out soon enough.

'You're ex-army?' Mac asked.

'Well, just about everyone in Cyprus is but yes, I did a little more than most. Twenty years I served. Does it show?'

'No, not that much,' Mac replied. 'It's just that you remind me very much of someone. He was my sergeant for quite a few years until I retired. He was ex-army and he knew how to use a gun too which was just as well as I'm totally useless. He used to joke and say that I shouldn't bother using the shooting range and that I should find a nice big barn to shoot at instead. He was right too. Have you known Dave long?'

'For nearly fifteen years and I was his sergeant for ten of those,' Yanni replied. 'He's a good policeman. He really cares about the job. I mean, just look at him tonight. Some kid tries to kill him and he's sad that he's dead. I am too if I'm being honest.'

Mac could see that Yanni had been quite affected by having to shoot someone dead.

'There was nothing else you could have done,' Mac said. 'If you hadn't shot him dead then it would be Dave and me who would be in body bags tonight.'

'Thanks, I think I needed to hear that,' Yanni said softly.

They were interrupted by the arrival of their drinks. Two large pints of Keo were placed on the table as well as two large shot glasses filled to the brim with a clear liquid. Mac guessed that it wasn't water.

Yanni picked up his shot glass and looked at Mac expectantly. Mac picked up his and they clinked glasses.

'Slainte,' Yanni said just before he downed his.

Mac downed his in one too as it was only good manners. He was prepared for it to be something akin to battery acid but, afterwards, there was just a pleasant warmth as it went down and the distinct flavour of currants in his mouth.

'How do you like zivania?' Yanni asked.

'It's good, no I mean really good. It's not what I expected at all.'

'Another one?'

Mac nodded. He could feel the relaxing warmth of the spirit coursing pleasantly through his veins.

Mac waited until Yanni had ordered the round before asking, 'How do you know how to say 'Cheers' in Irish?'

Yanni grinned as he said, 'Well, Larnaka's a holiday town and I always liked the Irish best. They're really good fun and just out for a good time, the crack I think they call it. Dave told me about you and so I said 'Slainte' just as the Irish always do.'

'Yes, you're right there,' Mac said with a smile. 'If there are two things the Irish excel in its drinking and having a good time.'

Two more shot glasses appeared on the table. Mac picked his up.

'How do you say, 'Cheers' in Greek?' he asked.

'Yamas,' Yanni replied. 'It means 'To our health'.'

'Well, I'm lucky that I've still got any health after tonight, so here goes. Yamas!'

Chapter Eighteen

Mac felt as though his eyelids had been glued together. When he finally got them open, he looked over at the clock but his vision was blurred and he couldn't make out the time. He rubbed his eyes and tried again but he still couldn't make out what time it was. He stared at the little clock until he finally realised that it was on its side. He turned the clock through ninety degrees and discovered that it was eleven thirty.

He felt a momentary panic at it being so late. Shouldn't he be doing something?

He then remembered the events of the previous evening and decided to cut himself some slack. He gingerly sat up. After all the zivanias he'd drank with Yanni he reckoned that his head should be falling off by now. However, he felt surprisingly okay. He was a bit on the slow side though and it took quite a while for him to go through his morning routine. It was twelve thirty by the time he finally managed to get himself out of the door.

He sat down at the first available table and ordered a large orange juice and coffee. He was glad that he was able to wear sunglasses. He'd looked in the mirror on his way out and, as one of his old sergeants used to put it, 'Maguire, your eyes look like piss holes in the snow.' The memory made him smile.

He felt better after the orange juice and even better once he'd gotten some caffeine inside him. He checked his phone for messages. There was just the one from Dave.

'Heard you had quite a night with Yanni so you will need some time to recover. We'll be busy all day chasing up some leads. We can catch up this evening at Yanni's place as it should be open by then. Call you later Dave.'

Mac smiled as he remembered his night with Yanni. It was just what he'd needed after nearly being killed. He supposed it was also just what Yanni had needed after killing someone. Yanni had been excellent company and they'd swapped police stories all night. He couldn't remember how many zivanias he'd put away but it had been quite a few. He vaguely remembered them closing up the café around them as they sat there and the waitress then giving them both a lift back in her little Seicento. He hoped that they'd left her a good tip.

Thinking of the café gave him an idea. He thought that walking might be the best way of clearing the cobwebs from his brain. He'd attempt the walk to the Kyrene cafe. He had no idea exactly how far away it was but he'd give it a go. He finally managed to raise himself from his seat and he set off.

He walked around the back of the fort and towards the sea. He passed by an armed policeman who was standing by a 'No Entry' sign. A car, ignoring the detour sign, passed by him only for the policeman to send it back.

As always, he leant on the glass wall and just gazed over the sea for a while. He then turned and looked around. There were no backgammon players on the pavement. Just past where he was standing a crime scene tape ran right across the road. Another one did the same about forty yards further on. The outline of a blood pool could still be clearly seen on the surface of the road. Mac's eyes followed the dark trail of blood that had run between the cobblestones and the events of the evening before ran through his head like a movie.

The gun being pulled and aimed; Dave dragging him to the floor; the echoes of ricochets right above his head; the sound of his heart wildly pumping in his ears; the soft thud of bullets impacting the shooter; the

167

gun slowly, slowly falling from a dead man's hand and the motorcycle falling to the floor, its engine still idling.

Mac awoke from his trance and looked around him. For a second or so he'd felt quite disoriented. While it probably had more to do with the quantity of zivania he'd drunk the night before than anything else, he knew that he'd have to keep an eye on himself. Not long ago, after being involved in some explosions, he'd had a bad time and discovered that he'd been suffering from Post-Traumatic Stress Disorder. It had been quite scary until he finally went to a doctor who told him what it was. He had reassured him that it would probably go away by itself. It had but Mac had kept a close eye out for it ever since. Even more so now, after the events of the previous evening.

He had to go down to the lower walkway to continue his journey. He stopped after a few yards and looked at Yanni's bar. He could clearly see the bullet marks on the wall. He noticed that only his head and shoulders would be visible from the bar and this gave him an idea. He sat down on the low wall separating the walkway from the sea. His eyeline was just about level with the street above. All you'd see from Yanni's Bar would be the top of someone's head.

About sixty yards further on he was able to go up a ramp and get back up to street level. He stopped at the next bench and sat down. The first bench was within the cordon so this was bench number two.

He sat and looked at the sea as mesmerised as ever by its colours and movement. A small blue tourist boat scudded by. It looked quite full. Some of the passengers, mostly children, were waving to the people on the shore as they sailed by. Mac did his due diligence and waved back.

He roused himself and made it quite easily to bench number three. He sat down again and looked at the restaurant with the windmill. As always it looked quite full. He had to think for a while to figure out what day it was. It was Saturday. He guessed that might be why he hadn't gotten any updates from the team in the UK. It was the weekend. Weekend or not he knew that the police team here in Cyprus would be working flat out.

If only he could help them in some way.

He realised that, not being built for an action-man role, the only way he'd ever really helped was by using his brain. He still had that, even though it felt as if it was only running at half speed at the moment.

Use the walk to think about the case, he told himself, but don't think too hard.

He often found that he got the best results by thinking his way around things rather than attacking the problem head on. He set himself a question.

Why did the shooting happen?

He got up and walked on. Before he'd reached bench number four, he'd thought of another question.

Why now?

He sat down on the bench and thought some more. He wondered whether this might be the more important question at this point. He just let the thoughts come.

It had all started with the motorcycle flying around the corner before stopping some five or six yards past them. Mac remembered the squeal of brakes. The motorcyclist had been going at speed and therefore, as the bar was just a few yards from the corner, he couldn't have been anywhere in a direct line of sight of the bar. He'd had to brake so hard because he'd overshot. If he'd pulled up opposite where he and Dave had been sitting, he'd have been only feet away and it would have had a much easier shot. He and Dave would almost definitely have been killed.

169

If the shooter had been a professional, he'd have come around the corner more slowly, ensuring that he could stop at the optimum spot to get a shot off. However, the shooter was an amateur and the adrenalin had been coursing through his veins while he was waiting. He came around the corner too fast and overshot.

He ran the scene through his head again and again. A picture of the bright-eyed dog popped into his head. Of course, the little electric tricycle!

It might well be that Dave and he owed their lives to the man who had parked the tricycle where he did. It would have blocked his view and the shooter wouldn't have been able to see them until it was too late.

So how did he know that they were there in the first place? Mac decided that the shooter must have had an accomplice.

He pictured the scene in his mind. If he'd have been the spotter, he'd have sat on the wall on the lower walkway, just as he'd done a few minutes ago, and kept watch. He wouldn't have been noticeable from that vantage point. He could have followed Dave from the station or even Mac from his apartment. The motorcyclist must have been parked up somewhere nearby, the back of the fort perhaps, while he waited for the call.

He made a mental note to ask Dave if a phone was found on the killer.

If he'd have been the spotter, he'd have walked briskly away the second that the call had been made. He hadn't seen any CCTV cameras on the Piale Pasa but he'd ask Dave anyway.

Again, the question 'Why now?' popped back into his head. He got up and started off for bench number five. He was oblivious to his surroundings now as he let his thoughts take him over. Halfway between benches he stopped and stood like a statue.

Why now? Was it because they were getting close to discovering something vital? While that had to be part of the calculation was there something else?

Mac carried on walking before stopping again after a few yards.

What would be gained if he and Dave had been killed?

It wouldn't have stopped the investigation although it would certainly have slowed it down. Yes, that was it.

Time. That's what would be gained.

He noticed that he was quite close to the next bench so he walked the extra few yards and sat down.

That might explain why Antonis, the wannabee gangster, was used. Ever since Dave had described him Mac had wondered why anyone would use him for a job like this. He'd never killed before, so how could whoever put him up to it be sure that Antonis would succeed at his very first attempt?

Mac smiled. It didn't matter. If Antonis had missed, then they would still be chasing their tails looking for him. His guess was that 'the man', as he'd started calling whoever it was that was running this show, had plans for Antonis afterwards. He'd bet that, if Yanni hadn't killed him, then the man might have done it anyway. There would be no loose ends that way and the police would waste time looking for a live shooter when they should be looking for a corpse.

So, the man might have needed time but time to do what? Is there a deadline of some sort that must be met?

Without thinking about it he got up and started off for the next bench. He pictured Harold Jones in the centre of a circle and around him on the rim of the circle there were the things that they knew about the case so far; Scarparis the smuggler, his car trips to places unknown, the land he'd bought, Lefkhod Logistics, the disappearing money, the Tornado Pub, the fire alarm system at the Libretta and finally the fair-haired man from Newcastle.

Was he 'the man'? Mac thought. He was certainly the only candidate that they had so far.

He sat down on bench number six.

Then there were the cleaners. Finding out about the glitch in the alarm system had muddied the waters somewhat. Whoever killed Harold Jones must have been aware of the glitch so it was either a cleaner, a hotel employee or someone they'd told about the alarm who had killed Harold Jones. Loukas Liourdis and the way he'd romanced hotel staff popped into his mind. It was hardly a unique MO so perhaps that's how the killer knew. Even if one of the cleaners had unwittingly given information to the killer, they probably wouldn't want anyone to know about it, and especially not the police.

A panoramic view of the sea lay in front of him but he was totally unaware it. Once again, he got up without thinking and slowly walked towards the next bench.

He had a number of facts but no one fact seemed to have any connection to another. He'd been in this situation many times before and something his old boss, Rob Graveley, had once told him came back to mind. The case they'd been investigating at the time had been confusing to say the least. They'd found out quite a lot about the murder victim but none of the facts seemed to fit together and the team had been getting frustrated.

'Calm down lads,' Rob had said. 'We're in danger here of going off in all directions. I want you all to have a really good think and come up with the five things that you'd like to know about the case, just five no more, so make sure every question you write down is a crucial one.'

They'd then selected the most popular questions and concentrated on just answering those. Mac thought that it had been a good way of focussing their efforts and it had certainly worked in that case. He remembered asking Rob afterwards what he would have done if the five questions they'd identified hadn't solved the case?

'I'd have asked you for five more,' he'd replied with a deadpan expression.

So, what were the five things that Mac would want to know more about?

He sat down on bench number seven and gave it some serious thought. He identified some questions he'd like to ask but, when he counted them on his fingers, there were eleven of them in all. He needed to get rid of six of them.

He always thought better when walking so he got up and started off for the next bench. By the time he reached bench number eight he'd got it down to seven.

What he really needed, he thought, was a pen and some paper.

He looked around him and was surprised to see that the Kyrene Snack Bar and Café was just a short walk away. His stomach rumbled and he realised that he was ravenously hungry. He walked towards the café and saw a board outside that said 'Full English served until 2 p.m. €5' with an appetising photo underneath. He looked at his watch. It was now fifteen minutes past two. He felt somewhat deflated as he sat down outside the café. He realised that he'd picked the same table that he'd sat at the night before.

A waitress came out to him and smiled. She was in her forties and she had long curling black hair and a face that mirrored her smile. Thankfully she wasn't the waitress who had served them and who had given them a lift home. There was a fair bit of last night that he couldn't quite remember and he was a little worried that he might have done something embarrassing.

She asked him what he wanted. In truth he didn't know.

'I saw the Full English Breakfast on the board there but it's gone two now,' he said mournfully.

'That's no problem, Mr. Maguire,' she replied with a smile. 'And what would you like with your Full English breakfast?'

'Coffee will be fine,' Mac replied now looking forward to his breakfast. 'Can I ask how you know my name?'

'I was here yesterday evening when you were in,' she said, 'I was working behind the bar. I've had to order more zivania this morning because of you and Yanni.'

She said this with a teasing smile so Mac wasn't quite sure whether she was being serious or not.

'I was alright...wasn't I?' Mac asked hoping that he'd get an answer that he wouldn't find too embarrassing.

'You and Yanni were fine, real gentlemen actually and, after what you'd been through last night, I think that you both deserved a drink,' she replied as she lightly touched his hand with hers. 'I'll get you your coffee.'

Mac felt better on hearing this. He decided to let his mind idle until he'd had something to eat and he once again got lost as he looked out over the ever-changing sea. He was so entranced that he almost jumped when the waitress came back with his coffee.

'Breakfast won't be a minute,' she said.

In fact, it was two and Mac's stomach rumbled until it arrived. He felt as if he hadn't eaten for days and it went down very quickly. A few minutes later he was wiping his plate with the last fragment of toast. Every morsel had been entirely wonderful and he felt a million times better for having eaten. He sat back in a satisfied stupor.

Once he'd let the breakfast go down, his mind inevitably returned to the case. He asked the waitress for another coffee as well as a pen and some paper. He set to work. After some scribbling outs and several amendments, he eventually listed his five questions –

Where is Costas Skarparis?

Why were two hectares of rocks worth twenty five thousand euros to Harold Jones?

What part does Lefkhod have to play in all this?

If the shooting was all about delaying the investigation to enable something to be achieved, what was that something?

Who is Richard Gatling really?

He sat back and looked at what he'd written and decided that they'd do for a start. He looked at the last question and a thought occurred to him. He took out his phone and went onto the internet. He quickly found what he was looking for. He smiled. He was now fairly sure that 'Richard Gatling' had been an alias as that had also been the name of the man who had invented the Gatling Gun. He thought about Martin and wondered if he'd made any progress with the photograph that he'd sent him.

At that point his phone went off. He had an email but it wasn't from Martin, it was from Colin Furness.

Mac,

Finally had some luck on the financial front. Around fifty million followed a circuitous route via the Far Eastern markets but ended up back in the UK. It went into a charitable trust fund called the 'Evagoras Arts Trust'. The only information I've got on it so far is that it was set up to assist UK based museums but exactly how we don't know. Kate is following this up right now.

As for the rest of the money we've got some good leads. I'll be working over the weekend so I'll let you know if I come up with anything else.

This made some sense to Mac. Harold Jones had wanted to be remembered and he supposed that this arts trust might help with that. However, this latest information only generated more questions. Why the attempt to cover up where the money came from by sending it halfway around the world? And why did only fifty million pounds make its way into the trust? Where was the other two hundred and fifty million or more?

He was wondering how Kate and Tommy were going to investigate the trust when he had a sudden thought. He knew that he'd been slow that morning but there was someone who he definitely owed a phone call.

He sighed as he looked for the number.

What exactly was he going to say?

Chapter Nineteen

Kate was woken by a loud thud. She sat up and saw the heavy leather-bound book *Collected Letters of Robert FitzWarren, 6th Viscount FitzWarren of Holles, Volume Three* on the floor by the side of the bed. She must have fallen asleep while she was reading it. She turned hoping that she hadn't woken Toni only to find that she wasn't there.

'Breakfast!' she heard Toni shout from the kitchen.

She sat down at the table and smiled as Toni presented her with her favourite – Eggs Benedict with mushrooms – and a kiss.

'You were reading in bed last night,' Toni said. 'A page turner was it?'

'Not exactly,' Kate said as she tucked into her breakfast. 'It was something to do with work and I got interested. I didn't keep you awake, did I?'

'No, I slept well. What's the book's about then?'

'It's a collection of letters sent to an early nine-teenth century aristocrat,' Kate replied. 'He was into collecting classical art and the letters are from people all over Europe offering him paintings or statues or talking about the art objects that they've managed to get their own hands on. Mostly by stealing them from other countries I'd guess.'

'Like the Elgin Marbles?' Toni asked.

'Exactly, I read about that on the internet last night too. They were taken in order to preserve them, or so the man who stole them said. He might have had a point back then but they've got a perfectly good museum in Athens now so why have we still got them?'

'You sound quite passionate about it,' Toni said.

'I don't suppose that I've ever thought about it before but, reading the letters, you get this sense of entitlement from all these colonial macho males striding

177

around the world taking whatever they wanted and thinking that they had every right to do so,' Kate explained.

She didn't tell Toni that this had resonated with her so much because they reminded her of her own father.

'So, what does that have to do with work then?' Toni asked.

'We found the book in Harold Jones' library. It had lots of notes in the margins and I even found a section in the book on Cyprus. These were mostly letters from someone called Captain Edworth Holwell Bassingbourne, believe it or not. He seems to have been employed by this Viscount FitzWarren to search out and buy classical art for his proposed museum. From what I've read he seems to have been more of a pirate than anything else. Anyway, Harold Jones seemed to be particularly interested in him for some reason.'

'Isn't there a FitzWarren Museum in Cambridge?' Toni asked. 'I'm sure that I drove by it a couple of weeks ago.'

'Yes, that's the one but it didn't exist when the letters were written. This Captain Bassingbourne was one of the men who the Viscount hoped would provide the exhibits for the museum when it opened.'

'So, what happened to him?'

'Who, Captain Bassingbourne?' Kate asked. When Toni nodded, she continued, 'He went down with his ship before he could get his art treasures home, a sudden storm in the Mediterranean just off the coast of Turkey.'

Toni was silent for a while.

'Do you really think that some letters written nearly two hundred years ago might have something to do with your murder?'

178

'I've absolutely no idea,' Kate replied. 'Maybe it's just clutching at straws but...'

Kate was interrupted by her phone. She picked it up and looked at the number. It was Colin.

'Have you found something?' she asked hopefully.

'Good morning to you too Kate,' Colin replied sounding quite pleased with himself. 'Yes, I have actually. I've found where the fifty million went.'

'Well, go on then,' Kate prompted him.

'The money ended up in something called the 'Evagoras Arts Trust'. It was apparently set up to assist museums in some way. The only other information I've got is the name of the person running the trust. He's called Peter Neville and he's a partner in a firm of solicitors in Cambridge called Carr, Neville and Baxter.'

'Hang on, just let me get a pen,' Kate said.

Toni already had a pen and notepaper to hand. Kate thanked her with a smile. She wrote the details down and then confirmed them once again with Colin.

'I know it's Saturday and all that but I thought that you might like to know,' Colin said.

'Thanks. What are you going to do now?'

'I'm off to bed, it's been a long night.'

'Oh, just a quick question,' Kate said. 'Have you any idea what a capital E with an exclamation mark next to it might mean?'

'Well, it could be mathematical notation I suppose. 'E' might be Euler's Number and the exclamation mark might be a factorial...'

'I found it in an old book that Harold Jones was interested in. It seems to be in his handwriting but I don't think that it would be mathematical.'

Colin didn't say anything for a moment.

'Oh, of course, how stupid of me! One of my old tutors at college used to write that occasionally when he felt that I'd actually got the gist of what he'd been teaching me for once. It's short for 'Eureka!' It's old Greek for 'I found it', I think.'

'Thanks Colin. I'll let you get to bed. Oh, and don't forget to let Mac know what you've found,' Kate said.

'Thanks for reminding me. I'll send him an email now,' Colin replied. 'I'll give you a ring when I'm up and about again.'

Kate was deep in thought for a while. Then she gave Toni a look.

'I take it that we're not going shopping this morning as planned?' Toni asked.

'Well, I would like to chase this up,' Kate said. 'Oh damn, talking of shopping Tommy's supposed to be going into London with Bridget today. He was really looking forward to it.'

'Need a sidekick?' Toni said with a smile.

'Really?' Kate said with an even bigger smile. 'That would be so much fun.'

She found a number for the solicitors but when she rang all she got was a recording saying that the firm was closed and to call back on Monday. She rang up the station and asked the duty sergeant if someone could find the home phone number and address for a solicitor called Peter Neville.

She and Toni got dressed while they waited. They were nearly ready to go by the time the information arrived. Kate rang the number straight away. She got lucky. Peter Neville was not only in but told her that he'd be free to meet them in around an hour or so.

'Where are we going then?' Toni asked as they walked out of the door.

'A place called Medingley. It's just outside Cambridge somewhere.'

'I've never heard of it,' Toni said.

'Neither have I. We can have an adventure then,' Kate said with a smile that proved to be infectious.

180

It took them just forty-five minutes to get to Medingley, a beautifully leafy thatched-roofed old-fashioned English village. The satnav took them directly to their destination. The house was hidden somewhere behind a row of trees and banks of shrubs. Kate knew that she was at the right place as an ornate sign next to the driveway said 'The Rectory'.

'Houses that don't have numbers are always going to be more expensive,' Toni said.

Kate guessed that Toni could be right. She also guessed that anything at all in this beautifully coiffured village would cost an arm and a leg. They parked on the road for a few minutes and discussed the pros and cons of living somewhere like Medingley. It was all theoretical, of course, as they knew that even two police salaries wouldn't buy much more than a dog kennel in this part of the world.

After fifteen minutes Kate started the car up and steered it into the driveway. The house was modern and quite big, at least six bedrooms, Kate reckoned. Half of the ground floor consisted of a huge window that went from floor to ceiling and inside she could see that some very expensive looking furniture had been scattered around. The front door opened as they got out of the car.

Peter Neville was grey-haired and in his fifties but he clearly looked after himself. He invited them inside and, as they went down a short hallway, Kate could see a well-equipped gym through a half open door. They followed him into a room that served as a home office.

He sat down and invited them to do the same. He looked totally at ease and not fazed at all at meeting the police on his day off.

'So, how can I help the police?' he asked.

'We believe that you're the sole trustee of the Evagoras Arts Trust. Is that right?' Kate asked.

'That's right but I'm afraid that's the sum of what I'm able to divulge about the trust,' he said with a serious expression.

'Presumably you'd need to get the permission of your client to allow us access to information about the trust, is that right?'

'That's correct but, even then, I must admit that I'd be reticent to provide any information directly to the police. We have a good reputation for confidentiality, so I'd strongly recommend to any client that they talked directly to you themselves.'

'Can you at least confirm that your client's name is Harold Jones?'

'I'm afraid that I can't confirm or deny that,' he replied.

'Well, we're a bit stuck then. You see Harold Jones can't give us permission as he's dead, we think he was murdered,' Kate said.

She carefully watched the solicitor's reaction. There was certainly some surprise in his face but it quickly disappeared. He then appeared to be deep in thought for a while.

'I have the bad habit of bringing work home sometimes and my husband really doesn't like it, so I hide it in my desk here.'

He took several folders out of a drawer. He pulled one out and placed it on the desk. Even though it was upside down Kate could make out the name 'Evagoras' on the front.

'However, as I said there is no way that I can directly divulge anything that's in that folder.'

Kate wondered what he meant by this. She got the point when he next spoke.

'Can you excuse me for a moment? I think I hear Paolo calling me.'

He smiled and left the room closing the door behind him.

Kate jumped up and opened the folder. She quickly took photos of the documents that were inside and then sat down again. She and Toni gave each other a conspiratorial smile. Just a couple of minutes later the door handle rattled warning them of Mr. Neville's return.

He sat down, smiled and said, 'As I've said, I'm afraid that I can't divulge any information. If I could help, I would.'

'Thank you anyway. We'll leave you to get on with your weekend,' Kate said.

She and Toni stood up and shook hands with him before he showed them back to the front door. They got in the car and drove it a couple of hundred yards down the road before they stopped.

'Well that was very nice of him to let us have a look at the folder,' Toni said.

'Yes, and he can also state with the absolute truth that he never told us a thing,' Kate replied.

She got her phone out and they both started quickly scanning the images.

'I'm not sure I understand it all but it looks like the trust is worth fifty-four million pounds and that all of that money is earmarked for a new wing at the FitzWarren Museum,' Kate said. 'FitzWarren again, that can't just be a coincidence.'

'Look, there's a sort of schedule here,' Toni said. 'The first payment to the museum is due to be released next week.'

'Yes, seven and half million. I wonder what they're going to do with it?' Kate asked.

'Well, let's go and ask them, shall we?' Toni replied. 'I'll drive as I know where it is. I believe that they also have a nice outdoor café there where we can get some lunch.'

'That sounds great.'

As they drove towards Cambridge, Kate looked over at Toni and wished that all her investigations could be as much fun as this one.

The FitzWarren Museum was truly impressive. Built of grey stone it looked as if an ancient Greek temple, complete with huge Corinthian columns and a triangular sculptured frieze on top, had been dropped into the centre of the city. They walked up the steps and into a huge foyer. The walls were covered with decorative marble punctuated by niches in which alabaster statues of naked Greeks and Romans were displayed. Marble columns flew up to a high vaulted ceiling where a huge round skylight flooded the room with light.

'I've seen palaces that would be shamed by this place,' Kate said as she looked around.

'Yes, it's really something, isn't it?' Toni replied. 'Come on, let's try her.'

Toni pointed towards a young woman who was loitering with intent near the entrance. She wore a dark trouser suit and had a name badge on her lapel. It said 'Charlotte'.

'How can I help?' Charlotte asked with a cheery smile as they approached her.

The smile disappeared when Kate showed her warrant card.

'Would it be possible to speak to the director or whoever it is that runs the museum?' Kate asked.

'I'm not sure,' Charlotte said looking hesitant. 'I don't even know who the director is if I'm honest. I just work here weekends helping people find what they're looking for. If you follow me, I'll take you to my supervisor. She might be able to help you.'

She took them around a corner to an older woman who was sitting at a desk. She talked to her for a while and the woman looked up at them and then picked up the phone.

'She's phoning the director now,' Charlotte explained.

She went back and waited while the older woman finished the conversation and then relayed the message back to them.

'He said that he can meet you in the café outside in about twenty minutes. If that's okay?'

'Tell him that will be fine,' Kate said.

She went back and told the woman that would be fine who then told the director the same thing.

They went outside and ordered some coffees. They sat at the table that was the furthest away from the counter to give them some privacy for the interview. The sun had come out and they sat looking out over a huge freshly mowed green lawn that was surrounded by trees.

'It's really nice here,' Kate said.

'We can have a bite to eat once you've spoken to the director, if you like?' Toni suggested.

'Oh yes please, the feta cheese salad looks really nice,' Kate said. 'And I might also...'

Toni never got to find out what Kate might have also have liked as Kate's phone went off again.

'It's Dan,' Kate said with a puzzled look as she put the phone to her ear.

Dan asked her where she was. He then told her the reason for the phone call. As the call went on Toni could see Kate's face turn pale. She knew that something serious had gone down. All she could do was hold Kate's hand and wait.

'My God,' Kate said softly as she put her phone down. 'That was Dan.'

'I gathered that,' Toni said. 'Something's happened, hasn't it?'

'Yes, it was Mac, he was shot at last night. He was with that Chief Inspector with the long name and someone tried to kill them both.'

185

'Are they okay?' Toni asked looking concerned.

'Yes, but only just. Dan said that the bullets missed them by millimetres.'

'Have they found the man who did it?' Toni asked.

'Oh yes, they were sitting outside a bar catching up on the case and, fortunately for them, the bar is owned by the Chief Inspector's old sergeant who's now retired. He shot the gunman dead. He saved Mac's life and the Chief Inspector's. Dan called me to warn me to be careful, this investigation is obviously hitting a nerve somewhere.'

They gave each other a worried look and held hands even tighter.

'Are you the two policewomen who wanted to see the director?' a man's voice with a distinct anti-podean accent asked.

Chapter Twenty

They both turned around and looked up to see a tall man who had long dark curly hair and a thick beard. He was in his late thirties and he wore denims and a black T shirt that said, *Art is not what you see, but what you make others see.*

Kate and Toni gave each other a quizzical look.

'Yes, I'm Detective Sergeant Kate Grimsson and this is Detective Inspector Toni Woodgate,' she said as she showed him her warrant card. 'And you are?'

'Den Strawberry, I'm the director of this pile,' he said nodding towards the museum. 'How can I help you?'

From his clipped vowels Kate decided that he was probably from New Zealand. Wherever he was from, he was certainly not what she'd expected.

'Have you ever heard of someone called Harold Jones?' she asked as he took a seat next to them.

'Sure, why has something happened to him?'

'You could say that,' Kate replied. 'He's dead, we think that he's been murdered.'

'Bugger!' he said with feeling. 'I heard that he was on the way out but getting murdered is bad luck. How did it happen?'

'He was pushed off a balcony in Cyprus,' Kate said.

'Cyprus?' he said with a mystified look. 'I wonder what he was doing there.'

'We're wondering about that too. Can you tell me what you know about Harold Jones and about any dealings that you've had with him?'

'Well, I can't really tell you very much about him personally. We only met a couple of times around six months ago and any contacts we've had since have been through his solicitor.'

'Would that be Peter Neville?' Kate asked. She noticed that he looked surprised at this, so she continued. 'We know all about the Evagoras Arts Trust.'

'Really? I thought that it was all supposed to have been kept top secret. Anyway, I don't suppose it makes that much difference now,' Den said with a shrug. 'According to Mr. Neville, Mr. Jones wanted everything to be kept under wraps until the deal was done. He told me that Mr. Jones hadn't got long to live but that he'd made plans to ensure that the deal would go through regardless.'

'What deal?' Kate asked.

Den paused and thought for a moment and then he shrugged his shoulders.

'I don't suppose it will hurt to tell you about it now, as far as I know it's a done deal anyway. Mr. Jones was buying the Dimetrescu Hoard.'

He said it as though it should mean something to Kate. It didn't.

'I'm sorry, I sometimes forget that there's another world outside the museum's doors,' he continued. 'Let me explain, I first heard of the hoard some twenty years ago when I was still at university, it's a sort of urban myth of the museum world. We know that it's partly based on truth, there really was a Constantin Dimetrescu who lived in Varna in the early nineteenth century. He styled himself 'Count Dimetrescu' although it's believed that he was really a merchant rather than an aristocrat. He must have been quite good at being a merchant though as he became very rich. He married late in life to a Greek woman and, after he spent his honeymoon in Greece, he became something of an Hellenophile. So, the port of Varna was a major trade hub in those days and he started buying ancient Greek art works from ships that were passing through. As his collection grew, he even went so far as to fund several voyages to Cyprus with the sole aim of collecting even more

188

items. It was said that he ended up owning one of the greatest private collections in the world. He corresponded with Viscount FitzWarren for a time and we have some of his letters here in our archive.'

'What happened to his collection?' Kate asked.

'Well, that's the question that people in the world of art and archaeology have been asking for nearly two hundred years,' Den replied. 'Unfortunately for Count Dimetrescu, he took his love of Greece a little too far. He joined a secret society called the Filiki Eteria. Varna is now in Bulgaria but, at the time, it was part of the Ottoman Empire which also ruled Greece. The Filiki were fighting for an independent Greek state and eventually got what they wanted when they started a war. However, before that happened some of the Filiki in Varna were betrayed and Dimetrescu ended up in an Ottoman prison where he died.'

'So, what happened to his art treasures?'

'Now that's the question. The reports at the time said that they were all lost when Dimetrescu's house was burnt to the ground not long after he was arrested. Some say that the Ottomans did it out of spite but there was another rumour that Dimetrescu might have arranged to have it done himself. The theory is that he'd somehow seen his arrest coming and had managed to get most of his collection to safety. So, if this was true, then the fire was just a cover. I must admit that it all sounded a bit far-fetched to me, so I was really surprised when I heard that Harold Jones was interested in Dimetrescu.'

'How did you hear about his interest?' Kate asked.

'He told me about it himself,' Den said. 'About six months ago he approached me and asked if he could have access to some of Viscount FitzWarren's private papers. As he wasn't an accredited academic researcher, I turned him down but he then waved a substantial cheque at the trustees and that got him what he wanted. He said that he was interested in looking at the letters that Dimetrescu had sent to the Viscount. So, he spent a week or so working in the archives and that was that, or so I thought. Then, about a month ago, Mr. Neville came and told me that Mr. Jones was buying the Dimetrescu hoard and that he wanted to present it to the museum.'

'So, what did you think of his offer?' Kate asked.

'I thought he was nuts if I'm being honest, Mr. Jones I mean not the solicitor. He was quite a strange bloke so, at first, I wasn't quite sure if it was some sort of joke.'

'So, what persuaded you that it wasn't?

'Well, I was told the story of how the hoard was found by the solicitor,' Den replied. 'Apparently, Harold Jones had found some clues in some old correspondence of Dimetrescu's that he'd managed to get his hands on and, from this, he'd been able to locate where the hoard was being kept. For nearly two hundred years it had lain in the vaults of a Swiss bank in Geneva. The bank had been paid a large sum of money at the time to keep the collection for perpetuity or until someone from the Dimetrescu family came to claim it.'

He smiled and shrugged his shoulders as if to say that he too knew that it was all sounded a bit unlikely.

'I was told that he'd also found the only direct descendent of the Count who was living in Austria. She was a schoolteacher there and she seemed quite happy to take the money for the collection. Well, who wouldn't? Anyway, I'm not a great believer in tall tales but there were these too,' he said as he pulled his phone out.

He got up some photos.

'This first one is a stele, a gravestone really. It shows a father and mother saying goodbye to their son. He's armed so it's likely that he died in a war. It's quite a common theme but I've not seen one quite like this before. And this one is a bronze krater, a massive bowl really. The decorations are of gorgon's heads and it looks as if it was made yesterday. They used these for mixing wine with water for their booze-ups. There are quite a few more but this is the one that floored me.'

He enlarged the photo and sat back in his chair while Kate and Toni looked. It was of a statue of a naked woman, her head tilted to her left. She had a cloth in one hand while the other shielded her sex.

She was beautiful, Kate thought, but not idealised. She had the face and body of a real woman.

'She's gorgeous,' Toni said.

'Yes, she is that,' Den replied. 'It's a bronze statue of Aphrodite, the Greek goddess of love and it's nearly two and a half thousand years old. It's either by Praxiteles of Athens or it's a bloody good copy. Here's another one with Harold Jones in the shot. You can see that the statue is near enough life size.'

'I take it that a statue like this is quite rare?' Kate asked.

'Rare? Non-existent would be more like it. If this isn't some photo-shopped joke, then you're looking at one of the most precious artefacts from the ancient world that has ever been discovered.'

'It would be expensive then?' Kate asked.

Den looked up to the sky and shook his head.

'We know that such statues existed in ancient times but none have made it through the years. If there was a war, and there always was a war, bronze spear tips and swords would be rated as being more important than a statue and so a lot of the bigger ones got melted down. So, this is a total one-off and she's in pretty good condition too. People say things are priceless when they really mean that it's just very expensive but this

191

really would be priceless. I couldn't tell you what it would sell for but a couple of hundred million wouldn't be anywhere near enough.'

Kate and Toni looked at each other.

'Mr. Neville mentioned that Harold Jones had paid over two hundred and fifty million for the hoard,' Den continued. 'From just these photos alone I'd say that he got a real bargain.'

So that's where the rest of the money went, Kate thought.

'You're due to be paid some money next week by the Evagoras Arts Trust, seven and a half million. What's that for?' Kate asked.

'That's to get the project primed. We've already got the architects on board and they've started on some designs but next week is when we'll really get going,' Den replied with a smile.

'What project?'

'The Harold M. Jones Wing of course. We're building a completely new wing to house the hoard and, looking at the photos, we're really going to need the extra space. The new wing will be right where we're sitting now. It'll put the FitzWarren Museum on the map, not just here in the UK but worldwide. I must admit that I get goose bumps whenever I think of it.'

Kate had to admit that he did look a little like an overgrown child thinking of Christmas. So, the wing was to be named after himself, Harold Jones' little slice of immortality.

'Once the money's in the bank I've also got to start work on the statue,' Den continued. 'The other stip-ulation of the bequest was that a life-size statue of Harold Jones was to be prominently displayed near the entrance to the new wing. A bit self-serving perhaps but a small price to pay for what we'll be getting.'

'Well, they say that you can't take it with you but it looks like Harold Jones did, in a sort of way,' Kate said.

Kate sat in silence for a while after the director had gone. Toni was content to sit and watch her while she thought. She had thought that the statue was gorgeous but the real thing was much, much better.

'Oh, I'm sorry,' Kate said eventually. 'I was miles away.'

'You reminded me of Mac just now. He does a lot of that,' Toni said.

'It must be catching,' Kate said with a smile. 'Although, talking of Mac, I think I'd better let him know what we've discovered. It certainly sheds some light on what Harold Jones was up to but there's one thing I just can't get my head around.'

'What's that?' Toni asked.

'Well, he was supposed to have been tracking down the hoard in Switzerland and then negotiating the sale of the hoard with someone in Austria. So, where does Cyprus come into it?

'

Chapter Twenty-One

Mac was thinking about that exact point after he'd finished talking to Kate. Dave had been able to confirm that Harold Jones hadn't left Cyprus since he'd first arrived there, so he certainly hadn't been spending any time in Austria or Switzerland. Not only that but he'd also confirmed that he'd only spent a couple of nights away from the apartment in the four months that he'd been on the island. He knew that from the interviews they'd done with the cleaners. They cleaned the rooms every day without fail and said that they would have noticed if a bed hadn't been slept in.

Kate had told him that the museum director had initially thought that the tale had been a bit far-fetched. Mac was still of that opinion. In fact, he smelt a rat.

He finished his coffee, said goodbye to the waitress and started back. What Kate had told him changed everything. He needed to give this some thought. He walked over the road to bench number eight and sat down again.

He pictured the circle but, instead of Harold Jones being at the centre, it was the statue of Aphrodite. He'd had a look at a picture of a stone version of the statue on his phone and he had to agree with Kate. It was very beautiful indeed.

The circle was clear in his mind; Aphrodite in the middle and around the rim there were Harold Jones, Scarparis the smuggler, the car trips to places unknown, the land he'd bought, Lefkhod, the disappearing money, the Tornado Pub, the fire alarm system at the Libretta and the fair-haired man from Newcastle.

So, did it make any more sense now? Mac thought.

Something was beginning to appear out of the mist. Mac tried not to think. He got up and started walking

194

again. He was so deep in thought that he walked right by bench number seven.

He didn't buy the story that the museum director had been fed. Harold Jones couldn't have found the hoard and negotiated the deal to buy it himself as he'd been in Cyprus for the past four months. Mac supposed that he could have hired someone to do it for him but that didn't ring true to him either. Harold Jones had been a secretive man and Mac couldn't see him delegating such an important task to anyone else, let alone allowing someone else to spend two hundred and fifty million pounds on his behalf. He'd been a skinflint all his life and, if he'd really found the hoard in a bank vault, Mac guessed that he would have sooner put a fake descendent forward rather than pay good money out. If he was right about this then what was the truth?

There was a link though, Mac thought. Lefkhod and Skarparis were in the business of moving things, something that the fair-haired man seemed to be very interested in as well.

He sat down on bench number six but got up almost immediately and set off again. His thoughts kept coming back to the centre of the circle. The bronze statue. That was the key, he knew it. But why?

Just before he gained bench number five, he had an epiphany. He stood as still as a statue while tourists walked around him. He had no idea how long he would have stood there for but for a kindly German tourist who asked if he was alright.

He smiled and said that he was better than alright. He rang Dave and asked him to meet him right away at Yanni's bar. He asked if he could bring someone with him.

He smiled all the way as the pieces in the jigsaw fell into place in his mind. He was still missing a few pieces but he thought he could make out the overall picture now. He walked past the restaurant with the windmill without noticing and only came to a stop when he saw the fort in front of him.

He sat down on bench number one and rang Kate. He told her of his suspicions and he was glad that she didn't think he was completely mad.

Mac knew that the bar was open as the back-gammon players were back. As he came nearer, he could hear shouting as they banged the counters down. They threw the dice quickly and smiled and grimaced in turn. It looked to Mac as if they were making up for lost time. He stopped by where the blood pool had been but there was nothing there to remind him of life lost, a life wasted. It had all been cleaned away.

He went inside, shook Yanni by the hand and helped himself to a sparkling water. He wanted to keep his head as clear as possible. He asked Yanni if he could join him outside.

'So how are you my friend?' Yanni asked with a big smile as he sat down. 'We had quite a night last night.'

'That we did and it was just what I needed,' Mac replied.

'Yes, me too.'

'I've asked Dave and Andy to meet me,' Mac said. 'And hopefully they'll be bringing someone else along as well.'

They didn't have long to wait. Dave and Andy appeared from around the corner. They were walking quickly and the woman following them was struggling to keep up. Mac watched her as she walked towards him. She was in her late twenties and had long jet-black hair tied up in a ponytail. She was wearing a Stone Roses T-shirt that had seen better days, denims and scuffed trainers. She wore large black rimmed glasses and a bemused expression.

Mac waited for them all to get seated before he asked, 'Have you discovered anything new since we last talked?'

'Not really,' Dave replied with a shrug. 'We've searched Antonis Komodromos' flat but found nothing. To be honest it was too clean and I had the feeling that someone had beat us to it. None of his friends or associates could add anything of value. They said that he was clearly excited about some-thing but they couldn't say what.'

'Tell me, did you find a phone on the shooter?' Mac asked.

'No, why?'

'In that case I guess that there might have been two of them,' Mac said.

'Two of what?' Andy asked.

Mac told them about his theory.

'I think that someone was watching us when we were sitting outside the bar. I guess that, when you turned up, he called an accomplice on his phone who then gave the signal to Antonis to set off.'

'I hadn't thought about that but, yes, what you say makes sense,' Dave said.

Mac turned to Yanni.

'What's the name of the man with the electric tricycle and the little dog?' he asked.

'Oh, that's Old Marios,' Yanni replied. 'He's been using the bar for nearly thirty years now. Even though he can't walk very far he still visits us every day for a few beers. Why did you want to know?'

'Well, buy him a few drinks on me the next time you see him,' Mac replied. 'I think that his little tricycle might have helped to save our lives. I think that might be one of the reasons that Antonis overshot, the tricycle blocked his view.'

As they were thinking about this the young woman coughed to let them know that she was still there.

'Oh, I'm sorry,' Dave said. 'Mac this is Doctor Evangelina Sofokleous, she's the assistant director of the local Archaeological Museum.'

'Please call me Eva. I'm sorry but I was working on something when I was picked up,' she said looking somewhat flustered as she glanced down at her stained T-shirt. 'Why am I here exactly?'

Dave and Andy looked at Mac.

'Before we get to that let me tell you what I've just learned from Kate Grimsson in the UK.'

Mac told them. He noticed that Eva's ears pricked up when he mentioned the Dimetrescu Hoard.

'So, Mr. Jones was building his own memorial,' Dave said, 'but what was he doing here in Cyprus then?'

'Now that's the question,' Mac replied. 'Eva what did you think of what I've just told you?'

'What? The Dimetrescu Hoard do you mean?' she said with some surprise.

Mac nodded.

'Well, I first heard about it when I started studying archaeology and I was really interested in the idea that it might still exist. After all most of the hoard was stolen from here in the first place but it's just a story, isn't it? I mean, it would be wonderful if those artefacts could have really lasted two hundred years, but, personally, I'd file it right alongside all those stories about Elvis still being alive and the moon landing being a fake.'

'I'm glad you said that,' Mac said turning to look at Dave. 'Before I tell you what I think this is all about, I'd just like to confirm what you've learned from the car trips that Harold Jones made over the last few months.'

'Well, we found another car rental company which hired cars to him when he first came to Larnaka,' Andy said. 'He had some sort of disagreement with them over a scratch on the bodywork after a couple of months and stopped using them. We did an analysis of the mileages that both car rental companies recorded. Most of the trips were between eighty-six to a hundred kilometres or so which would be consistent with a round trip to the Pano Lefkara area where he bought land. There were a couple of longer trips recorded too, the longest of which was nearly four hundred kilometres. He was reported to have been seen in both Paphos and Polis Crysochous, so it's possible that he could have driven to one or both of those.'

'Thanks Andy. Eva have you ever heard of a man called Captain Edworth Holwell Bassingbourne?' Mac asked.

'Oh, yes. He was another robber and an even worse one than Dimetrescu. He filled a ship up with some of the best of our ancient art works and then managed to sink it near Turkey. They said that he was greedy and overloaded it.'

Mac took his phone out and checked it for emails. There was one from Kate just as she'd promised. He opened it up and found the photo of Harold Jones standing in front of the bronze statue of Aphrodite. He placed it on the table so they all could see. Eva snatched it up and looked at the photo intensely.

'She's not real, is she?' she asked.

Mac could see that the picture excited her.

'I think that she just might be,' Mac replied.

'But...but I've never ever seen a statue like that,' Eva said waving her hands about. 'There are some stone ones, mostly damaged in some way, but I've never seen a bronze statue or any statue of that age that was so complete. It can't be real, can it?'

While saying that it couldn't be real there was clearly some hope in her voice that she might be wrong.

Mac was thoughtful for a moment and the table fell silent. When he looked up all four faces were looking expectantly at him.

'I'm making some assumptions here but here's what I think might have happened...

The only hobby that Harold Jones had, besides making money, was history, specifically the ancient history of Cyprus. Why he took this up is still a mystery. Just before he was diagnosed with terminal cancer, he found something in an old book he'd bought. It was called *The Collected Letters of Robert FitzWarren, 6th Viscount FitzWarren of Holles*. In the early eighteen hundred's the Viscount was planning to build his own museum, now known as the FitzWarren Museum in Cambridge, and he was after some exhibits to put in it. In one section of the book the Viscount swaps letters with fellow collectors and he purchases quite a lot of art works that way. However, he also funded an expedition to Cyprus, led by this Captain Bassingbourne, in the hope that he could emulate Dimetrescu and get his hands on something special.

The Captain spent the better part of a year here going around the country and buying artefacts from farmers and local people who had found them on their land. It wasn't illegal at the time and it's likely that he'd greased the palms of the local Ottoman officials anyway. What he found went well beyond the Viscount's hopes and he wrote back saying that he would be heading home with his treasure trove at the first opportunity.'

Mac paused and took a sip from his water. No-one said a word.

'He died trying to get back home but Harold Jones found a line in Bassingbourne's last letter that excited him. It excited him so much that he wrote 'Eureka!' by the side of it.' Mac swiped to another picture of a page in a book and said, 'Bassingbourne said that and I quote '*The bulk of the ancient relics have been packed and loaded and I will advise my Lord of the whereabouts of such others in correspondence sent by another route in case of pirates or inclement weather*'. This oblique reference interested Harold Jones enough to send him scurrying to the FitzWarren Museum to search for that other letter and he used the Dimetrescu Hoard as a cover story to get access. I think that he found that letter. Bassingbourne had hinted that not everything he'd found was on board the ship that sank and the letter was insurance in case he didn't make it back. It was that letter that sent Harold Jones all the way to Larnaka.

I'd guess that the letter contained directions or a map detailing where Bassingbourne had stashed the rest of the art works he'd stolen. Harold Jones figured that there was a good chance that they might still be there as there'd been no mention of them since.'

Mac let this thought sink in.

'I'd guess that the description or map wasn't overly specific as Harold Jones had to make many trips to the area around Pano Lefkara before he found what he was looking for. I'm guessing from the terrain that it must have been a cave of some sort. I'm also guessing that Bassingbourne had left the cave secure, probably by blocking the entrance with a big stone. He would have had men, ropes and sets of block and tackle available from his ship so it wouldn't have been too difficult. I think that's what Mr. Pitsillides heard that first time. It was some heavy machinery that Harold Jones had borrowed from Lefkhod to open up the cave. Once they'd confirmed what was in it, they closed it up again. Then Harold Jones made his plans.'

Mac stopped again and took another sip from his drink.

'As he'd already used the Dimetrescu Hoard story as a cover, he thought that he might as well persevere with it. He also got Lefkhod involved again. I'd be sur-prised if the people he used weren't flown in from Bulgaria without a clue as to what they were getting involved with. The cave was opened again and the art works inside, including the statue, were then safely packed into shipping crates. They were then taken away and the cave was once again blocked up. No-one had heard or seen a thing, apart from Mr. Pitsillides that is, but even he hadn't a clue as to what was really going on.

For a terminally ill man I think that his persistence was amazing but, in the end, there was only so much that Harold Jones could do. I think he got in some help, perhaps someone he'd used before.'

'The fair-haired man,' Dave said.

'That's right,' Mac said. 'I think that his role was to shepherd the consignment of art works and make sure that they got safely off the island. Once that happened then they could be taken by truck to Switzerland where they would be magically found in a bank vault. Harold Jones could then openly take them to England as legally purchased items and his future reputation as a generous patron of the arts would be secure.'

'So where are they now?' Dave asked.

'They're still on the island somewhere, I'd guess,' Mac replied, 'and that's why we were shot at. If we'd have been killed then someone else would have had to take the investigation over and, by the time they got up to speed, the art works would have been well on their way to Geneva. Even if we'd survived, they counted on us taking our eye off the ball by concen-trating only on the shooter and they knew that this would lead us into a literal dead end. I think that it might be well worth knowing when the next batch of Lefkhod containers is due to be shipped out.'

'Do you think that the art works might be in a shipping container?' Dave asked.

'I'm not sure,' Mac replied. 'That seems a little too simplistic somehow but we're going to need to check every container anyway.'

Dave got his phone out and rang Mr. Stassinos at the Lefkhod office in Limassol. He got no answer. He rang the police station and asked them to find his private number.

'Come on, let's get on our way,' Dave said. 'I want to be there when they start checking the containers.' He then turned to Eva. 'Thanks for your help. I'll get someone to drop you back.'

'You can forget that,' she said with determination. 'I want to be there too. If you do find something then you'll need me to verify it.'

Dave thought on this for a moment before concluding that she had a point.

'Okay, come on then,' he said.

As they drove on Mac couldn't shake the feeling that they were on a wild goose chase. However, an idea was forming in his mind.

He smiled to himself. He was now expecting that they'd find exactly nothing in those containers. However, if that was the case, then he hoped that it would be quite a lot of nothing.

Chapter Twenty-Two

Andy drove fast, lights flashing, as they sped towards Limassol and the port. On the way Dave managed to contact Mr. Stassinos who said that he'd meet them at the Lefkhod office with someone from the Customs Ports Authority. He also confirmed that the next shipment of containers was due to sail at two o'clock the next morning.

Mac had often noticed that, when a few of the pieces started to fall into place in an investigation, others quickly followed. Now one more piece fell into place. They were about halfway there when his phone pinged. He had an email and it was from Martin!

Mac,

Sorry for the delay, I had problems with the police database yesterday. As it turned out I needed have bothered as your man wasn't on it anyway. I'd already tried all the social media sites I could think of and he wasn't on any of those either. In desperation I started searching the news sites and I was about to give up when I came up with this photo (see attachment). He's at the back on the right and his name is John Allen. The photo is a few years old but he's the best fit for your photo that I've come across,

Best of luck

Martin

Mac opened the photo. He was surprised to find that it was one that he'd seen before. It showed the leaders of the Pentonville Crime Syndicate who, up until a few years ago, had been one of London's most feared crime families. He remembered now that he'd heard that name before. John Allen had long been rumoured as being an enforcer for the syndicate and a ruthless one at that. They'd never been able to catch him at it though which is why Martin couldn't find him on the database. He was also from the Newcastle area.

'We may have identified our mystery man,' Mac said as he handed his phone to Dave. 'If he is who we think he is then you'd better warn your men to be very careful. He's a professional and he'll stop at nothing.'

'I'll do that right now,' Dave replied as he got his own phone out.

'By the way I notice that his hair is darker in the photo so he might have been using a hair colourant,' Mac said. 'He might not be quite so blond anymore.'

'I'll ask the team to create a new image with darker hair as well,' Dave said, 'and I'll make sure that we also attach a warning. No-one is to approach the suspect without back-up.'

While Dave was once again busy on the phone, Mac looked out of the window and wondered if this dash to the port might prove to be a fruitless exercise. He had a strong feeling that they were nearing the endgame. Whatever John Allen had planned, Mac guessed that it wouldn't involve hanging around on the island for very long. He thought of his idea again and guessed that there might be a way that they might catch Mr. Allen in the act.

They met Mr. Stassinos outside the Lefkhod office. He introduced the man with him as Cosimo Mavros, the head Customs agent for the port. They first showed Mr. Stassinos the photo of John Allen. He identified him as being the man he'd known as Richard Gatling.

'So, is that right? You'll need us to check all the containers going out tonight?' the Customs agent asked.

Mac thought that he looked somewhat sceptical about the proposition as indeed did Mr. Stassinos.

'If possible,' Dave replied. 'How many are there?'

'Well, it's just a small load so they're only using a feeder boat tonight,' Mr. Stassinos said. 'There'll be just under two thousand containers in all.'

'What's a large load like then?' Andy asked with a puzzled expression.

'Well, the biggest ships can take around fifteen thousand containers,' Mr. Stassinos replied.

'Well, thank God we haven't got to deal with that many,' Dave said. 'We suspect that someone will be trying to smuggle some illegal goods out tonight. Would it be possible to check every container?'

The Customs agent shook his head and said, 'Well we could, we've got some cargo scanning equipment available, but it would take days to scan a whole shipment. What are we looking for, drugs or tobacco?'

'Neither, we believe that they're trying to move some stolen art works,' Dave replied. 'We know that this includes some stone monuments and some bronze items, including a life-size statue.'

'Well, a life size metal statue should be easy enough to spot on a scanner,' the Customs agent said as he turned to the Lefkhod manager. 'Is there any way that we can cut down the number of containers we'd need to check?'

Mr. Stassinos had a look at his computer.

'Well, luckily most of the containers in this shipment are filled with agricultural products; olives, cheese, potatoes, citrus fruits and so on. They're usually loaded up and sealed on site so I guess it might be straight-forward to check the seals on those. If we rule these out, then I'd guess that might leave around a hundred and fifty or so to scan.'

'Well, that will still be a lot of work and we'll need to get going immediately if we're to stand a chance,' the Customs agent said.

'What about the container ship, has it docked yet?' Dave asked.

'Yes, it came in a couple of hours ago,' Mr. Stassinos said. 'It's called the Evropeĭska Zvezda, the European Star in English. Its home port is Burgas, Bulgaria.'

'We'll need to keep everyone onboard in the dark as far as this is concerned,' Dave said. 'We're not sure whether the crew are in on this or not.'

'No problem. It's unlikely that anyone on the ship will notice the checks but, if they do, I'll tell them that it's just a training exercise,' the Customs agent said. 'We did something similar last year so it shouldn't raise too many suspicions.'

'Good then,' Dave said. 'Let's get on with it.'

It was now three-thirty so they had just over ten hours before the ship was due to sail. It took a while to get the containers moving through the scanner. At first the three policemen and Eva crowded around the scanning screen as the operator told them what they were looking for. Mac asked the operator if he could make a note of something as each container was viewed. Dave didn't ask why. Mac reckoned that he was getting the idea.

After an hour or so they decided to work in shifts and so Mac and Eva drifted off to the canteen for a cold drink and a sandwich. While they were eating Mac told Eva about his involvement in the case and how they'd gotten to this point.

'That's really bad luck, your first night on holiday and you get involved in a murder case,' she said. 'Although I have to say that you don't look all that unhappy about it.'

'I don't suppose I am really,' Mac admitted. 'In my former life I used to have cases on the go all the time, I'd sometimes have input into five or six at the same time and I really liked that. It's been a bit quiet at times since I've retired so, if I'm being honest, I never turn down any chance to be involved, even if I am on holiday.'

Mac squirmed in his seat as a twinge of pain hit him. It wasn't all that severe but he hadn't been expecting it.

'You've got a bad back,' Eva stated. 'I know the signs too well. My grandfather lived with one for years.'

'You're very observant and right, of course. I've been surprisingly well since I've been in Cyprus but I've done a lot of walking today,' Mac said. 'Perhaps too much.'

'You should rest for a while,' she said as she looked around the room.

Towards the back of the canteen she saw that there were a couple of long padded benches.

'Come on,' she said as she stood up.

Mac followed her. She moved a table out of the way and gestured towards the bench. Mac looked at her and then looked around the canteen. There weren't many people around and the bench was well out of the way. Another, much more severe, twinge decided the matter. He did as he was ordered and lay down. He then waited for the spike of pain that usually came soon afterwards. It came and with such force that he couldn't help letting a grunt out. He felt somewhat embarrassed afterwards.

'You really need to rest. I'll tell Dave,' she said.

She then went towards the serving counter where she had a conversation with the woman who'd served them their drinks. She glanced over at Mac and nodded. She gave Eva something and she walked back towards Mac.

'Here,' she said. 'Hold your head up.'

He could see that she had a pack of hi-viz jackets in her hand. She placed the pack under his head. He lay back and relaxed. The hi-viz jackets made a reasonably good pillow.

'I'll see you later,' she said.

Mac closed his eyes. He was just going to lie there for half an hour or so. He reckoned that should take the edge off the pain. Seconds after closing his eyes he realised how exhausted he was. However, he also realised that he needed to do something first, just in case he slept for too long. He got out his phone and spoke to Dave and told him about his idea. He wasn't too surprised when Dave said that he'd been thinking along the very same lines.

He then lay back and almost immediately fell into a deep sleep.

Dave thought for a moment after speaking to Mac. With a man like Allen involved they might need more help. He decided to phone a friend. Just in case.

Chapter Twenty-Three

Kate got Martin's email just after they'd finished eating lunch at the museum. She told Toni what Martin had said.

'Can we pop by the station before we go to the super-market?' Kate asked. 'Martin said that he'll be there for the next hour or so.'

Toni, of course, agreed. She loved Kate's passion for the job, it mirrored her own.

While they were on their way back Kate got a call from Mac. He told her of his suspicions.

'Mac thinks that the art works in the photos that we saw in the museum aren't in Switzerland at all,' Kate said as she put her phone away. 'He thinks that they're about to be smuggled out of Cyprus. It looks like this whole story about the Dimetrescu Hoard was just a cover.'

'Well, it did sound a bit unlikely, didn't it?' Toni said. 'Is there anything we can do to help him?'

'I wish there was. We can only go through Harold Jones' notes again and see if he mentions anything about how he intended to get the statue and the rest of the items out of Cyprus.'

'We can always do the shopping tomorrow,' Toni said with a smile.

'Thanks,' Kate said as she gave her partner's hand a little squeeze.

Martin was not alone when they walked into the Major Crime Team's room. Colin was talking to him and they seemed to be getting on quite well.

'Hello, you two,' Kate said. 'Thanks for the email, Martin. Has Mac got back to you yet?'

'Yes, he emailed me and said that there's been no sign of Mr. Allen as yet but the Cyprus police have put his photo out. He's on his way to Limassol where they're going to check some containers.'

Kate told them of Mac's suspicions.

'I've discovered something too,' Colin said. 'I've found that the bulk of Mr. Jones' wealth was transferred into bearer bonds. Now, if Mr. Jones had really been buying the hoard then that might have made some sort of sense as the bonds could have been used as payment.'

He stopped as he saw some puzzled looks.

'I'm sorry, bearer bonds are a sort of security but there are no records as to who owns them. They're not so common these days for obvious reasons such as money laundering. Basically, you can redeem the value of the bonds just by being in possession of them.'

'So, it's more or less the same as having a two hundred and fifty million pound bank note?' Toni asked.

'Yes, that's about it,' Colin replied. 'Now that sort of fits in with him buying this fabulous hoard but, if Mac is right, then you have to wonder where that money is now and what it's being used for. On that thought I was wondering if you had a copy of the will?'

'Sure,' Kate said.

She dug out the copies of the two wills and gave them to Colin.

'Coffee anyone?' Toni asked.

They all put their hands up.

'I'll give you a hand,' Martin said.

Kate watched Colin as he read the will. It was only two pages so it didn't take him long. When he'd finished, he read part of the second page again before he burst out laughing.

'I think that I might just have discovered where all the money went,' Colin said pointing to the last paragraph of the will.

She read it again. She'd found it a somewhat eccentric request when she'd first read it but now it made some sense.

'My God,' Kate exclaimed. 'If you're right then that makes Harold Jones the most miserable sod who ever lived. I'll get the keys to the house.'

They quickly drank their coffees while Colin told Toni and Martin of his suspicions.

'Let's go and have a look, shall we?' Kate said tossing the keys in the air.

'This is all rather exciting,' Colin said as the car sped towards Knebworth.

'It reminds me a bit of Scooby Doo or something,' Martin said with a smile.

'I bags being Velma,' Toni quickly said.

Everyone laughed. Kate did indeed feel as if she was on an exciting adventure. They'd know for sure in a matter of minutes if Colin's theory was correct.

They pulled up in the driveway and Kate fumbled with the keys before opening the door. They all followed her into the downstairs room that Harold Jones had used as a bedroom.

'It's quite specific,' Kate said as she read from the will. 'Mr. Jones will be buried in a dark blue blazer with brass buttons that bears the badge of his old university. It's located in the wardrobe of the room he sleeps in and it's the only blazer in the wardrobe. Before the lid of the coffin is screwed down the undertakers are required to take a video of Mr. Jones wearing the blazer. The video shall run until all of the coffin screws have been fully tightened. On production of the said video the undertakers will be paid a bonus of five thousand pounds by Mr. Jones' solicitor.'

'He doesn't make any other stipulations then?' Martin asked.

'No, just that one, apart from him being cremated that is,' Colin said, 'and that's what gave me the idea. Shall we have a look then?'

They all stepped back and watched as Colin opened the wardrobe and searched for the blazer. It wasn't hard to find. As the will said, it was the only blazer there. It was encased in a clear plastic bag.

'It looks new, doesn't it?' Colin said as he slipped the blazer from the bag.

He felt all around the lining. When he reached the bottom of the blazer his smile grew.

'Sounds a bit crinkly to me. Has anyone got a knife?'

'I've got some nail scissors,' Toni said.

'Perfect.'

He lay the blazer on the bed and held up the lining and very carefully cut it open. He put his hand inside and pulled out three ornately printed documents. He examined them and then smiled.

'If you've ever wondered about it,' Colin said with some satisfaction, 'then this is what two hundred and fifty million pounds looks like.'

Chapter Twenty-Four

The threads of a truly weird dream disappeared from his mind like water down a plughole as he slowly awoke. He had a strange taste in his mouth. He opened his eyes and looked upwards. For a few seconds he wondered if he was in yet another dream. He was staring up at a corrugated metal roof and wondering where the ceiling of his apartment had gone. He looked to his right and remembered where he was. He was still in the canteen. With a shock he also noticed that it was dark outside. He looked at his watch and found that he'd slept for over five hours.

He took his time sitting up and was glad that all he felt was the usual background pain. He rubbed his face with his hands and looked up. Someone was coming towards him. It was Dave and he had a cup of coffee in each hand. He gave Mac one and sat down.

'You must have read my mind,' Mac said as he gratefully took a sip. 'I'm sorry, I didn't think I was that tired.'

'Don't apologise, remember that you're supposed to be on holiday,' Dave replied. 'Anyway, you haven't missed much.'

'Any empty or part empty containers yet?'

'Yes, we've had three so far and the Customs agent was quite surprised by that,' Dave said. 'He said that, with the price of shipping a container being what it is, exporters usually send full containers only. He told us that sometimes half empty containers can't be helped if the shipment's really urgent but he thought that three was a little on the high side.'

They fell silent for a while as they both sipped their drinks and thought.

'That idea that you came up with, I must admit that it made immediate sense to me. I've spoken to the

Marine Police who are looking into it now. If, as you say, Skarparis has the statue and the rest of the art works on his boat then that might explain the number of half-empty containers,' Dave asked.

'They're bulky items and they might not have gotten past the normal customs checks so, from their viewpoint, it must be safer to intercept the container ship somewhere at sea and unload the art works there,' Mac replied.

'So, they meet the container ship and offload the art works which are then inserted into the partially empty containers which will then become needles in a massive haystack as they're driven to Switzerland,' Dave said. 'If you're right, then it's good that we thought of it now. Even a few hours delay and it might have been too late.'

'For once we may have gotten lucky,' Mac replied, 'and in more ways than one. The only reason I could see for the shooting was that whoever is running the show needed time. It was Colin Furness who connected the dots to the arts trust and after that Kate who found that the money was destined for the museum. It wasn't much of a leap after that. I just hope that I'm right.'

'Me too,' Dave said.

'I been wondering if the ship's crew are in on it,' Mac said. 'If it was me, I'd try and keep them out of the loop. The less people who know the better. I think that I need to ask Mr. Stassinos a question though.'

They finished their coffees and ambled back to the scanning bay. They were still hard at it. Mac noticed that another scanning operator had taken over. He also noticed that Andy and Eva weren't taking much notice of what was being shown on the scanning screen. In fact, they seemed to be much more interested in each other. Mr. Stassinos was slumped back in his chair, his eyes closed. Dave gently shook him.

'Ti?' he said as he sat up.

He looked up at Dave and Mac and then rubbed his face with his hands.

'I can't believe I fell asleep,' he said.

'Well, it's not exactly the most exciting process to watch, is it?' Dave said. 'We need to ask you another question. Has anyone ever been late with a delivery and had to ferry it out to the container ship while it was still at sea?'

'Well, it's very unusual but yes. I think it's happened twice in the time that I've been working here, so that's twice in eight years,' Mr. Stassinos replied. 'It's usually to do with just-in-time deliveries of some sort. The financial penalties for a failure to deliver can be far more costly than hiring a boat but, as I said, it's unusual. It's unusual because both the logistics company and the ship's captain would have to agree before any such arrangements can be made.'

'I doubt that Lefkhod would have any objection in this case but, when you say the captain has to agree, what do you mean by that?' Mac asked.

'Well, if the sea conditions aren't right then it might be unsafe to load anything anyway,' Mr. Stassinos replied.

'And what's the sea like tonight?' Dave asked.

'Fine, so there'd be no problem there,' Mr. Stassinos said, 'but there might also be a problem loading items from a smaller boat. On the two occasions I mentioned before all the items were pharmaceutical products and were fairly small but for something like a bronze statue....'

He stopped dead and was clearly in thought.

'Now that might well explain it,' he continued. 'The European Star rarely makes runs to Limassol and the reason for that is that it's a geared container ship. By that I mean that it's got its own cranes so it can operate from smaller ports that don't have any crane systems. Ships like that are a bit more expensive to build and run so it's a bit of a waste of time sending it to a port like Limassol.'

Mac hadn't stopped to think about how they'd get the art works from the deck of a fishing boat up onto a container ship.

'So, what you're saying is that they would have no problem picking up a heavy item such as a bronze statue?' Mac asked.

'No, the ship's cranes would be capable of lifting several full containers at once so something like that would be no problem at all,' Mr. Stassinos confirmed.

'Where exactly is the European Star headed?' Dave asked.

'It's going to Antalya in Turkey first and then back to Burgas.'

Dave pulled out his phone and got up a map of Cyprus. The ship would have to go west around the island and then head north.

'So, the ship won't pass too far away from Paphos or Poli Crysochous if it's heading for Antalya?' he asked.

'That's right,' Mr. Stassinos confirmed.

Dave made a call. He was on the phone for several minutes.

'I've just spoken to the Marine Police again and they've said that they're getting a fast patrol boat ready for us,' Dave said. 'It's going to pick us up at the Marine Police Headquarters just the other side of the port at one o'clock.'

'We're going on a boat trip?' Andy asked.

'Well, if Mac's right we might just get to meet Mr. Skarparis after all,' Dave said as he looked at his watch. 'It's nine thirty now so if you want to get some rest now's your chance.'

217

'The benches in the canteen are very comfortable if you need to lie down,' Mac said with sincerity.

'I'm not that tired,' Andy said, 'but I could do with something to eat.'

'Me too,' Eva quickly said.

'Okay, if you both get something to eat now then Mac and I will get something later on,' Dave said. 'We still need to keep an eye on the scanning operation just in case.'

Mac watched them both go. They walked closer together than was strictly necessary, their shoulders touching at times.

'They seem to be getting on very well,' Mac said.

'Yes, I'd noticed that too,' Dave said. 'Well, it's been a while since Andy's been in a relationship. I don't think he took it too well when he broke up with his last girlfriend but, if I'm being honest, I never thought that she was that serious about him anyway. I think that, while she liked the idea of having a policeman for a boyfriend, she didn't like the reality of it all that much.'

'Yes, I know that can be a real problem for some policemen but, luckily, it's not one that I ever had. I met my wife when I was just twenty and I'd only just started in the force. She never seemed to have a problem with the job. I asked her once and she said that was because it wasn't just a job with me, it was part of who I was.'

Dave was thoughtful for a while.

'I can't even imagine what it must be like to lose your wife,' he said.

'Let's just say that I wouldn't recommend it to anyone,' Mac said. 'I was really down when I spoke to someone about six months after Nora died and, strangely enough, she was someone who had been a victim in a case of mine from many years before. Anyway, she was a trained counsellor and she said that, instead of concentrating on her death I should try thinking about her life and of the time that we had together. She was so right. I was gifted with thirty wonderful years and that's what's important.'

Mac noticed Dave bend slightly and touch the wooden table leg. The operator turned and said something to him in Greek.

'Another part-empty container,' Dave said looking relieved at being able to change the topic. 'That makes four now.'

Mac thought that he'd be kind to him and change the subject even further.

'Who's going on the boat tonight?' he asked.

Dave looked at him with some surprise.

'I've asked someone I know if they could come along but apart from that I hadn't really thought about it to be honest. If this John Allen is on Skarparis' boat, then it might not be as straight forward as I'd like. If he was behind the attempt on our lives, then he might just put up a fight. That being the case Eva will have to stay here.'

'Is it one of those really fast patrol boats?' Mac asked.

'Yes, I'd guess so.'

Mac remembered some years ago being on one as they chased a rich murderer trying to flee the country in his yacht. The chase had been exhilarating with the patrol boat cresting the waves and seeming to fly through the air before slapping down hard on the water again.

'I'll keep her company,' Mac said.

'Are you sure?' Dave asked.

'Oh, I'd love to come along for the ride and see if my little theory is correct but, if there's any sort of a chase, I'm afraid that I'd be useless. My back would feel like raw meat after a few minutes and I'd just get in the way or worse.'

Dave could see that Mac was sad and frustrated at not being able to go but they both knew that it was the right decision.

Mac's phone went off.

'It's Kate,' he said as he got up and walked a few steps away.

Dave looked over at him and was surprised to hear him burst into laughter. It was a short call and Mac had the broadest of smiles on his face as he walked back towards Dave.

'What was that all about?' a curious Dave asked.

'The team in the UK has made a discovery,' Mac replied. 'Remember the cover story about the Dimetrescu Hoard? Well, it seems that Colin Furness found that the bulk of Harold Jones' estate had been turned into bearer bonds. The bonds have no record of ownership so whoever has possession of them can cash them in. This might have made sense if there really was a hoard and a relative that needed to be paid but, as we know, that's a load of tosh. So, what were the bonds going to be used for then?'

Mac paused for a moment.

'Colin had an idea when he read a copy of the will,' he continued. 'The will had a strange stipulation, it stated that Harold Jones had to be wearing a particular blue blazer before the coffin was sealed. The whole process was to be filmed and the undertakers were to be given a five thousand pound bonus by Harold Jones' solicitor if the stipulation was adhered to.'

'That is strange but people do have a sentimental attachment to certain things, I suppose,' Dave said.

'I don't think that Harold Jones was the sentimental type and obviously neither did Colin,' Mac said. 'Anyway, they went to his house and, in the lining of the blue blazer, they found over two hundred and fifty million pounds worth of bearer bonds.'

'You're joking!' Dave said in astonishment. 'What a miserable excuse for a human being he was. He leaves everything to his only grandchild in his will and then arranges to have all his money go up in smoke when he gets cremated.'

'They say that you can't take it with you but you have to admit that Harold Jones gave it a really good try.'

Chapter Twenty-Five

As Toni drove them back towards the station, Kate couldn't help glancing at the large brown envelope that lay in Colin's lap.

'So, what happens to the money now?' Martin asked.

'Well, according to his will it belongs to his granddaughter,' Colin replied. 'It's evidence for the moment but, once it's released, she'll be more than two hundred and fifty million pounds better off.'

'What about Harold Jones' last wish though?' Martin asked.

'Well, he only stipulated that the blazer should be burnt with him,' Colin replied, 'and that's still hanging in his wardrobe ready to be incinerated with him inside it. So, the funeral directors will still get their bonus.'

'So, how long do you think we'll need to keep the bonds for?' Kate asked.

'Well, that's up to you really but, if it was up to me, I'd release them about an hour after Harold Jones was cremated,' Colin replied with a smile.

This made Kate laugh.

'That's really good advice. I'll mention it to Dan.'

Back at the station they asked the duty sergeant to log an item to go into the evidence safe.

'How should I describe it?' the sergeant asked.

'A large brown envelope containing three bearer bonds of various denominations,' Colin said.

The sergeant entered this into the computer.

'And does the item have any monetary value?'

'Yes.'

'And how much would that be?' the sergeant asked.

'Two hundred and fifty million pounds,' Colin replied.

The sergeant started to enter this but then his head snapped up and he gave Colin a questioning look. When Colin's face stayed absolutely straight, he looked around at Kate's and then Martin's. In desperation he turned to Toni who he knew quite well.

'DI Woodgate is this man pulling my leg?' the sergeant asked.

'I'm afraid not, Ken,' Toni replied. 'It really is worth that much.'

The sergeant looked mildly horrified.

'Okay but please don't go spreading it around,' he said picturing a ram raid on the station in his head.

'Don't worry we won't,' Colin said. 'Hopefully it won't be in there too long.'

The sergeant took the envelope up and held it as if it could explode at any moment.

As he walked away Colin said, 'Don't lose it now, they'll take it out of your wages.'

Kate couldn't suppress a giggle but the sergeant clearly didn't see the funny side of the remark.

They all stood there looking at each other wondering what they should do next.

'Pub?' Toni suggested.

No-one disagreed.

'We can always go shopping tomorrow,' Toni said with a smile to Kate as they headed off towards the Magnets.

Toni and Martin went straight to the bar to get the drinks in.

'So, you found just over three hundred million pounds in all,' Kate said. 'Do you think that's all of it?'

'Well, there's at least ten to twenty million pounds knocking around somewhere if not more,' Colin said. 'I'd guess that this John Allen would have to be paid somehow but, from the little I've learned about Mr. Jones, I'm betting that the deal was strictly cash on delivery. With any luck Mac and the Cypriot police will

223

throw a spanner in the works as far as that's concerned.'

'What about the money in the Evagoras Arts Trust?'

'Well, it's stipulated in the trust documents that it must go to some museum or other,' Colin replied. 'Where the money ends up will be down to the trustees but I'd guess that the FitzWarren will be in with a good shout.'

'So, the FitzWarren Museum will be disappointed but they still might get something while Chelsea Jaskolski will be two hundred and fifty million better off,' Kate said. 'And, hopefully, this John Allen will end up with nothing.'

'That's about it,' Colin said.

'I take it that this the end of the case for you then?' Kate asked.

'Yes, I suppose it is now that we've found most of the money,' Colin replied. 'It wasn't the hardest case I've ever dealt with but it was interesting. So, I'll be going back home tomorrow and after that I've got a few days off to spend with Sarah and the kids.'

'You sound as if you're looking forward to it,' Kate said.

'Oh, I am,' Colin replied. 'You know there are times when Sarah has a deadline to meet and the kids are being even louder than usual and I think that a little bit of peace and quiet would be nice. Then, when I get exactly that, I find that I miss them all dreadfully. That was why I was so glad that this case came up. That plus the fact that I'd never been to Letchworth before. Ah, here comes the neck oil.'

Toni and Martin handed out the drinks.

'I think we've earned this,' Toni said as she took a sip from her glass.

Everyone else did the same.

'So, when are you going to give Mrs. Jaskolski the good news?' Colin asked.

'I don't know,' Kate replied. 'Monday probably.'

'Well, give her this just in case,' Colin said as he got a card out of his wallet. 'It's my friend's card. Tell her that she can trust him. I know we're not supposed to recommend things but that's a hell of a lot of money and she might need some good impartial advice.'

'Thanks,' Kate said as she put the card in her handbag. 'What would you do if you had that much money?'

'Now that's a question!' Colin said. 'I certainly wouldn't let it affect our lifestyle, I love my job and Sarah loves hers too. We like where we live and the kids are in a great school so I'd probably put a few million in the bank, just in case, and then set up some sort of charitable trust with the rest.'

'What's that exactly?' Martin asked.

'Well, it's a way of ringfencing money that you want to go to some sort of good cause,' Colin replied. 'In the main, it's also a way of making sure that the money is exempt from being taxed so you can imagine that these types of trusts are abused from time to time.'

'I've heard of the Peabody Trust,' Toni said. 'Is that one?'

'Yes, now that's a really good example,' Colin said with some animation. 'George Peabody was a really interesting chap. He was a financier who set up a charitable trust in the 1860s and left it all his money when he died. It's still going today, mostly around social housing I think.'

'Well, I think I'd blow a good bit of it on having a good time first,' Martin said with a smile.

'Ah, the folly of youth!' Colin said. 'Although, being honest, if I was a few years younger I'd be carrying your cases.'

'Are you going to have breakfast here before you go home tomorrow?' Kate asked.

'Well, as I'm not the greatest cook, I think that I'll be filling up before I trudge my weary way home. So yes.'

In truth, Kate had enjoyed working with Colin and she found that she was a little sad it would soon be over. She glanced over at Toni who smiled and nodded back.

'Good we'll meet you here then. And after that we'll finally have to do our shopping,' Kate said as she smiled back at Toni.

'But first let's celebrate a bit,' Colin said. 'It's not every day you save such a wad of cash from going up in smoke. Here's to it going to a good cause.'

They all clinked their glasses together and said, 'A good cause!'

Chapter Twenty-Six

The last container had been screened. They'd found just one more part-empty container so at least they had an idea as to how much room the statue and the other art works might take up. It was quite considerable. Mac and Dave were still by themselves as Andy and Eva seemed to be taking their time. It was now eleven thirty.

'Do you fancy something to eat?' Dave asked.

'I'm not really hungry but a coffee would be nice,' Mac replied.

As they walked towards the canteen Mac asked, 'Just how big is Skarparis' boat?'

'Yes, I've been thinking about that too,' Dave replied. 'I'd doubt that his boat would be big enough by itself, so I'd guess that he's got some help. We've been looking for one of his associates who we know has been heavily involved in some of his scams in the past. Apparently, he, and his boat, have also gone missing.'

'So, you'll be looking for two boats then,' Mac said. 'Have you any idea how the Marine Police will go about following the container ship?'

'I'll give the Captain a call when we get to the canteen and see what his plan of action is,' Dave said.

Andy and Eva were deep in conversation when they arrived at the canteen. They sat opposite each other with their heads almost touching. Her hand was on top of his. Things seemed to have been moving very quickly between the two of them. They both sat bolt upright when they saw Dave and Mac approaching. They reminded Mac of two children who had been caught in school slouching at their desks and who had been told to sit up straight. Eva looked a little flustered but she was also glowing with excitement.

In fact, she looked quite beautiful, Mac thought.

'Do you need us to take over?' Andy asked.

'No, they've finished,' Dave replied. 'We found five part-empty containers in all, definitely far more than usual.'

'They've finished?' Andy said as he looked at his watch. 'Oh, I'm so sorry. I didn't think that we'd been here that long.'

'Don't apologise, Mac and I had a nice chat and you didn't miss anything. I going to ring the Marine Police and find out what they're planning for tonight. While I'm doing that, I think that a couple of coffees might go down well,' Dave hinted.

'Sure,' Andy replied with a smile as he bounced up and made his way to the counter.

Dave walked a few yards away and pulled out his phone.

'I'm sorry too,' Eva said. 'It was my fault, I kept him talking.'

'I doubt that Andy needed much persuasion,' Mac said. 'What are you going to do now?'

'I've no idea but I don't want to go home. I want to see how it all turns out.'

'Yes, me too,' Mac said, 'and, as I'm not going on the boat, it would be nice to have some company.'

Andy returned with two coffees. They sat in silence while Dave finished his call.

'The Captain said that he wants us over at the Marine Police station in an hour or so,' Dave said.

'You sound like you're looking forward to it,' Mac said.

'I am,' Dave replied. 'We'll find out tonight whether you're right and whether we'll be able to prevent a part of our history being stolen from us.'

'What are they planning on doing, did they say?' Andy asked.

'The Captain said that we'll shadow the container ship from a safe distance using radar. They've got fast patrol boats stationed near Paphos and Poli Crysochous keeping an eye on anything coming out. There are lots of small ports and jetties all along the coast where Skarparis could be tied up so they think that it might be easier to locate the fishing boats using radar as they come out to meet the container ship. Most boats don't fish at night and, even when they do, they don't usually go that far out so the Captain's confident that it shouldn't be too hard to spot them.'

Dave took a sip from his coffee before continuing, 'They're fitting machine guns to the boats now just in case.'

'Machine guns?' Eva said with a worried look. 'Is it going to be dangerous?'

'Hopefully not but you never know,' Dave replied. 'If the identification of John Allen as our mystery man is correct then we're going to be dealing with a hardened and very violent criminal. It's just insurance really.'

Eva didn't look convinced.

'What are you going to do, Mac?' Dave asked.

'I've already slept for hours so there's no point in me going back to my apartment,' Mac replied. 'I'd like to wait for you at the Marine Police station if that's possible, perhaps near whoever is communicating with the boats so that we can hear what's going on.'

'We?' Dave asked.

'Well, I'll need a translator,' Mac replied looking over at Eva.

She gave Dave a determined look. When his wife Eleni gave him that look it always meant that any further discussion would be totally pointless.

'Okay, I think that might be arranged,' Dave said.

Before they left the canteen, Mac told Andy and Eva about the discovery of the missing two hundred and fifty million pounds.

'God! What a hateful man,' Eva exclaimed.

'He was that,' Mac replied. 'However, thanks to Colin Furness, Harold Jones' wicked little plan didn't succeed.'

'Let's hope that his other wicked little plan fails too,' Dave said.

Mac didn't reply but he said a silent prayer that Dave and Andy might come out of it in one piece.

The Port and Marine Police Headquarters building was larger than Mac had expected. It was right on the water's edge. Ships of all different sizes were tied up around the dock and looking across the harbour he could see four huge container cranes only one of which was in use. It was loading up a ship that had layers of containers stacked high on its deck. Mac guessed that this was the European Star. It was supposed to be one of the smaller container ships but it still looked quite big to him. Two patrol boats were moored at a nearby jetty one of which had its lights on. People were moving about on it readying the boat for departure.

'Your ride?' Mac asked as he took in its sleek lines.

It looked as if it was going fast even when it was standing still.

'It looks like it,' Dave said.

Mac could see that Dave was excited and he once again wished that he could be making the trip with him. If it had just been the effect on his back, he would have taken the chance but, if something happened to him and it adversely affected the operation, then he knew that he'd never forgive himself.

They were met in the lobby by Captain Michael-ides of the Marine Police who ushered them into a large room that had about twenty chairs lined up in rows.

A briefing room, Mac surmised.

This was confirmed when they were joined soon afterwards by the crew of ten officers. They were all in uniform, dark blue trousers, crisp white short-sleeved shirt with epaulettes and a peaked cap. Mac had been told that two of them were frogmen. They were also joined by a young man dressed in an Army uniform. When Dave saw him, he jumped up and went over to him. He gave him a big hug and kissed him on both cheeks.

Mac guessed that this was the 'someone' who Dave had invited along. He certainly knew the young soldier well and Mac wondered what part he might have to play in the proceedings.

The Captain asked Dave to outline the case. Eva translated for Mac. He could see that they all got very interested when he mentioned the art works and even more interested when he told them about John Allen. He warned them that he might not give up easily.

The Captain then got up and gave the briefing. Eva skipped all the jargon and coordinates but Mac still got the gist of the plan. They were going to follow the container ship keeping behind it so that they could track anything coming from the east by radar. They now had three patrol boats stationed along the coast between Paphos and Poli Crysochous who were hoping to pick up the fishing boats en route.

Once they were reliably identified, two of the patrol boats would track the fishing boats as they tried to make a rendezvous with the container ship. The other would stay on station just in case there might be more than two boats involved. They would all wait until the container ship and the fishing boats had come to a dead stop before making any move. The three patrol boats would then corral the fishing boats so that they wouldn't be able to escape. Two of the boats had police frogmen on board, just in case they were needed, and all had machine guns fitted. Everyone on board would need to wear bulletproof vests.

He then introduced the young soldier.

'I know that we have machine guns fitted but when Dave heard that we were dealing with a professional and very violent criminal this young man here popped into his mind and, personally, I'm more than glad to have him along. I'd like to introduce you to Lieutenant Jason Kyriakou who's a firearms specialist with the army. In other words, he's a sniper. I'm hoping that we won't need his skills but I'm glad that he's decided to join us tonight.'

Everyone looked at the young Lieutenant with interest.

Mac did too. The name sounded familiar as did the young man himself. Of course, he must be Yanni's son!

The Captain then concluded by looking at his watch and saying that they would be sailing in thirty minutes.

The briefing room quickly emptied.

Captain Michaelides said something to Dave and Andy and then waited for them at the door.

'We need to go and get our bulletproof vests,' Dave said. 'The Captain also said that the comms room is just down the hallway, turn right and it's the second door on the left. They'll be expecting you.'

'I'll be with you in a minute,' Andy said as he looked over at Eva.

Mac didn't even try to make an excuse. He just put himself on the other side of the door as quickly as he could.

As they waited in the hallway Mac asked, 'That young soldier, he's Yanni's son, isn't he?'

'Yes, he's the youngest in the family and he's also the one that takes most after his father,' Dave replied. 'He's representing Cyprus in one of the shooting competitions in the next Olympics.'

Remembering how Yanni had grouped his shots around the shooter's heart Mac thought that, if he really did take after his father, then Dave did well in bringing him along.

After about two minutes had passed a clearly pleased looking Andy emerged. He said his good-byes to Mac and then chased after Dave and the Captain as they disappeared around a corner. Mac went back inside. Eva was leaning against the wall. She looked both sad and happy at the same time. She sat down heavily in one of the chairs.

'This is all so crazy,' she said. 'I've only known him a few hours and now I'm more worried about him coming back than the statue.'

'You don't always need to have known someone for a long time to feel something for them,' Mac said. 'Anyway, I'm sure that he'll be fine.'

'Yes, I'm just being silly, aren't I?' she said trying to convince herself.

'Come on, let's find the comms room and then, hopefully, we'll be able to locate a coffee machine.'

The comms room was both larger and busier than Mac had expected. They were introduced to the young woman who would be across all communications with the four patrol boats. She had a loop of plaited hair on either side of her head and a pair of purple glasses perched on a small snub nose. She wore a discrete pair of headphones that had a small microphone jutting out from one side. She remind-ed him of someone but he couldn't think who.

'I'm Marina,' she said in English, 'and, before you ask, I have no idea if my name was responsible for me joining the Marine Police.'

This pre-emptive strike was conveyed with light-ness and a smile. Mac and Eva introduced themselves.

'Is there anywhere we can get a coffee?' Eva asked.

'There's a machine. Come on, I'll show you,' Marina said as she stood up. 'Nothing will be happening for a good while yet.'

While they were gone Mac searched in his head for who Marina reminded him of. He knew that it would only annoy the hell out of him otherwise. For the first time in many years he thought of Jill Tavistock and wondered why. She certainly looked nothing like Marina. She had long blonde hair and Mac had been chasing after her for some weeks before she finally agreed to go to the cinema with him. This was a couple of years or so before he'd met Nora and he'd still been a teenager. When they were in the cinema and the lights went out, she'd been expecting him to jump on her. In truth, she'd been hoping that he'd jump on her, but she was to be disappointed. Mac had gotten so engrossed in the film that he'd almost forgotten she was there. That was his first and last date with Jill Tavistock.

So why think of her now? He smiled as it came to him. The film had been a new sci-fi movie called Star Wars that everyone had been going on about. It was Princess Leia that Marina reminded him of. He was once again struck by the roundabout way that his mind sometimes worked. He was still thinking about this when Eva and Marina returned with the drinks.

'So, what happens now?' Mac asked as Marina took her position behind the computer and put her head-phones back on.

'Not much, if I'm being honest,' Marina replied. 'All the boats will be keeping radio silence for as long as possible. We've prepared a list of code words for just about every contingency that we can think of. So, what you'll hear is a code word identifying the patrol boat and then another code word which will be the message. I'll put it on the speakers so that you can hear it too.'

They sat there in comfortable silence for a while.

'So, what made you want to be an archaeologist?' Mac asked as he turned to Eva.

She gave this some thought.

'I think it was when I found an old one shilling piece in my back garden when I was ten years old. I'd been watching a programme on TV showing archaeologists on a dig and how they carefully dug into the soil and found things, so I thought I'd give it a go. I was so thrilled at finding that shilling that it made me wonder what other treasures were concealed under the earth. That wonder has never left me.'

'I take it that you're a local girl?'

'Oh sure. I come for a little town called Pyrga. It's about thirty kilometres west of Larnaka.'

'Pyrga?' Marina said looking surprised. 'I come from Kornos.'

There then followed a quick-fire discussion in Greek that ended up with them both bursting into laughter. The two women then stood up and hugged each other.

Mac was confused and his face must have shown it.

'I'm sorry Mac,' Eva apologised. 'Kornos is only about five kilometres away from Pyrga and it appears that we're related. What is it, second cousins?'

'Yes, my mother is a cousin of your father's,' Marina said with a smile.

'Cyprus is a small country,' Eva said with a shrug.

The speakers came to life. As Marina had said they heard a man's voice say just two words in Greek.

'He said 'Blue' and 'Tide',' Eva explained.

'That's the Limassol patrol boat, it's making its way out to sea now,' Marina explained. 'The other boats are 'green', 'red' and 'yellow'.'

'Is there any chance that those messages could be picked up?' Mac asked.

'Well, years ago I believe that it was possible but all of our messages are encrypted now,' Marina replied. 'We alter the frequencies as well, so they'd be lucky to pick up any of our messages in the first place. Even if they did, all the words would be garbled so it's quite secure.'

Mac was about to ask why they were using code words but he stopped himself. He didn't want to embarrass Marina. He guessed that they were being used as an extra level of security to ensure that other policemen couldn't spill the beans.

Mac looked at his watch. It was now one thirty. The European Star would sail in half an hour. He was now feeling somewhat anxious. It was his idea that had started all this off and, while he hoped he was right, that wasn't what he was worried about.

He'd gotten quite fond of Dave and Andy and he felt that they might need their bulletproof vests. He couldn't shake the feeling that John Allen might not be the kind of man who would go down without a fight.

Chapter Twenty-Seven

Dave and Andy followed the Captain onto the boat. He found them some seats inside the wheelhouse. They were seated just behind the steersman and so they had a good view out of the huge glass windscreen. The ride was smooth as they made their way out to sea.

'We'll be going to a point about four kilometres south of Limassol and a couple of kilometres to the west,' the Captain explained. 'We should have no trouble picking up the European Star and following her at a distance. We'll keep that distance until she starts slowing down then we'll go dark and move closer in.'

'What will trigger any action?' Dave asked.

'That will be the call of the patrol boats that will be following the fishing boats,' the Captain replied. 'Once they've verified that the fishing boats have pulled alongside the container ship and are static, then they'll move in. One will stay central while the other will cover the bow side, the front of the ship. We'll come around the stern of the ship and cover the other side. The fishing boats will then be corralled and will hopefully have nowhere to go.'

Dave sincerely hoped that it would be as easy as the Captain was making it out to be.

'How will we know when the other boats have started moving in?' he asked.

'You'll hear the code word 'Nike'. Once we hear that then we'll start on our approach to the container ship,' the Captain said.

'Nike, the goddess of victory,' Andy said.

'Is she really? I thought they were just sneakers,' the Captain replied.

He said this with a slight smile that let Andy know that he was having his leg pulled.

They eventually came to a stop and nothing happened for quite a while. The crew went quietly about their business and Dave could see the frogmen getting their gear ready on the deck outside. The Captain was called over by the radar operator.

'We've located the European Star,' the Captain turned and said. 'She's exactly where we thought she'd be, so we'll start shadowing her now.'

The engines started up again and they slowly made way. Dave could see nothing except night through the window but he guessed that they knew where they were going. He turned to look at Andy who had a soppy smile on his face.

'You're very quiet,' Dave said.

'I'm just thinking,' he replied with a shrug of his shoulders.

No need to guess about what, Dave thought.

'How do you think it will go?' Andy asked.

'I've no idea, for once it's someone else who is running the show,' Dave replied.

Andy got the idea that Dave didn't seem all that happy about that.

The boat moved slowly on for another half hour or so before the radio squawked into life again. They then heard the words 'green' and 'red' followed by 'hotel'.

'They've picked up two fishing boats that are heading towards us and they're tracking them now,' the Captain said. 'It looks as though they've come from somewhere just north of Paphos.'

'Are they sure that it's them?' Dave asked.

'They're fairly sure. Some fishing boats go out at night but they rarely, if ever, take the heading that these two have. If they carry on the same heading then they'll make rendezvous with the container ship in about an hour or so. If you hear the code word 'golf' then that means that they're still being tracked and are still on course for a rendezvous.'

Dave picked up the word 'golf' twice in the ensuing forty-five minutes. Once again, the radar operator called the Captain over.

'The container ship is slowing down,' the Captain said. 'It looks like the game is afoot,' he said in English with a big smile.

Now both Dave and Andy felt their legs being pulled.

'What do you want us to do?' Dave asked.

The Captain looked surprised at this.

'Nothing, you're only along for the ride.'

While Dave could see the logic in the Captain's statement, he couldn't help feeling frustrated at just being an observer.

'You might as well relax,' Andy said, 'we're literally out of our depth here.'

This made Dave smile and, of course, he knew that Andy was absolutely right. They would literally be all at sea if they tried to help. He looked at the crew, they all knew their jobs and they were doing them. His only job for now was not to get in their way.

'The container ship's come to a total stop now,' the Captain said. 'We're turning all lights off so we can get closer without them noticing us.'

A few seconds later the only light was that reflected from the radar and navigation screens. Dave only knew that they were getting near when the engines throttled back and the boat slowed right down. He could now see the green and red running lights of the container ship with the bulk of the ship itself a darker shadow against the night sky. An area of the deck was suddenly illuminated and some small figures could be seen moving around.

'I certainly hope that the crew of the ship aren't going to get involved,' the Captain said. 'They'd definitely have the benefit of the high ground.'

Dave could see what he meant. The ship loomed high above them as they came ever closer.

'Nike, Nike!' someone on the radio shouted.

'Action stations!' the Captain shouted. 'Full ahead.'

The engines roared into life and they got up to full speed. As they rounded the stern of the ship, all the boat's searchlights were turned on. Dave saw two fishing boats, one of which had a cable going up the side of the container ship while the other seemed to be trying to back away and escape. Their route was cut off by their arrival. The two fishing boats were now trapped by the three patrol boats who all had their powerful searchlights pointed right at them. It reminded Dave of a floodlit football match.

Captain Michaelides picked up the mic. The external loudspeakers roared into life.

'This is the Marine Police. Turn off your engines immediately and prepare to be boarded. All hands are to come on deck and lie face down,' the Captain ordered his voice echoing from the side of the ship.

A few did exactly what they'd been told to do but Dave noticed that at least two men on the nearer boat ducked for cover.

'We may have a problem,' the Captain said into the radio. 'Green boat, get as close to the container ship as you can and we'll do the same. Two men have taken cover. Let's see if we can get a clear shot at them if we need to.'

The boat went sideways until it was almost touching the rough metal side of the container ship. Dave looked up and could see a number of the European Star's crewmen looking down at them. They looked more puzzled than anything else.

There were several short bursts of gunfire and the boat's searchlights went out. The Captain shouted at everyone to get down. Dave and Andy were already on the floor when they heard a bullet crack the windscreen and fly over their heads.

'Machine gunner, can you get a clear shot?' the Captain asked into the radio mic as he crouched down behind the bulkhead.

'No, there's no clear shot,' a frantic voice replied. 'They're hiding behind some crates. Shall I fire anyway?'

'No, don't fire!' the Captain ordered all too aware of what might be in those crates. 'Lieutenant, can you hear me?'

'Loud and clear.'

'Can you get a shot off?'

'I'm in the same position as the machine gunners but I'm going to climb on top of the wheelhouse now and see if that gives me a better angle...' the Lieutenant replied.

There was another burst of gunfire aimed at the machine gunners.

'Gunners are you alright?' the Captain asked.

'We're fine but we still can't get a clear shot.'

They then heard some muffled sounds right above their heads as the Lieutenant got into position. Then there was silence.

They waited in the dark as another volley of shots could be heard. This time it wasn't aimed at them. The searchlight on the green boat now went out.

'I've got a shot,' the Lieutenant said calmly.

'Then shoot,' the Captain said.

They heard the sounds of two faint gun shots and then there was silence.

'The two shooters are down,' the Lieutenant said in a matter-of-fact way.

'Are you sure?' the Captain asked looking some-what incredulous at this news.

241

'Yes, two head shots,' the Lieutenant replied. 'It's not what I'd usually aim for but it was all I could see of them. I saw the bullets hit.'

The Captain half stood up and took a quick look. Men on both boats were holding up white cloths, some of which he could see were their shirts. They were waving them as hard as they could. A couple of men made for an inflatable motorboat that was tied to the stern of the far fishing boat. They stopped and stood as they watched the motorboat gently float away from them. The rope had been cut by the frogmen.

'Boarding parties get ready,' the Captain said into the radio.

All three patrol boats moved tentatively closer to the two fishing boats. Grappling hooks were thrown and these were used to close the gap until the boats were actually touching. Men in helmets and bullet-proof vests who were carrying assault rifles vaulted onto the decks of the fishing boats. Dave half expected the sound of more gunfire but an eerie silence ensued.

'All secure on boat number one,' a voice on the radio eventually said. 'Two casualties to report, both very dead.'

'Boat number two secure also,' another voice said. 'No casualties here.'

'You can exhale now,' the Captain said to no-one in particular.

Dave did just that anyway.

'Get the container ship on the radio,' the Captain ordered. He then picked up the mic. 'This is the Cyprus Marine Police, Captain Michaelides speaking. I'd like to speak to Captain Sokoloff please.'

He didn't have to wait long.

'Captain Sokoloff here,' a heavily East European accented voice answered. 'What the hell is going on down there?'

'We'd like to board the European Star and talk to you. Will you let our men on board?'

'Of course, we'll let a ladder down for you right away,' Captain Sokoloff replied.

The Captain turned to Dave and Andy and said, 'It's my bet that the crew aren't in on the scam but I'll send some armed men up first just in case.'

'What's going to happen to the fishing boats?' Dave asked as he looked at the wooden crates stacked on the decks.

'We've brought some pilots along who will take charge and make sure that both boats make it safely back to Limassol.'

'Do you think they'd mind if we went along with them?' Dave asked.

'You want to make sure that the cargo arrives in one piece I take it?' the Captain said with a smile. 'Of course, but you might as well sit down and relax. It will be a while before they'll be ready to go.'

Dave got up and looked up at the seat he'd just been sitting in. There was a bullet hole in the backrest. He and Andy exchanged looks.

Dave sat back down in his chair. He was all too aware of where the hole was, it just about lined up with his heart.

Chapter Twenty-Eight

Mac and Eva were on their fourth coffee when the radio came to life.

'That's the green and red patrol boats saying that they've picked up the two fishing boats and are following them,' Marina explained.

While they were waiting Mac had learned that Eva had gone to Durham University in the UK to do her doctorate and that she had worked there for almost two years. She'd left a job that she'd really liked when the one in the Larnaka museum turned up, mainly because she'd been so homesick.

'And it rains a lot in Durham too,' Eva said.

'That's true,' Mac replied.

'If I'm honest, I've been wondering lately if I made a big mistake. I mean the museum here is tiny and, while I've got a fancy title, it doesn't really mean very much. There are only about six of us in the team and two of those are part-time. We can't get the funding we need and it's turned into a bit of a backwater for me.'

'What if those art works really do exist though?' Mac asked.

'Now that would be a game changer,' Eva replied with some excitement. 'It would turn our little museum into something special. We'd have something that no-one else in the world would even come close to having.'

'The statue?'

'That's right. Paris has the Mona Lisa, Florence has the David statue and we'd have Aphrodite,' she said dreamily.

'Do you think it could be that big?' Mac asked.

'Oh, I really shouldn't say things like that,' Eva said with a concerned look as she crossed herself. 'Counting my chickens and all that...'

The radio came to life again.

'They're still following the fishing boats,' Marina said. 'It looks like they'll make rendezvous with the European Star in less than an hour if they keep on their present heading.'

Just as she finished talking Marina suddenly stood to attention.

'Commander Vassiliou,' she said.

Mac turned around to see a tall grey-haired man standing behind him. He wore black trousers and a white shirt that contrasted with his tanned weather-beaten face.

'I'm off duty now so please just call me Theo,' he said to Marina as he pulled a seat over. He offered Mac and Eva his hand and then sat down.

'So, you're Detective Chief Superintendent Maguire,' Theo said. 'I looked you up on the internet before I came out. You have a very impressive CV. It seems that we were in luck the day that you decided to come to our island on holiday.'

Eva turned and looked at Mac with a somewhat puzzled expression.

'And Dr. Sofokleous,' Theo continued, 'it seems as if your skills might be put to the test if Mr. Maguire here is right. In case you're wondering I'm in charge of the Marine Police on the island. This might be one of the most important actions during my time as Commander and so I asked them to keep me updated at home but I just couldn't get comfortable there. So, I thought I might as well come in.'

Mac smiled as he knew the feeling all too well. He couldn't count the number of times when he'd hung around the station waiting for news of a raid or an arrest, sometimes when it wasn't even one of his cases.

'We've got two of our patrol boats following two suspect fishing boats and another patrol boat shadowing the container ship,' Marina said as she sat down.

Theo just nodded at this.

'We have our best people on this,' Theo said after a pause. 'We mostly deal with smuggling; alcohol, tobacco, counterfeit goods and so on but this one is different. They're trying to steal our past.'

More coffees mysteriously appeared. Mac didn't say no.

'So, DCS Maguire have you had much to do with the Marine Police before?' Theo asked.

'Please call me Mac. I mostly worked in London when I was in the force and we have a Marine Policing Unit there. They're responsible for policing the River Thames which runs right through the city and yes, I've worked with them on quite a few cases over the years.'

'Oh yes, of course,' Theo said his face breaking into a smile. 'I visited that unit some years ago and they took me out on one of their boats for the day and then out to a local pub for the night. It was a very good visit.'

Over the next half-hour or so three more senior officers joined them. There was some conversation at the start between them but it quickly stalled. There was a tense atmosphere as they all just sat there and looked at Marina.

The radio burst into life once again.

'The container ship is slowing down,' Marina said. 'The fishing boats are about ten minutes away now.'

'Can you ask green boat to leave their wheelhouse mic on?' Theo asked.

'Sure,' Marina replied.

She passed the message on and another tense silence ensued. After about five minutes it was broken by the radio. Eva whispered a translation to Mac.

246

'We can see that both fishing boats are stationary and one has already tied up to the container ship,' a voice said.

Another voice said, 'We're going in.' Then more loudly 'Nike, Nike!'

'All lights are now on and we can clearly see men on board the decks of the two fishing vessels,' the first voice continued. 'We seem to have caught them by surprise. One of the fishing boats is trying to back away but blue boat has arrived and blocked them off.'

'Blue boat is the one that your police friends are on,' Marina said.

Another voice that sounded quite tinny could be heard in the background saying, 'This is the Marine Police, turn off your engines immediately and prepare to be boarded. All hands are to come on deck and lie face down.'

There was silence for a moment before the sound of gunfire could be heard.

The first voice shouted, 'Gunfire, get down! Gunfire's being directed at blue boat. They've knocked their searchlight out.'

Mac found that he and Eva were suddenly holding hands. Eva squeezed his hand tight as they heard the sound of yet more gunfire.

'It looks like two men with machine guns but we can't get a clear shot at them.'

Another tense pause followed. It seemed to last for hours to Mac. He could hear Eva whispering something in Greek. A prayer, he guessed.

They heard more gunfire and then there was silence. It seemed to last for an eternity before it was finally broken.

'They're now saying that the two shooters are both down!' the voice said jubilantly. 'The sniper blue boat took along with them took the two shooters out with two shots. It doesn't look as if anyone else is up for a fight.'

There was another pause before he carried on, 'We're boarding now. We've got men on both of the fishing boats. They're saying that we have two casualties, the two shooters, who are both dead. No injuries reported otherwise. They're also saying that both of the boats and their cargo are now secure.'

Mac sat back in his chair and exhaled. Theo turned and shook hands with Mac and Eva and then the other officers finishing up with Marina.

'That could have gone worse,' Theo said with a big smile to Marina. 'I'm going back to bed. Please tell them that was a job very well done and that we'll have a full debrief later today. I think we'll all need some sleep before that.'

He left the room a very happy man. The other officers were smiling too as they too drifted away.

'Are you going to wait for them to come in?' Marina asked. 'I'd guess that the patrol boats will be back around six o'clock or so.'

Mac and Eva glanced at each other. Mac looked at the clock on the wall. It was nearly four o'clock.

'Yes, why not? Another few hours won't hurt,' Mac said knowing that sleep would be out of the question anyway.

'I'll stay too,' Eva said. 'I'd like to check the cargo to make sure that there's no bullet holes in it.'

While that might be true Mac suspected that she might want to check Andy over as well.

'I take it that they'll be tying up at the jetty outside?' Mac asked.

'Yes, that's right,' Marina replied, 'but I'm afraid that I won't be around to see it. I'm off duty at five and I'm going straight to bed.'

They had yet more coffee. Mac was well over his usual caffeine intake and vowed that this would be his last one for a while. He looked out of the window and could see fingers of light starting to break up the darkness. It wouldn't be long before the sun came up.

'Fancy some fresh air?' Mac said.

'Yes, please,' Eva said. 'It feels so stuffy in here now.'

They said their goodbyes to Marina and went outside. Mac was still in a T shirt and shorts and it felt chilly when he stepped outside. He didn't mind though as it blew away some of the cobwebs and made him feel more awake. They both leaned on the fence and looked out over the dock. The jetty where the boats would tie up was just to their left. On the other side of the dock a crane was busy building another wall of Lego bricks on the deck of yet another container ship.

'So, what will happen to the art works now? Assuming that's what's in the crates,' Mac asked as he crossed his fingers just in case.

'I've been thinking about that. If we can arrange some transport then I'd like to get them back to the museum as soon as possible. I'm hoping that they've been well packaged but, even so, we'll have to be very careful how we open them up,' Eva said. 'Oh, it's Sunday today, isn't it? I'd completely forgotten. It feels like a lot longer than a day since Dave and Andy asked me to go along with them. I wonder if transport will be a problem, I'd hate to have to wait until Monday to see what they're bringing back.'

'I doubt that will be the case,' Mac replied. 'I'd guess that the police will arrange the transport themselves as they'll want to get the art works somewhere safe as soon as possible.'

'I'll need to call the whole team in but I'd guess that they won't mind. I must admit that I can't wait,' she said with an excited smile.

She turned and gave Mac an appraising look.

'That man Theo, the Commander, or whatever he is, said that you're on the internet and that you used to be a Detective Chief something or other?' Eva asked. 'Is that right?'

'A Detective Chief Superintendent,' Mac replied. 'Yes, that's right. The teams I worked with were involved in investigating some pretty high-profile murders so yes, a lot of them are featured on the internet.'

'I'd honestly never have guessed,' Eva said. 'What happened?'

'Well, I had a back condition that was slowly getting worse and the pain was getting near to being intolerable. I kept it to myself and took whatever painkillers I could get my hands on. I was able to cover it up for quite a while but then my wife died and I just couldn't control the pain anymore. It became all too apparent and I was forced to retire.'

'Oh, I'm so sorry,' Eva said. 'I didn't know...'

'No, please don't be sorry. It is what it is and talking about it helps,' Mac said. 'Anyway, I'm coming to terms with it now. After six months of moping around my daughter and my best friend Tim persuaded me to set up a detective agency in the town where I live. My first case put me in contact with one of the local police detective teams and they allowed me to help them out. I've been helping them out ever since and it's been an absolute godsend.'

'Yes, you can never tell what life's going to throw at you,' she said.

'But it can throw good things at you as well as bad,' Mac said. 'Dave needed an archaeologist and found you and, because of that, you met Andy.'

She was silent for a while. They watched as the light grew ever stronger and the clouds started to turn pink and then gold.

'This thing with Andy, it's crazy, isn't it?' she said softly.

'Is it?' Mac asked.

250

'Well, I've only just met him and, I mean things don't ever happen that quickly, do they?'

Her upward inflection at the end of the sentence let Mac know that she was asking him a real question.

'I can only talk from experience. From the very first second I met my Nora, I knew that she would be something special in my life. Of course, I never guessed that we'd be married within four months which was just about as quickly as you could get married in those days unless the bride was pregnant. If you meet the right person it can take a little time to convince yourself but, deep down, I think you know.'

She thought on this for a while.

'It might be a bit awkward meeting Andy again,' she eventually said. 'We were quite close for a few moments yesterday, at least that's how it felt but here in the cold light of dawn, I don't know. It seems like a long time ago now. How long have you known him?'

'Not much longer than I've known you really but I think that he might be a kind man.'

'I could really do with one of those but what makes you think that?' she asked.

'It was just a small thing really,' Mac replied. 'The day after Harold Jones fell to his death, I had to go to the police station to make a statement. Afterwards, Dave and Andy dropped me back at my apartment. I was curious and asked them if I could have a look at the crime scene, Harold Jones' apartment. They said I could which was nice of them. However, the forensics team had asked us to put latex gloves and those elasticated shoe covers on so as not to contaminate the crime scene too much. I can't bend down and so I was a bit stuck with the shoe covers. However, Andy picked this up really quickly and he bent down and put the covers on for me. As I said, it was a small thing but it was a kind thing too.'

Eva gave him a peck on the side of the cheek.

251

'Thanks Mac, for some strange reason that's made me feel a lot better,' she said.

She was smiling but then he noticed that her expression changed. She looked quite sombre.

'I found it quite exciting at first, you know listening as the patrol boats were moving in, but when I heard the gunfire my knees started knocking and I felt sick if I'm being honest. I mean this wasn't some movie, this was really happening. You and Dave were shot at too, weren't you?'

'Yes, we were but it's not something that happens a lot,' Mac replied. 'I'd bet that Dave has gone years without anyone taking a shot at him and then it happens two days running. Being a policeman's not like most jobs, you can never predict what's around the corner.'

She gave this some thought and Mac wondered if she was making some sort of a decision.

'Are you hungry?' she asked.

'Starving now I come to think of it,' Mac replied.

'Come on, let's find some breakfast.'

Mac followed her and wondered what her decision had been. He guessed that he'd find out soon enough when Andy finally returned.

Chapter Twenty-Nine

By six o'clock Mac and Eva were once again leaning on the fence looking over the dock. It was daylight now and the morning sun shone on yet another container ship that had docked since they were last there. It was having its cargo slowly unloaded, brick by brick.

Breakfast had consisted of a cold cheese pie from a vending machine washed down with sparkling water. While it was about as far from a Full English breakfast as you could get it had hit the spot for now.

Three large police vans passed them and pulled up by the jetty.

'For the prisoners, I'd guess,' Mac said.

Eva didn't say anything. She seemed to be locked into her own thoughts so Mac stayed quiet.

Just before six thirty, a patrol boat motored into the dock. It slowed down and tied up at the jetty. Six policemen climbed out of the vans and walked towards the boat.

Mac and Eva went closer. They leaned on the fence that stopped unauthorised access to the jetty. It was as close as they could get to the boat.

One of the boat's officers shouted something towards the policemen standing on the jetty. They all laughed. A few minutes later four men were led off the boat. They were all in handcuffs and they didn't look at all happy. They were led into one of the vans that then drove off.

Mac guessed that it was on its way to the Central Prison in Nicosia. He turned and noticed that Eva was looking at the boat intently. The boat was emptying now and she was searching the faces but she was to be disappointed.

'They're obviously on one of the other boats,' Mac said.

She nodded and gave Mac half a smile.

They watched as another boat came in and saw more handcuffed men being led off into a police van. Dave and Andy weren't on that one either. A few minutes later the third patrol boat came in. Three men were escorted off the boat and into the remaining van. It drove off. They watched closely as the boat emptied.

There was still no sign of Dave and Andy.

He glanced at Eva. For all of her avowed uncertainty about Andy she looked quite worried at not seeing him.

At last there was a face Mac recognised. He waved at him.

'It's the Captain who briefed us earlier,' Mac said.

Captain Michaelides came over towards them. He looked a happy man. He must have noticed Eva's worried look.

'Don't worry, your friends are okay,' the Captain said. 'They decided to get a lift home on the fishing boats. They should be here in half an hour or so.'

'Thanks,' Mac said. 'It went well then?'

'Yes, except for the gunfire that is. We were lucky there. They got the searchlight and a few bullets went through the wheelhouse as well. One of them went right through the windscreen so there goes my no-claims bonus,' he said suppressing a smile.

'I'll bet that you're glad that you took Lieutenant Kyriakou along with you,' Mac said as he watched the young soldier walk down the jetty.

'Well, as much as I'd like to take all the credit it was your friend Dave's idea that we take him along and yes, his shooting was incredible,' the Captain replied. 'He took the two shooters down with two shots. Our machine gunners couldn't get a clear shot which is probably just as well for you, young lady, as they were hiding behind your crates. At least

254

your art treasures are in one piece and not full of bullet holes.'

'Yes, thanks for that,' Eva said with real sincerity.

Mac congratulated the Captain and shook hands.

'At least we know that they're alright,' Mac said as they watched the Captain walk away.

Eva tried to give Mac a smile and almost succeeded.

It took forty minutes before they saw the first fishing boat chugging into the dock. As it came closer Mac could see Dave standing on the deck. He was leaning on a stack of wooden shipping crates. Mac waved to him. He waved enthusiastically back. As soon as the boat tied up Dave jumped onto the jetty and came over to the two of them.

'You're still here?' he asked with some surprise.

'We were listening to it all on the radio. It sounded exciting,' Mac said.

'Too exciting for me,' Dave replied with a shake of his head. 'Getting shot at twice in two days was no fun, believe me.'

This gave Mac some pause for thought. He'd have a quiet word with Dave later.

'Anyway, we hopefully got what we came for,' Dave said as he turned towards Eva. 'I'll bet you can't wait to get those crates open. I've asked for some police trucks to come and unload them for you, they should be here in an hour or so. Where do you want them to go?'

Eva wasn't really listening. She was looking towards the entrance into the dock.

'Where?' she said looking puzzled. 'Oh, to the museum. We've got a big workroom there and I'm planning to start opening them up as soon as they arrive.'

'Good,' Dave said as he gave Mac a knowing look.

Eva stood to attention as the second fishing boat appeared. As it neared, they could all see Andy standing on the deck. He was smiling as he waved at them.

Mac was wondering what Eva was going to do. He could almost hear her heart thumping just by standing next to her.

Andy jumped down onto the jetty and walked quickly towards them. Mac turned to find that Eva had climbed over the waist high fence. She ran towards Andy and then slowed down. They looked at each other and Andy said something. Eva didn't reply. She simply put her arms around his waist and hugged him tightly, her head buried in his chest. He kissed the top of her head.

So, she's made her decision then, Mac thought. For some reason he felt that it was the right one too.

Dave and Mac turned away and gave each other a slightly embarrassed look.

'Well Eleni's been on about it for ages,' Dave said. 'She said that Andy should get a nice girl so that we can go out as a foursome.'

Mac turned and took a little look at Andy and Eva who were still embracing.

'It looks as if she'll get her wish,' he said.

They dropped Eva at the museum and Mac and Dave had to wait a few minutes while Andy said his goodbyes. He then climbed into the back of the car.

'Is everything okay?' Dave asked as he started the car up.

Andy's smile said it all.

'Oh, Eva said that she'll call us as soon as they're ready to start opening the crates.'

'I'm absolutely exhausted but I wouldn't miss that for anything,' Dave said. 'I just hope that they were worth getting shot at for. Come on, I'm starving.'

Dave drove them to a little café that was tucked away down one of the back streets. It looked bright and modern. They sat at a table outside that was under a colourful awning. Mac was beginning to wonder what sort of food they did when Dave answered his question.

'They do a good Full English here,' Dave said. 'If ever I was in need of one, it's now.'

The Full English was indeed very good, in fact as good as the one he'd had at Kyrene. However, the view of the dusty street outside couldn't match their magnificent views over the sea.

Mac had noticed that, whatever the circumstances, a good breakfast always made it a little better. They all sat back in a companionable silence as their food went down.

'I still can't believe that we pulled it off,' Dave said with a shake of his head. 'Of course, it was mostly down to Jason, Yanni's son. If he hadn't got those shooters then we could have had a real problem on our hands.'

'That was a good idea of yours to bring him along. How on earth did he manage it though?' Mac asked. 'I mean it was dark and, while the sea wasn't rough, the two boats must have both been moving at the time.'

'I asked him exactly that,' Dave replied. 'He said that he was using thermal imaging sights on his rifle so the fact that it was dark was actually an advantage for him and he didn't seem to think that the shots were that hard. In fact, he said that, for a sniper, it was pretty much point-blank range.'

Mac shook his head in wonder.

'Tell me, was John Allen on board either of the boats?' he asked.

'No, I had a look at the two shooters before they put them into body bags but neither of them was him,' Dave replied. 'They weren't from around here either, too pale.'

257

'It's my bet that he brought in some muscle from one of his old gangs in London,' Mac said. 'Forensics might be able to prove that from their clothing.'

'Do you think that he's still on the island?' Andy asked.

'I doubt it,' Mac replied. 'There's a reason that he's never been caught, he's smart and he gets others to do his dirty work for him. I'd guess that he's in Bulgaria waiting for the European Star to dock.'

'Well, Mr. Allen's going to be in for something of a shock then,' Dave said with a smile.

'There's still one thing that bothers me though,' Mac said.

'What's that?' Dave asked.

'Who killed Harold Jones?'

Chapter Thirty

They were still chewing over Mac's question when Andy got a call from Eva. The crates had arrived and they were going to start opening them up soon. They quickly finished their coffees and drove to the museum. They passed by an old honey-coloured building with beautiful arches at the front and Mac expected the car to slow down. It didn't.

The museum proved to be a fairly modern white building situated down an anonymous side street. It too looked anonymous, more like a small office block than anything else. A sign that would have easy to overlook said 'The New Archaeological Museum' in both Greek and English. Mac carefully made his way up the steps while Dave showed his warrant card to three police officers who were guarding the museum entrance.

Inside there was more space than Mac would have thought, more space than exhibits anyway. It felt musty and dusty and he could now understand why Eva had called it a 'backwater'. They looked at each other, unsure of where they should go, when a young girl waved at them from a doorway. They followed her into a large open space in which a crate was being manoeuvred into position by a ceiling lift. The buttons controlling the lift were being pressed by Eva. Around her stood a small crowd. One young man standing near her was armed with a jemmy while another had a hammer in one hand and a chisel in the other. A couple of women in their forties and a short bald man in his sixties stood a little further back and watched.

Eva was concentrating on getting the crate in position and never noticed them come in. Once there was some slack in the chain the young man with the jemmy unhooked the crate from the ceiling lift. As she moved the hook out of the way she noticed the new arrivals and her face lit up.

'Oh, you're here,' she said with a smile that Mac was sure was at least eighty per cent for Andy. 'I'm afraid that we just couldn't wait, we've already opened the first crate.'

She led them over to a wide table that had sturdy metal legs. Five stone relief sculptures lay flat on its surface.

'These are stelae,' Eva explained, 'basically ancient gravestones and they're very important as they usually contain a fair amount of information about the deceased.'

She pointed to a stone that showed a bearded man in a cloak who had a helmet on and a spear in his right hand. A woman held his left hand while two young boys looked on. It was so beautifully carved that the folds in his cloak made it look almost real. The woman's mournful expression left no doubt as to who was dead.

'This one's wonderfully intact and we have an inscription which basically says that the stone was made in memory of Heliodorus, a dyer of wool who lived in Kition, from his wife Eirine,' Eva said as she gently touched the stone. 'I'd guess from what he's wearing that he must have gone off to war and never come back.'

She looked sad and Mac noticed that she sneaked a glance at Andy. He wondered if she was thinking about him being shot at just a few hours ago. She turned and looked to see how the two young men were getting on. They had the top off the crate and were now gently removing pieces of hard polystyrene and wads of bubble wrap.

'Whoever packed these did a really good job,' Eva said. 'We're hopeful that all the items should be in as good a condition as possible.'

One of the young men said something to Eva and she took the controls of the ceiling lift. She lowered the hook towards the crate and strong padded leather straps were arranged around whatever was in the box. Eva very gently raised it and they could all see a stone horse's head. The horse's mouth was open, the muscles in its jaw were tense, the nostrils were flaring and the ears were pricked up. The mane stood up straight from the neck to suggest that it had been braided.

Although the statue ended at the neck, Mac could see an excited horse pawing at the ground and ready to charge at whatever enemy awaited it.

Eva carefully lifted it onto a nearby table and set it gently down.

'Shall we try the big one now?' she said with a gleeful smile.

The 'big one' was a crate about fifteen feet long and six feet wide. Eva and one of the other women joined the two young men in levering the top off. To make it easier to get at whatever was inside they took one of the side panels off too. Mac could see lots of polystyrene inserts and masses of bubble wrap. They carefully took away the packing piece by piece, checking that whatever was inside didn't move. They uncovered a part of the crate's contents and they all stopped and stared in something like veneration. They took a few steps back so that everyone could see.

Mac could see a head. It was a woman's head and she looked as if she was staring straight at him. Her wavy hair was bunched at the back of her head and a ribbon held the rest in place. Her face was serene and composed with just the hint of a smile on her full lips.

'God but she's beautiful!'

Mac had said the words aloud without realising it but no-one disagreed with him.

Eva came over to them. She had tears in her eyes and Andy had no difficulty in supplying her with a shoulder to cry on.

'I just can't believe it!' she said as she looked again towards the statue.

'I guess that it will take you quite a while to unpack her,' Mac said.

'It will,' Eva replied as she wiped away a tear. 'We'll have to go very carefully.'

Dave picked up on what Mac was saying.

'Shall we leave her to it?' he asked. 'I'm in need of my bed right now.'

Mac nodded but Andy said as nonchalantly as he could, 'I think I'll hang around for a while.'

This made Dave and Mac smile.

'I'll see you tomorrow at the station then,' Dave said.

As they drove back Dave said, 'I'm going to pop into Yanni's bar for a quick drink and to tell him what's happened. I can drop you off first if you like.'

'A drink sounds like a good idea to me right now,' Mac replied.

While Dave went inside Mac sat down at the same table and looked at the bullet holes in the wall behind him. One was just a few inches to the left of his head. He looked at where the shooter had stopped and, in his mind, he drew a line from there to the bullet hole. He was pretty sure that it went right through his head.

It had been a strange sort of holiday, he thought, but, even though he'd been shot at, he found that he wouldn't have changed it for anything.

Dave brought out two large bottles of beer and a beaming Yanni. He'd just had a quick visit from his son before he had to return to his army unit.

Dave told Yanni exactly what had happened.

'So, my little Jason really saved the day then?' a proud Yanni asked. 'He didn't say anything at all about it when I saw him just now.'

'Well, Jason never was one for boasting,' Dave said. 'He did a great job though. If it hadn't been for him, some of the wonderful things that we've just seen in the museum might have been riddled with bullet holes.'

Yanni looked like he was going to burst with pride.

'Another beer?' he asked.

No-one said no. When he returned, they moved on to discussing the finer points of the case.

'So, even though you've got the boats and the art works, you're still no closer to finding out who killed the old man?' Yanni said.

'That's right,' Dave replied. 'We'll start again on that again tomorrow after I've had a nice long sleep.'

As Dave said the word 'sleep' Mac felt the fatigue wash over him. He suddenly needed his bed. Dave offered him a lift but Mac insisted that the walk would do him good.

He walked around the back of the fort and down a side street. As he passed by the little restaurant a group of lounging cats once again followed him with their eyes but otherwise didn't move a muscle. Tired as he was a thought was beginning to form in his head but it wasn't quite there yet. He didn't try to chase it down, he knew from experience that it would come when it was ready.

At the end of the street he crossed the road and headed towards the square. He walked on and then stopped and looked around. It was already hot and the honey-coloured stone of the church tower seemed to glow in the sunshine. People were coming and going or just sitting down and letting the world go by. Another tour group stood outside the church while a stream of tourists took selfies of themselves and the church.

Mac smiled. After all the excitement of the previous few days it was nice to know that nothing else had changed. He wearily made his way to his apartment.

His room had been cleaned and looked as fresh as the day he'd first arrived. He took his medication and then put the air conditioning on. He pulled the curtains making sure that they were fully across. He undressed and then lay back on the bed. A few seconds later he was deeply asleep.

He awoke feeling disoriented as images flashed through his mind; boats, gunfire, a man in a prison cell, blood on the ground and the face of a beautiful woman. He quickly realised that these thoughts weren't the product of one of his lucid dreams but were real, flashes of the strange events of the past few days. He looked over at the clock. It had just gone twelve. He had no idea whether that was twelve midnight or noon.

He sat up and then stood up. His old friend the pain was still there but it was better than he'd expected. He opened the curtain. It was night. He sat on the bed wondering what to do next. He decided that he needed a cold drink. He poured himself a large glass of orange juice and took it out onto the balcony.

It was blessedly cool outside and the café below was in the process of shutting down. He sat and watched the waiters as they cleared up and stacked the chairs and tables away. Soon the square was quiet and he looked at the illuminated tower of the church as though he'd never seen it before. While he was doing this the thought came back to him.

The fire door alarm was the key. Harold Jones' killer had known about it but how? There was something else too but what was it?

He allowed his thoughts to run free as he sat and let the peacefulness of the night envelop him. However, there was something, something from very early on in the investigation. The thought was still vague and unfocussed. As he sat there the thought slowly emerged and came into view. He sat up and smiled.

Of course, he thought, how hadn't he seen it before?

Chapter Thirty-One

He had no trouble going back to sleep and he woke up at six thirty more than ready for the day ahead. Before he did anything else, he checked that the thought was still there and that it still made sense. It did. He reminded himself that it might be nothing but he knew that he was going to ask Dave to check it out anyway.

He had a leisurely breakfast in the square before texting Dave. As he sat there, he realised with a start that it was already Monday and nearly a week of his holiday had already gone by. Tim would be flying in tomorrow afternoon but Mac had a feeling that there was a chance that the case might be done and dusted by then.

Andy picked him up. He looked a happy man.

'How did the unpacking go?' Mac asked.

'Really well,' Andy replied. 'They got the statue out in one piece and it's absolutely unbelievable, wait until you see it.'

He'd only seen the statue's face so far and that was unbelievable enough.

'I take it that they're carrying on with the unpacking today?' Mac asked.

'Oh yes, and later on the Mayor's coming to have a look and then they're holding a press conference,' Andy replied. 'I was thinking about it as I watched them yesterday. It will probably be a big boost for tourism in Larnaka but it means more than that.'

Andy paused while he thought.

'Eva told me that Larnaka has been in existence for well over three thousand years and I got a real sense of that as I looked at the statue and the rest of the art works as they were being unwrapped. It was like seeing my people's history written in stone and bronze.'

'That's very well put,' Mac said.

'Well, it was Eva who said it first,' Andy admitted with a smile. 'But it's how I feel too. If I'm being honest, I felt close to tears myself at times. It's been a very strange few days.'

It has that, Mac thought.

Once at the police station they walked into the office. Dave was at his desk and Andy pulled up a couple of chairs.

'Did you sleep alright?' Dave asked.

'Like a baby,' Mac replied.

'Yes, me too,' Dave said. 'I slept straight through and woke up at five this morning. I was able to make Eleni and the kids breakfast this morning which made a nice change.'

Mac noticed that Andy had said nothing about how he slept but his smile said a lot and Mac drew his own conclusions.

'I'll be calling for a team briefing soon but I thought I'd see if anyone had any ideas first,' Dave said. 'I'm just hoping that we won't have to start from scratch again.'

Mac told him of the thought that had come to him during the night. Andy got the details up on the computer.

'That is strange, she lives not too far from you,' Andy said. 'That's a bit up-market for a cleaner perhaps. Shall I send a car around to pick her up?'

'Yes, let's do that,' Dave replied.

Just over an hour later Mac watched as she was brought into an interview room. He went next door where he could watch the whole thing on TV. Andy got a young detective to sit with him and act as a translator. He watched the woman as she waited for the interview to start. She was in her early thirties with black hair cut quite short. She was striking rather than conventionally pretty and she wore a long pale blue skirt and a high-necked blouse over which she wore a thin cardigan which covered up her arms. She

267

looked nervous and kept pulling down the ends of the sleeves of the cardigan which made Mac wonder. Dave and Andy sat down opposite her and the interview began.

'Miss Orphanides when we sent a car around for you just now the policemen were told that you were at work,' Dave said. 'They were also told that your place of work was the Cyprus Express newspaper office and that you were employed there as a journalist. They went to the newspaper office and there you were. Why didn't you tell us this when you were interviewed?'

'I didn't think it was important,' she muttered.

'You've been working as a cleaner for three days a week at Libretta House for a couple of months now. Can I ask why?'

She shrugged and said, 'I needed the money.'

'Yet your editor said that he knew nothing about this. You told him that you were on a story, didn't you?'

'I lied,' she said as she once again pulled at the sleeves of her cardigan.

'Even with the fans on it's quite hot in here,' Dave said. 'Wouldn't you like to take your cardigan off?'

Mac smiled. Dave had noticed it too.

'No, I'm fine,' she replied with a worried look.

'Miss Orphanides, I'd like you to take your cardigan off, if not I'll get one of my men to do it for you.'

She looked up at the policeman standing by the door and her shoulders slumped. She took the cardigan off and even Mac gasped. Her upper arms were covered with bruises. They were purplish-blue in the centre fading to yellow at the edges. She pulled up her blouse and there were more bruises on her stomach.

'How did you get those?' Dave asked softly.

'Harold Jones gave them to me,' she replied her face showing her disgust.

'What happened?'

'It all started a couple of months ago when an old woman came to see me at the newspaper. She'd waited for hours and wouldn't talk to any other reporter. She told me that she had a journal with her that had belonged to her father. She said that she was going to die soon and that she wanted me to have it. I asked her why but she just told me to read it. So, I did.

The journal she gave me recorded the life of a policeman who'd worked under the British in the 1950s. Most of it was routine stuff but it still gave me an interesting insight into life at the time. About two-thirds of the way through I discovered why the old lady had given the journal to me specifically. Part of this policeman's duties were to attend punishment beatings and hangings. In the journal he described the last hanging that took place in Larnaka.'

'That was Nicos Leonidas, the poet, wasn't it?' Dave asked.

Mac remembered the hanging room at the fort and the photograph of the impossibly young man on the wall.

'It was,' she replied. 'It was never made public but the hanging was a botched job. The hangman was called Harry Jones.'

Mac remembered that he was the famous English hangman who had executed the prisoners in Nicosia Prison.

'This Harry Jones had been in a local bar for most of the night before and the hanging took place very early in the morning. He was so drunk that he got the length of the rope wrong and, instead of the prisoner breaking his neck, he just dangled there, twitching, for more than ten minutes. Can I have some water, please?' she asked.

Talking about the hanging had clearly upset her, Mac thought. He wondered why. He also wondered about Harry Jones who, he'd been told by his old sergeant, had never made a mistake.

She took a sip of water and continued, 'In the back of the journal there was an old photo. It showed the hangman, a representative of the British Governor and the policeman. On the back of the photo a message was scrawled. It said, 'I saw the hangman last week in Kalograion. He's old but it was him.' It was dated a couple of days before she gave me the journal.'

She paused and took another sip of water.

'I looked up Harry Jones the hangman on the internet and I thought that the old woman must have gone mad. He died in the early nineties so there was no way that he could be walking around the streets of Larnaka. I looked at the photo again. Harry Jones would have been in his mid-forties at the time of the hanging but this man looked much younger and so I dug some more. I discovered that there had actually been two hangmen named Harry Jones and that they'd worked together on several hangings in the UK as well as some here in Cyprus.

It turned out that the older Harry Jones had gotten sick and couldn't make the hanging and so the younger Harry Jones had been forced to do it by himself. I don't know if he got drunk simply because he needed some courage as he was having to handle the hanging all by himself. Anyway, afterwards they kept the whole thing covered up but Harry Jones the younger was never used as a hangman again.'

'I take it that you were able to identify Harold Jones as being Harry Jones the young hangman?' Dave asked.

'Yes, I started following him around and I took some photos. I then had someone do a comparison

270

using facial recognition software. They were fairly certain that he was the same person.'

Mac thought of Harold Jones' face. It was bony and with little flesh on it. He figured that it might not have changed that much as he got older.

'I take it that some of your photos were taken at Psarolimano?' Dave asked.

She nodded, 'I regret it now but I was scared and I hoped that telling you about Harold Jones meeting that man would take the spotlight off me a little.'

Dave had to admit that it had worked too. While Harold Jones' meeting with Skarparis had diverted attention away from the apartment and the people who worked there, it had also led to them discovering the plan to smuggle Aphrodite and the rest of the ancient art treasures out of the country.

'Go on,' Dave said.

'I also took samples of his fingerprints from his room and had someone try to match them to those on some old documents related to the hangings both here and in Nicosia. He found a match.'

'That was good detective work and it must have cost you some money but why did you go to all that trouble?' Dave asked. 'Was it just for the story or for some other reason?'

This was exactly what Mac wanted to know.

'It was both,' she said with sigh. 'Nicos Leonidas was my grandfather.'

Now it all made sense to Mac.

'Why did you go to Harold Jones' apartment the night he died?' Dave asked.

'I was going to publish the story soon and I wanted to see what he had to say about it. I told him that I wanted to see him in his room and the old goat must have thought I fancied him or something. When I got there, he had a bottle of wine open and he was all smiles but when I told him why I was there and what I'd uncovered about him he went absolutely crazy. He said that he wasn't going to let a Greek whore ruin his reputation then he started hitting me with his stick and swearing at me. I thought he might argue or something but I honestly hadn't been expecting that. I backed off and pleaded with him to stop but he just kept hitting me. He was strong for an old man.'

Another sip of water.

'I found myself on the balcony and with nowhere else to go. He only stopped to shout 'Help' a couple of times which I thought was a bit rich as it was me that needed the help. He then tried to push me over the balcony but I managed to fall to the floor and he went over instead.'

She took another sip of water.

'I didn't even look to see what happened to him, I crawled away from the balcony and then ran off as fast as I could. The fire door was propped open so all I had to do was close it after me and then run down the fire escape to the street. I went home, took some pain-killers and then had the most horrible night of my life. If I'm honest it's a relief to tell you what really happened.'

'Have you any evidence to back your story up?' Dave asked.

'Here,' she said as she took out her phone.

A recording started playing. An old man's voice said, 'Good evening dear...' It was Harold Jones. She'd recorded the whole thing.

Miss Irena Orphanides was more than surprised when she was told that she could go after a police photographer had taken some photos of her injuries. She was trusted to hand her passport in at the station as soon as she could manage it.

Mac sat with Dave and Andy afterwards while they had a coffee.

'Now that wasn't at all what I was expecting,' Andy said.

'You can say that again,' Dave said. 'It's been a strange case all round. We investigate a murder only to find that we've uncovered what is possibly the biggest art theft of all time and nearly get our-selves killed. Then we find out that it wasn't murder anyway but a sort of accident. Mac, that was a good idea of yours to check her out, with everything that's happened I'd almost forgotten about her.'

'Me too but I remember thinking that it was slightly strange at the time and it stuck in my head,' Mac said. 'Not the fact that she volunteered information about Harold Jones meeting someone at Psarolimano but it was the way she described the man he was with. Her description was so detailed that you knew it was Skarparis straight away. If she was just his cleaner then why would she have been so interested in someone she saw with Harold Jones? It just struck me as odd.'

'And of course, we now know that she could describe him so well because she'd taken a photograph of him,' Dave said. 'She's a journalist so she must have had an idea of who he was and what he gets up to.'

'I dare say that she was hoping it would keep you off her back until the bruises went away,' Mac said. 'Anyway, she needn't have worried, that recording puts her in her clear. You can hear her pleading with him to stop hitting her and then, after he shouts for help, he clearly whispers 'Die, you Greek bitch' just before going over the balcony himself. Are you even going to bother sending it to the prosecutors?'

'I'll have to but I can't see any way that they'll proceed with a prosecution,' Dave replied. 'The evidence strongly suggests that it wasn't murder, besides which, she's the granddaughter of one of our most famous

273

poets, a poet that Harry Jones executed at that. I'd guess that there isn't a jury on the island who would convict her when they hear the whole story.'

'So that's that,' Mac said.

'Yes, that's that,' Dave said. 'Now you can finally get on with your holiday. Isn't your friend flying in tomorrow?'

'Yes, that's right.'

'So, how come he didn't manage to make it for the first week?' Dave asked.

'Well now, that's a story in itself,' Mac replied.

He told them the story of how Tim had managed to mistake Herefordshire for Hertfordshire.

'That sounds like an easy mistake to make,' Dave said with a smile. 'So, what are you going to do now?'

'My plan is to have a very quiet day and probably an early night,' Mac replied. 'I'll call Michalis tomorrow and I'll get him to take me to the supermarket so there'll be a full fridge for when Tim gets here. After that I'll meet him at the airport.'

'You'll certainly have a tale to tell him, won't you?' Dave said.

'That I will,' Mac replied. 'That I will.'

Fourteen months later

Mac had received the two invitations in the same envelope a couple of months before and had immediately accepted both over the phone. Just over a year after their first visit he and Tim were once again staying at Libretta House and had once again booked themselves in for a three week stay. Tim had made sure that he didn't accept any new work coming up to the holiday just to be on the safe side.

It was Saturday morning and they were waiting in the lobby for Michalis to pick them up. It was a hot day but both Mac and Tim were wearing white shirts, ties and trousers. They both held a suit jacket over one arm. They were on their way to the first engagement.

Michalis was dead on time.

'You're both looking very smart,' he said as Mac and Tim climbed into the old Mercedes.

'We're going to the opening of the new wing at the Archaeological Museum,' Mac replied.

'I've heard that people have been trying to get tickets for that, offering good money too,' Michalis said as he pulled away. 'It would be nice to see such a wonderful part of our history but I suppose I'll have to wait until it's open to the public and join the queue.'

Mac pulled out his invitation and read it carefully.

'You can come in with us if you want,' he said.

'Really?' Michalis asked with some surprise.

'Yes, it says here on the invite 'Mac Maguire and Guests'. I've only got one guest so I guess that I'm allowed to take another one in as well.'

'I've got a tie and jacket in the back,' Michalis said excitedly. 'I always keep them there just in case.'

'Okay then, it would be a pleasure if you'd join us, wouldn't it, Tim?'

'It would indeed,' Tim replied. 'It would be a little thank you for that 'night out' that you gave us last year, you know the one that turned out to be a long weekend. Now that's something that I'll never forget. I'm hoping that next Saturday will be just as good.'

Next Saturday was when Mac's second engagement was going to take place. It was a wedding and he was very much looking forward to it.

Michalis dropped Mac and Tim outside the museum and went off to find somewhere to park the Mercedes. The sign outside was large and colourful and it now proudly proclaimed, 'The Aphrodite Archaeological Museum of Larnaka'. Policemen were on duty to hold back curious onlookers as a gaggle of dignitaries made their way inside. They waited for Michalis to appear before they made their way inside. The outside of the museum was the same except for the fact that it had been cleaned so that it now was now a gleaming white. The inside, however, was unrecognisable to Mac. Instead of a wide-open space there was a row of desks where entrance tickets could be bought and, on the right, the 'Aphrodite Gift Shop' which was fully stocked with items of all sorts bearing an image of the now famous statue.

A uniformed young woman led them through the next room, which was the Pre-Historic Gallery, and then into the Late Bronze Age Gallery where drinks and snacks were foisted on them, not that Mac or Tim complained. He looked around and saw that Eleni was waving to him. He went over to her just as Dave returned with some drinks.

'That was a lovely evening last night,' Mac said.

'Are you sure that your friend Tim there hasn't got any Greek in him?' Dave said with a smile.

This made Mac laugh.

Dave and Eleni had invited Mac and Tim to the taverna for some food and drinks and he'd finally got to meet their daughter Christina. He'd found her to be a very bright young woman who was especially knowledgeable about where all the best shops were in his native city. He'd enjoyed chatting to her but then some bouzouki players had arrived and a space was cleared for dancing. A round of zivanias had appeared from nowhere and, with Eleni's encouragement, Tim had gotten up to dance with her and Christina. He'd surprised them all by not doing too badly either. However, this was one occasion when Mac had found a bad back to definitely be an asset.

As his Nora had once told him, 'God may have given you the odd gift but a sense of rhythm definitely wasn't one of them.'

'Where's Eva?' Mac asked.

'She's doing some last-minute alterations, I think,' Eleni said. 'I take it that you heard about the old Director retiring and her being made the new Director of the museum?'

'Yes, I did and she deserves it...'

Mac was going to say more but Tim and Michalis joined them. Andy joined them a few minutes later. Mac had to look twice as he looked very unlike his normal self being dressed in a very smart suit and tie.

'Is Eva okay?' Eleni asked. 'Does she need any help?'

'No, I think everything's fine now,' Andy replied a little breathlessly. 'She's just putting some make-up on.'

Eleni went off to the ladies to join Eva. As Mac watched her walk away his eyes caught a couple that were standing a little apart from the rest of the crowd. She was dressed in a beautiful blue gown while her husband looked a little uncomfortable in a black suit and tie. They both looked nervously around. Mac guessed that was because they didn't know anyone there. He'd met them in Stevenage just after he'd returned from Cyprus the year before. He went over to them.

'Mr. and Mrs. Jaskolski, how are you both?'

They both smiled and visibly relaxed at meeting someone familiar.

'Mr. Maguire, how are you?' Chelsea said with some relief. 'There's a lot of people here, I wasn't really expecting something this big.'

She had a major part to play in the proceedings and she looked somewhat jittery about it.

'I'd like to introduce you to someone,' Mac said. 'Come with me.'

He introduced them to Dave, Tim, Andy and Michalis.

'So, it's you we have to thank for all this then?' Dave asked.

'No, not really,' Chelsea said looking embarrassed. 'It was just well, what my grandfather had been trying to do just didn't seem right, trying to steal all those ancient things. He'd wanted to have a museum wing built so I thought, I've got the money now, so why don't I do just that? When Mr. Maguire here told me what had happened, I contacted the museum and spoke to Eva about it and she was great. I feel as if I've made up for my grandfather's actions a little now.'

'You've called the wing after your mother,' Mac said as he looked up at the discrete sign over the entrance.

The Becky Jones Wing.

'That was Eva's idea too,' Chelsea said. 'It will be nice that mum will be remembered.'

'And Mac was telling me that you've founded a charity in her name too,' Tim said.

278

'That's right, the Becky Jones Foundation. My job now is to travel around the country and hand money out to deserving causes. It's the best job I've ever had,' she said with a wide smile.

'He also told me that you were still living in the same house and that your husband here is still working,' Tim said.

'What else would I do?' Jan said. 'We've put some money in the bank but we're going to give everything else away. It's not really our money anyway, is it love?'

'The neighbours think we won the lottery,' Chelsea chipped in with a smile.

A flushed and excited Eva interrupted them.

'Hello everyone. The Mayor and the President have arrived. Mr. and Mrs. Jaskolski, we need you now.'

Chelsea and Jan followed her to the entrance to the new wing. A wide red ribbon was stretched across it. Mac noticed two late attendees slipping in at the back of the crowd. It was Yanni and his son.

Speeches were made by the politicians who, thankfully, had the sense to keep them short. Then Eva got up to say a few words.

She first thanked the police for the part they had played in ensuring that the contents of the new wing hadn't left the island. Mac turned and saw Commander Vassiliou and Captain Michaelides standing proudly in the crowd. She also thanked her team for all their hard work in conserving the finds. She then thanked the architect and the builders for the fine job that they'd done on the new wing and in record time too.

'I'd lastly like to thank Mr. and Mrs. Jaskolski for their astoundingly generous gift without which everything you see around you now would still be a dream. I'll now ask Mrs. Jaskolski if she would like to cut the tape and declare the Becky Jones Wing of the museum open.'

279

Eva had done a fine job but she looked more than glad that it was nearly over. She handed Chelsea a pair of gold scissors and the tape was duly cut. The crowd applauded and they then slowly followed Eva and her team into the new wing.

Yanni and Jason came over.

'Jason's bus was late,' an excited Yanni said after all the hugs and handshakes. 'I didn't think that we were going to make it.'

They followed the crowd inside. The new wing had been specially designed to hold all the ancient art works and it consisted of two parts; a huge wedge-shaped room that was wide as you walked in and then gradually tapered as you went further along. Through the entrance into the next section Mac could see her. They'd positioned the statue so they she appeared to be looking straight down the length of the new wing. He decided to detach himself from the rest and walk on.

It was the first time that he'd seen her properly. Eva had sent him photos but they weren't the same. The face, serene and with that faint smile, looked down on him as he neared the statue. She had a cloth in one hand but it didn't obscure her body. Her breasts were taut and her nipples hard as though she was aroused. He walked into a large round room that had windows all around and a translucent skylight above. She stood in a clear glass tube that didn't get in the way of you taking everything about her in. He walked around to the front of the statue. Her right hand was held down, guarding her secrets. One foot was flat on the ground while the other was on tip toe. She was in motion, caught in a bronze freeze-frame. There were seats all around the side of the wall so he sat down and continued to look.

A little later Eva and the crowd caught up. They all marvelled at her for a while and then went on their way back to the Late Bronze Age gallery where more food and drinks were being served. As the room emptied Eva noticed him still sitting there. She sat down beside him.

'So, what do you think?' she asked.

'I was going to say that she's beautiful but she's well beyond that,' Mac replied. 'I don't think that I have the words really. What do you think?'

Eva thought for a while.

'She's a goddess but she's a woman first,' she replied as she looked adoringly up at the statue. 'She's got the figure of a real woman and she's not ashamed of it. She smiles at her lover but she's playing a game too. If you want her, you'll have to win her but it won't be easy. Her smile hints that the prize will be well worth it though.'

'Yes, that's about it,' Mac said with admiration. 'Tell me, are you looking forward to next week?'

'I'm kind of half looking forward to it and half dreading it,' Eva replied. 'Of course, my mum and sisters are going crazy about it as we haven't had a wedding in the family for a while. To be honest, I think my mum had given up on me getting married at all. It's crazy to think that I'll be Mrs. Kalorkoti in just seven days from now. It's crazy but it's really nice too. I'd just like to say thanks, Mac.'

'What for?'

'For your little story about Andy.'

'What? How he helped me on with the shoe covers?' Mac asked.

'I know it sounds silly but it made a difference and you were right. He is a kind man. I didn't realise how lonely I'd been until I got to know him. He's exactly what I needed and what I still need.'

'Well, I guess that he must be the right man for you, after all it was the Goddess of Love herself that brought you and Andy together.' Mac said looking up at the statue. 'You're lucky that you found each other. Don't ever forget that.'

'Don't worry, I won't,' Eva said giving Mac's hand a little squeeze. 'Come on, I'll buy you a drink.'

'I don't suppose you've got any beers in there. Those little glasses of fizz don't sit all that well with me,' Mac said.

'For one of our guests of honour I'm sure that it can be arranged.'

'Thanks, I'll join you in a minute,' he said.

He must have sat there a little longer than that as Tim came looking for him.

'Come on Mac, Eva's got us some cold beers.'

He stood up while still looking at the statue.

'What do you think she's saying?' Mac asked.

Tim turned and looked up at Aphrodite with a serious expression. He then smiled.

'She's telling me that I'm not dead yet,' he said with a wink.

This made Mac laugh.

'Come on, let's get those beers while they're still cold.'

As he walked away, he couldn't help but turn for one more look. His friend Tim, for all his jokes, could be very wise at times. Mac felt that this was one of them.

That's exactly what the goddess of love had been saying to him all along.

He wasn't dead yet.

THE END

Author's Note
On coincidences – Part of the plot concerns two hangmen both with the same name. I hope that you didn't find it too far-fetched as it is based on reality. Harry Allen, along with Albert Pierrepoint, was one of the most famous hangmen of his time. It is also true that he hanged nine of the men who are buried in Nicosia Prison in the 'Imprisoned Graves' as well as three others in Cyprus. The last execution took place in 1962. He was at times assisted with some of his hangings by a man who was also called Harry Allen. None of the hangings ever went wrong.

The character of 'Dave' Christodoulou was suggested by the notary who married my wife and I in Larnaka a few years ago. He was a lovely man in his fifties who, on seeing that we'd both been born in Birmingham, spoke to us in a flawless 'Brummie' accent and told us that he used to live just down the road from where we'd both been brought up. So, I thought, why not make the lead Cypriot detective Dave come from Birmingham too? I hope it worked.

On the statue – I've based the bronze statue on a real one, Praxiteles' Aphrodite of Knidos. You can find out more and see exactly what she looks like here - https://en.wikipedia.org/wiki/Aphrodite_of_Knidos She is definitely worth a look.

On Larnaka – Just about all of the locations are based on real places and the 'Eight Bench Walk' on the Piale Pasa was something that I tried to do most days while I was there. It was strange but I somehow knew that this book had be called that well before I knew exactly why!

I hope that you've enjoyed this story. If you have then please post a review and let me know what you think. *PCW*

Made in the USA
Coppell, TX
06 November 2020